ASK
THE *CHATTER* OF POP
PAUL MORLEY

Paul Morley, determined to make plenty happen, first wrote for a Stockport-based pre-punk fanzine called *Penetration* which usually featured Lemmy, Hawkwind and Ted Nugent. His article about Lenny Bruce was pasted up in the wrong order, but nobody noticed. His own magazine *Out There*, he designed himself – getting it professionally type-set, even the line about the elephant's hard-on. His article in the magazine about Patti Smith is one of the seven best ever written about her. *Out There* looked like no other fanzine. It was small, glossy and elegantly printed. 800 people read it, including *Sniffin' Glue's* Mark P who sent him an anti-glossy abusive letter, and Nick Logan, editor of the *New Musical Express*, who sent him a telegram. Employed at the end of 1976 to write for the *NME* from Manchester, then right at the make-believe centre of punk rock, his first published review was written on the 7.20 a.m. Inter City Train, going backwards towards London and his job interview with Logan. It was a review of Buzzcocks and Eater at Manchester's Houndsworth Hall. "Buzzcocks are the Ornette Coleman of new wave. Sex Pistols are the John Coltrane. And Eater, they must be the Acker Bilk." He started writing regular concert reviews for the *NME*, and much preferred it when he was sent to review The Prefects, Subway Sect and Buzzcocks rather

than Mott, The Edgar Broughton Band or Rush. To this day he feels that a group like The Prefects, performing their 11-second "Bohemian Rhapsody", or their 8-minute "The Bristol Road Leads To Dachau" summed up the cunning, hope, distortions and absurd brilliance of the pop ideal, while all the records and breathing of Phil Collins, Emerson Lake and Palmer and Dire Straits put together amount to little more than a stomach ache. Why doesn't everyone realise this? It was this thought that perhaps made Paul Morley start to ask questions. Looking back on punk rock, and what everyone thought then, he now says, "If life was less complicated and everything had gone according to plan, Subway Sect's "Ambition" would now be accepted as one of rock music's greatest number ones, and groups influenced by Subway Sect, like The Fire Engines, would now be more successful than Duran Duran."

As it is, he ended up interviewing Duran Duran as they prepared for superstardom, and Subway Sect suffered a lonely death. What went wrong?

continued page 128

DETAILS

First published in 1986 by
Faber and Faber Limited, 3 Queen Square, London WC1N 3AU

Printed in Great Britain by Redwood Burn Ltd, Trowbridge, Wiltshire
Typeset by Input Typesetting Ltd, London SW19

British Library Cataloguing in Publication Data

Morley, Paul
  Ask.
  1. Music, Popular (Songs, etc.)-History and criticism
  I. Title 780'.42   ML3470
ISBN 0–571–13813–6

Library of Congress Cataloging-in-Publication Data

Morley, Paul
  Ask.
  1. Rock musicians-Interviews.   2. Music and society
  I. Title ML394.M67   1986   784.5'4'00922 [B]   85–29401
ISBN 0–571–13813–6 (pbk.)

Interviews originally published in *New Musical Express* © Paul Morley
Commissioned and edited by Tony Stewart, Phil McNeil and Neil Spencer with special thanks to
Tony Stewart.
Wham! appears thanks to the editors of *Blitz*.

The photographs belong to Anton Corbijn at *Ze Famouz*: specially printed for this book.
Cover and page presentation by David Smart.
Research: Paul McDonald.
For support, thanks to Penman, Donohue, Bohn, Mackinnon.
Then, thanks to those who opened their mouths "from the dust of Crisp's bed-sit to the dust of
Bombay."
. . . . you can't help but wonder.

For Leslie Ronald who should be around, and Dilys and Claudia who thankfully are.

ORDER

+ in order of appearance

killing joke
jerry garcia
marillion
gary numan
martin fry
midge ure
bauhaus
adam ant
david sylvian
paul weller
mick jagger
clash
fire engines
depeche mode
chrissie hynde
peter gabriel
david bowie

OUT

The interview had begun. I'd asked the first question. Was it a good question? Was it a wise question? Do me a favour. It was a question. The interview had begun.

I sat between Sir Michael Tippett and Sarah Brightman. The television studio at London Weekend was filled with some of the most prominent names in the arts and the pops. Over there, Nic Roeg. Right behind me, Malcolm McLaren. Scores of faces I knew from TV and film, drama and documentary, their names tipped on my tongue. Just there, Andrew Lloyd Webber of course. Rushdie, Puttnam, Michael White. I was surrounded by those who are those – the ones that are supposed to lead us on – and in front of us, their mascot, our host, Melvyn Bragg. Bragg was to present Channel 4's Arts Review of 1984, and he would ask representatives of theatre, film, literature to pass cosy comment on the year's ups and downs. I'd been invited to sit among this particular version of the elite to sum up pop music. Put rock in its place, as you must do in such a situation – be the expert. Know it all. I could cope. Before we all trooped into the studio and found the bits of paper with our names on that told us where to sit, I'd taken in enough white wine to hum with brilliant confidence. I hadn't made my mind up what to say had happened and why, but I knew that as soon as Bragg got round to me I would make history. Whatever I said to Melvyn, that's what would have happened to rock music that year.

I started to prepare the "script" in my head. Go right for the valid, I told myself, and be irresistibly lucid. Impress all the posh people looking down on pop, with a fabulous definition of the emotional climate of rock. Prove within your four minutes and ten seconds that rock music might be getting more and more restricted by glum, expensive videos and the anxious predictability of the record industry, but it is still an area of great significance and expressiveness. Yes, sure, Sade and the polite people, Phil Collins and the light ones, might appear to be all that's up, making a present of the pleasant to the peasants I'll say, that'll knee them, but have you thought about the marching logic of The Redskins or the metaphysical halo around David Byrne of Talking Heads? Don't let them know, I mentioned to myself, that it's all a bit of a mess really and that the best things in pop are being pushed more and more into a corner, while the polite people clean everything up. Wrily admit that the real event of the year was the emergence of TV adverts for records, but that there were exciting stirrings of some smashing activity down in the depths that would knock apart mediocrity's grip on things. I could speak fast. I would get all this said. Pop splitting apart! On one side music for the adults in their thirties and forties who'd lived through the Stones and lived in comfort, something you didn't really need to take notice of; and then the real stuff, what it's meant to be, pop as the noised nervous grounding for the agitation and delight of the young. I'd move everyone to tears. I started to worry whether I could remember it all. Ask me a question Bragg!

I sat opposite Grace Jones. The microphone was dead centre between us. She gave me the look they always give at the beginning of an interview, a look mixed up of challenge, boredom, worry, confidence and, if you're lucky, concentration. The look that tells you the interview must begin. It's a horrible moment. Have you got it fixed what you want to get out of your subject? Do you know enough to help the conversation move into the right places with an inspiring rhythm? Can you stand an argument? Are you both in the right mood to take this seriously, and yet not? Does the person opposite believe in you? What are you going to talk about? At this point you wish you'd written down a list of questions that you could just tick off, one by one. But the best interviews don't come from planning. You just have to trip over the first question. Once you've tripped up, the next problem is to ease out into a kind of vacuum where the only thing that matters in the world are the words of the conversation, the strange pressure between the two of you that is somehow summoned up, the belief that you are digging right into the truth of the person's private vision. At that horrible moment at the beginning of the interview for no reason at all other than pride and the nervous twitch, you have to be on the verge of discovery.

Jones waited. I tripped.

Bragg started off with India, how it had been treated on film and televison. I affected my interested look in case the camera caught me: I was on the front row, desperately hoping I wouldn't have one of those silly attacks where your limbs suddenly shoot out, and so elbow Sarah Brightman in the ribs. My fine intoxication was beginning to wear off a touch, and no drink was allowed in the studio as recording dragged on. I'd forgotten what it was I was going to say – mustn't forget the middle-class saturation, the business dominance, the return of a new underground. What was that bit about ''pleasant?'' I started to go over new things to say in my head. There was no shape to my commentary, and all sorts of observations started to race around. Come on Melvyn. I'm ready. I'm going to go on about how a lot of the new pop stars who've triumphed these last few years aren't even very interesting as people, how the boring ones are taking over. But is that positive enough? I don't care. Just say what you have to say. Make the point at the end that it's going to get better, thus emphasising the inevitable illusion of pop. But do explain how in an attempt to create a fluid colourful drama of pop, magazines like *Smash Hits* and *Number One* have contributed to a rubbing away of life and imagination. They've allowed a forced glamour, an uncritical drenching of consumers, that ultimately mocks the deviance and suddenness of *what pop really is*. What pop really is? Should you take it for granted that this audience will know as much as you about *what pop really is*? Don't worry, they'll catch it from your anger and enthusiasm, realise straight away that pop is much more than a cackle of tish and a big bunch of statistics. Here's a good one, remember this – the industry, the system, the business, the pop media, whatever name is given to the organizations and events that have fastened popular music to the multi-media fabric, have cost pop its uniqueness . . . no, I'll never remember that. Just say, pop rests in pieces. Too much going on, too little that's charged up. But are you meant to be just isolating a few things that happened this year, the ones that make sense to the people who read Robin Denselow in the *Guardian* and Richard Williams in *The Times*, making subtle suggestions as to their significance, and suggesting that it all just keeps rolling on and it's not worth getting worked up about it, it's only what it is, and it's just something that takes up the times of lots of people? Am I meant to just take it for what it is, and work at some of those details in an expert post-Simon Frith way? Is there a place here for despair, disillusion, faith, mixed feelings? Do I just show off some wit and settle into a rut? Hurry up, Melvyn. Catch me now, and watch me go. You might get your money's worth. Any longer and I might get stuck into that terrible problem of dismissing Wham!, Sade and Billy Joel, saying how it could be this much better, in these different ways, and then have to discuss how an individual who takes in the music of Lou Reed and Captain Beefheart is actually going to get a chance for a better quality of life. That's really getting stuck. But can I damn the hugely successful new bland wave without arguing why it is a disturbing thing, why such colossal boredom should be eradicated; can I celebrate the kind of noises I want and need and say that what I get out of this music is morally, aesthetically, intellectually superior to the sound of Dire Straits? Won't it just be taken as one man's opinion and another's disgust and so what really, so what? Perhaps I should slyly adjust the sociological rock writer's detached reason, and analyse how the TV channels and radio stations are saturated with the most calculated and forgiving pop music, and announce that such developments cannot be healthy. I don't have to justify why I say the music on television and radio is predominantly banal, the coverage so locked into release schedules and so one huge advertising sham – one being the cool analyst, they will take it for granted that what I say is for real and as good liberals express disdain at the rampant mindlessness of rock. But won't that just confirm their prejudices; they won't see that you're criticising the structure, the formats, putting pop up as a symptom of a nation's accelerating reduction . . . and that attempting to fight their way through this controlling of the young by a huge herd of hi-tech hippies are explosive, entrancing pop groups who could stimulate and intensify feelings. If Melvyn came to me now, I might just about hit it spot on. The point is this system, that I honestly haven't got time to define right now, is happy to make the successes bigger, and pop a predictable channel, by swamping everything with more of the same and then some; and it's a crying shame that whatever it is we're involved in, we all want it to be mobile and surprising and something that allows the individual to be asserted, and even though pop is only what it is – and some of us might make it out to be more than that – it must still be better for it to be irreverent and more active than a stationary lump of pleasant. There! Surely the right mixture of the academic and the anguished. I'm ready Melvyn. Really.

Do you ever want people to know where you came from?

The interview had begun. I'd asked the first question. Was it a good question? Better than some I could think of. Where could we go from here? I climbed into her answer, all ready to work it out. Was it going to be the right question, one that when linked with all the others and all the answers would give me Grace the person, the creation, the worker, the fool, the Grace in love with herself or scared of the future or confused with the world or the laziest of them all? What was Grace and what had she experienced in the past, and was that nothing when set against what she is now and what she can be used for?

I asked the second question.

So tell me about your parents?

And she did. Then she talked about her grandfather. I was interviewing Grace Jones, trying to push her about my way.

The way you're talking about your parents, it seems they passed on some kind of wisdom to you. Would that be so?

In what way did it fuck you up?

You threw yourself on to the floor?

What did you learn for yourself?

What do you mean by the spice of life?

Have you got used to yourself?

What you have had to live with?

Were you scared when you first took LSD?

You floated on a cloud?

Did you ever come down?

Grace was now 18. I'd pushed her there easily, learnt vague details about her childhood and her first set of risks, her running away from home. We hadn't, though, got anywhere near the weightlessness of the best interviews. A little bit of despair settled into me, and I knew it would grow.

Bragg turned out of my way and to the year's films. In the middle distance I could hear the sound of satisfaction. As for me, I wasn't so drunk, and I wasn't so confident, and I'd forgotten everything that I was going to say. Let's go over it all again. I know, a cracking speech celebrating myself, thus highlighting the crass egocentricities of rock, clamouring on about that book you've always wanted to compile: the book that will be the seventh book of any use to the happy, hard-working goods-consuming citizen who seriously wonders about the wealth and wither of rock; the book that will match hard facts with ungovernable rage and be some kind of mark of the spirit. I'll be the salesman, thus emphasising one of the great factors of rock as mass market, and turn on a great show, to symbolise the flamboyance of pop. Don't stumble. No mumbling. For those who succumb to an interest in what popular music has been up to in the few years through to 1984, I am working on a book that will tell all without being too certain or too grand. The seventh rock book of any use, following the works of Lester Bangs, Richard Meltzer, George Tremlett, Nik Cohn. The trites and the heights of pop falling into smashing passions, scattered remarkably by a shy, aesthetic youth who began by interviewing Marc Bolan and Steve Harley and ended up telling Jerry Garcia he should get a hair-cut, Mick Jagger he should quit, and every rock star that wore a head band and banged his chest that he talked too much. From a patch in pop between punk's last stamp protest and the professional begging of the guilt-edged Band Aid, all the stuff about the last era of rock before it became for most people just a long list for Guinness, a decorative lightness, a mechanical rite lacking conflict and contrariness. Someone in the audience would publish this, or turn it into a musical! The seventh book of any use would emerge out of a time in pop when there was still pretence, hope, that the imagination could roam freely and without inhibitions. And that time must come again . . . calm down; it is still something that is just what it is: a series of happenings and existing parts that can be about the darkness of life, the daftness of life, the love of life . . . is that going too far? Think about it. Not long ago the economic value of the newly cherished youth market was not so harshly defined. Or is that just me being naïve? Go for the vivid . . . if it's always been such a business prison, then it seems the possibility of passing any Discontent, Abandonment, Extremity through this capitalist equipment is getting less and less. But should I go on and on about lost opportunities that might be imaginary anyway? Maybe what I'm here for is to convey some sense of why so many people are fascinated by pop, why they get so wrapped up and turned over – then I could drift over casually into where it goes wrong and why even that still remains something of fascination. Rock music is just here to give lots of people something to talk about! That's it. It must be my turn. No, it's Theatre. Shit. I'll never be this close to it. Mustn't forget. Rock gives us something to talk about, and that's why there's as much complaint as there is compliment, as much gossip as there is music. That's why there are so many music papers. ROCK MUSIC IS HERE TO GIVE US SOMETHING TO TALK ABOUT. Easy, when Melvyn comes to me, there's a great opening line: well, there's lots to talk about concerning rock this year, why else did someone invent the compact disc and advertise the new Sade album on television? Might get a laugh. But is it just a bit cynical? All this effort, swindling, submission, triumph, success, misfortune, just so that we can all chatter? It makes it easier for me, I don't have to get caught out. There'll never be coherence, completion, consistency; it's just one maddening crush, a jungle of pose, and nobody's any better or worse out of it than they've ever been or ever will be. Not bad. And then of course, the romantic side of it – that you must always grasp the provocative, gasp for delight, so really what you're talking about in rock is that you like this you hate that you win some you forget some you want that you need this and you know better than anyone else. Is it a bit *simple*? Too complex? Too certain? Too ambiguous? Get here Melvyn, before all this is lost for ever. Remember – rock music is here to give us something to talk about. That can include everything and nothing, the excitement, the dismay. I think in there it might even explain the problem of ageing, and why pop music has to be allowed to develop as something more than just the tool of businessmen. Rock music is about growing old? Is that where I got to? And in 1984 what it meant to be growing old was Dire Straits? Too pat. What's new? Just something else . . . to talk about? Read all about it.

If it's not age that you take much notice of, what kind of marks in time, or on the land, do you refer to?
Different romances?
Different careers?
Difficulties?
What would you risk for happiness?
Why did you want to act – the ultimate achievement for you, you don't have to be yourself?
It's a good escape for you?
Do you act all the time?
Do you act when you walk into a room full of people?
With tenure?
What do you think people's main preconception of you is?
What year was that?
Or do you just wait it out?
Amazonian? Bigger than life? A shining example?
People perceive you as something to worship?
Are you as common as muck?
Does it surprise you to hear that?
Do you look down on other people?

Do you feel sympathetic?
So you keep quiet about it in order to let it happen?
So are you saying that the only reality for you is yourself?
The centre of the universe?
You'd say so.
The religious element?
What happens during that time?
So you need other people in order to make what you do exist?
What kind of things embarrass you?
Why do you do what you do instead of lying for money or killing for glory?
Or do you lie for money?

Then it occurred to me, if pop's so exhilarating and life can never be the same again, what's happened to those people who bought the Who, Hendrix, Stones records in the '60s as surely something more than an investment for nostalgia – are they buying Sade, Phil Collins and Dire Straits? Is this the fatal flaw, or the reason we must never get complacent? If Melvyn, chatting now with Sarah, came to me next I would be in a muddle, having thought of loads to say, having forgotten it all, and getting bogged down in issues that only really matter to the truly anxious. He'd ask me what it was like for rock this year, and I would say – what has happened to the individuals who bought Captain Beefheart's ''Trout Mask Replica'' in 1968? Are they now listening to Foreigner, thinking Steven Spielberg's an example to us all, or what? Or are they reading Chekhov and listening to Cecil Taylor? And what if they are? Shouldn't they be out and about rushing through real dissent and independent research? Or is rock music the stuff that creates the new nostalgia that helps us settle into the control state with no care for protest? Rock is just about creating the stuff of nostalgia: additional trivia. If I said all that it would be *really* impressive. An audience would be moved nowhere. ''The stuff of nostalgia'' – edited straight out. Too confusing. If he comes to me now, I'm lost. Worrying about what actually happens to people after they've listened to Tim Buckley or read T. S. Eliot. Do we want rock to be better just to make people more *sensitive?* Sounds a little destructive to me. Have to stop fretting so much. If he comes to me now, just act casual. Don't appear lost. Well, Paul, what happened to rock in 1984? ROCK SHOULD BE THERE TO MAKE PEOPLE FEEL MORE INTENSE, EVEN CLEVER, AND IN 1984 IT WAS JUST ONE LONG JINGLE. Calm down. Weren't you thinking before about *talking* . . . Things happen in rock so that we may talk. Rock is an accumulation of competition. *What is it actually doing?*. Melvyn wanders past me, off over there, to Martin Amis or someone. I wipe the froth from my mind. Act casual. It must be my turn next. I start again to prepare my ''script''. Maybe I should just stand up and dance.

I suppose it's all to do with snobbery, Melvyn, and a set of images that bewitch, and begin again. And, of course, it's about types of ambition. Some things that happened this year you had to think about, some things you didn't. Rock: it's a form of life. This year there was undeniably a lot of waste. A massive investment in pop groups by record companies – a lot of that due to the hysterical expansion in this thing 'the promotional video' – means that records have to sell more and more copies to make ''real money''. This has led to a standardisation of product. It means that record companies are becoming more persistent and persuasive in the ways that they demand the attention of their audiences. Promising worlds and not even giving away cheap magic. The 1980s teen pop magazines, glossed into a daze with their hippy parodies of teenage excitement, further helped the pop record be less and less of a magical property and more a routine exercise. It was a year when record companies began to discover the beauty of market research, and acted accordingly. More colour photographs of pop stars posing as masters of a forbidden power were published than ever before. There was the script. It made me sound like one of those interchangeable writers in the Virgin Yearbook, professors of rock. Thank God I forgot that script immediately and started to panic again. I cannot be a professor of rock, Melvyn, and so instead must talk about the easy satisfaction that today's pop consumers are accustomed to. Does that sound like a professor? If he comes to me now I'll just have to say that, you know, the truth can be suppressed in many different ways and must be expressed in many different ways, and I've only got four minutes, and time flows on, for if it did not, it wouldn't be much of a gold prospect for those who sit at the boardroom tables. Applause.

Grace stared hard at me, waiting for the next question. I'd found out some things, but had she? That's often when the interview begins to push sense, when you feel that the other person is thinking things for more or less the first time. Are they hearing the questions? Grace was tending to go through the motions, toy with the questions, tease, prop up the same old answers. I'd have to get her to take this seriously. I'd have to get her to realise that a success for me – a truth! a laugh! one new value! – would be a success for her too. Anything else would be a waste of time.

She waited for the next question. This is a *difficult* moment. A good, inspiring atmosphere has been created, you're getting to the point where it can become intense and satisfying; the person opposite is starting to believe in you and one weak question can send it all tumbling down. You dread having to go through *the trip* once more. If you fumble or, worse, admit that you've dried up, you're finished. Pause. The subject stares, losing whatever confidence in you he or she had, fidgets. You must not lose them. You have to pull them back before they think of things beyond the interview, things more trivial and pressing, that are of no use to you. It's at moments like this that you ask how old they are, or what have they been reading lately. Such questions can ruin everything. The next question must snatch both of you back into a hard concentration. You have to get them with something forceful yet delicate, take them gently back into "the vacuum", cut them off. This is the moment. . . .

She waited for the next question.

The applause died down. Melvyn came towards me. My turn? No. Sir Michael Tippett, who was to talk about his latest, immensely civilised work. Sir Michael had been late arriving for the recording, as had one or two other made up experts. There had been a student demonstration at a number of the Thames' bridges, clogging central London traffic. Bragg had suggested that it might not be possible to complete all the recording, but everything was apparently running to schedule. During the show, Sir Michael had asked me what my business was. I quaked ever so slightly with that embarrassment adults often possess at being associated, and so seriously as well, with pop music. Sat next to this great man, who could perceive possibilities of a profound nature without succumbing to any ashamed worry, who could celebrate and confront the imagination with stirring inevitability, made me feel a bit of a twit. The more I gnawed at what I might say to Melvyn, the more I became conscious of the steady Tippett on my right. "I accidentally saw a pop programme on television the other day," he told me. "The Whistle Test, I think it's called" – embarrassed again at the show's daft name, as if I'd thought it up myself. "Mmmmm . . . three very odd looking little fellows dancing about. . . ." Bronski Beat I admitted, immediately deciding against trying to explain or justify, as you sometimes feel you must about something you're obsessed with to an outsider. "Luckily the television set was turned over for me – Cagney and Lacey. I much preferred that." I gamely grinned, and began to wonder whether I could constructively engage Sir Michael in a conversation about the energy of pop.

You see, Sir Michael, rock music is much closer to the line at the front when it comes to the urgency of enlivening people's souls and dealing with their doubts. You write that "imagination and desire nourish our ever-renewed hope" and it's something I completely agree with, and such things can come through rock; because of its huge audience it is important that we demand an uncompromising, dramatic drive from the music, and angrily despair when business considerations seem to demolish its chances. When I get embarrassed about being involved in rock music, it is because of the surface restrictions, the useless censorship wrapped around it by all sorts of collapsed, mad controllers. Rock can be such a potent combination of innocence and experience, and be the best form for its audience at conjuring up the times, the lost times, what can be, what must be. It's less abstract than your music, it can express collective feelings, dislodge, determine, refresh. It can be just as much a *renewal* as any art-form. Who is to say that the experience of listening to a piece of great pop music is any less enriching than anything else? Cannot the idiosyncrasies and affirmation of rock at its very best, crash through the impersonal exploitation that helps it come into being? You say that everybody needs to dream, that this need seems to be satisfied by the simplicities of popular art, but that behind the mass demand for entertainment lies somewhere the desire for something more important . . . but surely within rock there is someone searching for the new language, who respects the permanent, who understands *the dream* . . . who is acutely aware of what it means to be human. We're all susceptible to the same chaos, the same violence, the same unpredictability, and whoever understands and uses this, in rock or not, will come up with something direct, strong and inspiring. As much as rock helps create this age of mediocrity, it opposes it as well. Good and bad in everything, everywhere, Sir Michael, I would say, half playfully, half in earnest. What my business is, you know, is that rock music, poisoned by mediocrity more than anything because it is right there at the dead centre of money-making hypocrisy and hysteria, can be as living and as combative as anything.

And Sir Michael would turn to me and say, it is what it is, it comes and it goes, it sweeps round the edges and, my, haven't you got a lot to say about it. If it's my turn after Sir Michael, I might have to take the easy way out, praise Sade Inc. for the ravishing skill of the product, respect the Phil Collins versatility and pretend that all the rock professors' sayings are too complicated for me.

Meanwhile, Sir Michael talks to Melvyn. "I have gone on writing because I must, whether society has felt music valuable or needful. And I know that my true function within a society which embraces all of us, is to continue an age-old tradition, fundamental to our civilisation, which goes back into prehistory and will go forward into the unknown future. This tradition is to create images from the depths of the imagination and to give them form whether visual, intellectual or musical. For it is only through images that the inner world communicates at all. Images of the past, shapes of the future. Images of vigour for a decadent period, images of calm for one too violent, images of reconciliation for worlds torn by division. And in an age of mediocrity and shattered dreams, images of abounding, generous, exuberant beauty."

I'm moved to tears and it's still not my turn.

What are you thinking when you look at a rainbow?
Go on, tell me.
Tell me about the protective shell.
What does punishment do to you?
It's only words.
Are you guilty?
You don't seem to struggle at all with things like self-pity?
Did you ever imagine that would happen?
What did you feel when you were offered the role in the James Bond film?
In what way is doing a James Bond film a form of creative growth?
Like a cartoon?
You can control that?
What can't you stand about women?
Aren't you guilty of that sometimes?
Revenge?
What kind of things?
Just that?
Do you ever blush?
Can't you ignore that?
Being adored and worshipped?
What things do you adore and worship?
What gives you love and life?
Would you hate to feel cheated of experience?
Metaphysical as well?
What's the hardest work you've ever had to do?
None of it?
Where did you get all these thoughts anyway?
You've been absolutely dead lucky?
How many times a day?
What will you be doing when you're 75?
And taking it off?

Does Grace Jones have a sense of humour?
What's your favourite joke?
And then what?
Really?
So what?
I see. And that's that?
What?
Something to look forward to.
And proud to be alive?

. . . it's all a question of loyalties really, and then there are the wet dreams, the dry runs, forgeries, optimistic beliefs, the missed opportunities and oh just imagine each and every one of the first off surrealists spitting in their graves at all that runny stuff in the middle of the videos . . . oh, sorry Melvyn, just thinking aloud . . . when is it going to be my turn? We've gone through the lot now, haven't we? Except Opera. So I'm going to be the last. Supply the punchline. To get to the other side. Sure thing. But what am I going to say? "I'm afraid I'm not going to hear what you've got to say," explains Sir Michael to me, "I've got to be off now." What a shame. "Good luck." Yeah. We must face our predicament with realism and honesty? Bit melodramatic. Record sales were up 300% this year? Bit Paul Gambaccini. Off goes Sir Michael, leaving me in my mind and wherever else going over and over what I'm going to say.

I suppose popular music as some unreliable, well-rubbed folk representation of the state of the western upset acted out 1984 just as it should, Melvyn. Spoilt, greedy, trying to hide real fears and annoyances under a brash of quick steps and smiling eyes. If pop represents the times, well, look, a surface affluence and bravado, a secondary blur of untidy activity, and underneath, the knifepoint testing all our throats. So what we get is the brand newness of the '50s, the fancy ringing abandon of the '60s, the convention and contempt of the '70s, the crooked self-control of the '80s. If pop previously for its bombing ambitions and conspicuous cynicisms at least left things open to question and went some way to demanding excessive, unlikely responses, now the music is trying to tell people to shut up, with a last rush of Aid to the head, as if the straight handing out of cash can cover up a whole phenomenon of self-advertisement, blinding glamour, elitist imaginings and cracked principles. This recent, well, passionate, guilt-on-a-banner outburst deserves close examination. Penetrating this booby-trapped thicket of celebrity, fame, ego-moves, opposing all this stubborn commitment and neon honesty is obviously not good for one's health. But I'm prepared to appear slime just so that I can say that rock as a collective should feel guilty because of its self-congratulation, its reckless certainty and consistent narrowness of concerns and speculations. The fact that it generates such appalling amounts of money that it can now divert a tiny part of it towards what everyone is told is worldwide justice should not shame it as much as its betrayal of success. Rock, now that it has such a booming impact on public life, has squeezed out all the bits that could be there that would quicken our sense of time or alter the significance of events. I feel, Melvyn, that rock's subtle, enormous influence – that perhaps it once had in intangible areas – can create an interest, fascination and identification with the liveliest aspects of one's time and place. It's all imitation and petrification these days, except for those contorting themselves on the fringes and being made to sound and look more and more shrunken by the up-to-date supertechnical skills and techniques. What we need is illumination and action, rather than melodious consolation. And one more thing, distinguished audience – a big cheque, which barely covers the callous manipulators of commercial taste with a veil of contemporary humanity, cannot make up for the way that imagination is being buried these days, and what should concern the buttery liberals of rock is not hand-outs and self-reliefs but to find ways, through vigour, pertinence, and excitement, to charge up its captive audience, to forge self-belief and determination so that we can more and more question our masters, the masters that make the muck that is apparently to be cleared away overnight with paper money. Melvyn, I believe my uncertainties are more powerful than their certainties and I am speaking like this not to hide from mayhem but to try and find a way to truly confront it and . . . what are those huge hairy muppets doing dancing in front of me?

Surely I was next, not Dance. But no. For some reason this quaint, costumed dance routine, which is the finale of Bragg's Arts Review of the Year, is happening now. Well, the show is being recorded, they must be doing me next, editing later. That'll make it even harder for me, having to talk in front of this audience after they think it's all over. At least I've almost got something worked out for me to say. Responsible, yet quietly controversial. Nice. The Muppets are flopping to their finale. Here we go. The flippant and the glorious.

But no. "I'm sorry," explains Melvyn to the audience, as I work out a killer opening line. "We've only got the studio booked for 2½ hours, and because we were so late starting, we've got no time left. Apologies to Paul Morley, who you won't be able to hear."

Shit. The audience look around for Paul Morley. I do as well, as the buzz of what I'm going to say speeds faster through my head. It seems rock music didn't happen in 1984. Everyone stops looking for Paul Morley and moves off to the hospitality room. Shit. Almost the entire history of pop ran through my brain, forgotten for ever.

As I walk along the corridors of London Weekend Television, in my mind it's still my turn next. What's up, Paul? Well, Mel, there's loads of these people, idealistic, eccentric or just dumb plain. They earn their living in an unusual way, manufacturing music, singing songs. Some are worth bothering with, some are a waste of your time. Most of them talk a lot about themselves; they're often asked to open their mouths. Then, Melvyn turns away from me, looks into a camera. . . . "And to find out what's it's nearly all about, let's hear them talk."

Thanks, Melvyn. I couldn't think of anything to say anyway.

The interview was over. I'd asked the final question. Was it a good interview? Did it get through to Grace? Was it an intoxicating mixture of scepticism and benevolent curiosity? Was it almost a piece of fiction? Will the world know more about this unusual individual? Did you reach that uncanny, disorientating point where you *float*, right over the edge of a revealing all-round contemplation? Was it just a cover up? What appeared to be the trouble? Were you satisfied? Is it that much clearer?

Who can tell. It was an interview. It's all to be continued.

QUENTIN CRISP

June 6, 1981
Thus the action can be
likened to an odyssey
or pilgrimage. . . .

THE VOICE is a rarefied power of virtue and veneration, a sovereign creation that you could never imagine bickering or whimpering or indeed staying quiet.

It is a voice I first heard ingeniously represented by the actor John Hurt in the classic television portrayal of Quentin Crisp's life-so-far, *The Naked Civil Servant*; a voice I have heard many times since on radio and TV and lately record.

QUENTIN CRISP greets me at the front door of a terraced house in Chelsea – **"You are the music paper?"** – and I hear the voice for the first time neither disembodied nor alluringly distant. It is no disappointment.

"Years ago," it frostily sings, **"my agent said to me you must expect to become part of the fantasies of strangers. I said ho ho ho, but in some mysterious way you do. People very kindly say that in my early life I showed a great deal of courage, but I was actually stuck with it. There was no way I could behave as an ordinary mortal.**

"There is no sense of revenge now that I am accepted, because in order to revenge myself on the world I would have to think that I had been treated unfairly. If you think you've been treated unfairly you must think you deserve better, whereas I think I deserve nothing.

"I'm only glad that the world is kind to me. How can I say how grateful I am? My attitude is not 'oh you're too late now, I offered you my love 50 years ago and what did you do . . . I'm certainly not going out into the world now, I shall stay right here'. My attitude is that 'things' have changed – these things are nameless, there shouldn't really be fashions in morality but there undoubtedly are – and so I've emerged and looked around and everything seems to be all right. The war seems to be over after I've been in my shelter for 50 years. So I've got out.

"And so now that I'm out the best I can do is to seem grateful. Never to take either my wages or the friendliness of the world for granted, this is the only return I can give. I must make sure that never a day goes by without me acknowledging that I live by kind permission of the universe."

The room in Chelsea is exactly as I imagined it, and therefore it is exactly how you imagined it: not sombre or sad but simply splendidly slovenly. The dust collects around the edges of the room like down, paint on the walls peels with a flourish – Crisp removes housework from the list of life's troubles. **"You must first remove the unreal problems. . . ."**

Crisp sits opposite me, an unhurried, immaculate, fluorescent purple vision set in sharp relief to the soft-focus anachronism of the room.

Quentin Crisp rarely has conversations. He has interviews, especially now that he is promoting a book, a record and a stage show. I say to him that people already have the opportunity to know everything about Quentin Crisp that they wish to know; another set of interviews is perhaps unnecessary – and certainly he will supply similar chunks of answers.

"Somebody said to my agent, why does he always say the same things? And my agent said because they always ask the same questions. But then if I was the Prime Minister I would be asked the same questions, or if I was the Archbishop of Canterbury. You try to vary the answers a little. The last person who came was from a magazine for women, so the answers tended to be slightly cosier. But they're the same answers!"

You adapt, depending on the interviewer and eventual readership?

"You try and adapt. You hear yourself saying something which is a quotation from an obscure poet and you think that really won't do . . . when you're being interviewed on television you try to think what the interviewer will want the interview to be like. If you are on Mr Cavett's show you're in the entertainment business. But you can be in an interview where you are in the human interest bracket, and then you must not be funny all the time, you must be funny occasionally. A brave laugh!"

You imagined this interview would be for young people?

"Yes. When we spoke about young people and music I thought that this is what you had come to hear, and so I thought, well I'll go on about this instead of thinking I don't want to talk about it. It's the least I can do. You bothered to come here. If you were a friend I would think, what would they like to talk about? I would ask you 'And how is your allotment coming along?' It's like being a music hall comedian: you say the lines the audience hopes to hear, and indeed you are being provoked to say the lines the audience hopes to hear. I mean, everybody must now be used to the fact I don't clean my room,

I must admit I felt a little uneasy. If I had heard how Jaz had let Youth know that I'd arrived, I wouldn't have bothered with the interview. I would have run away. The photographer, neutral as always in these situations, told me later what was said – what was said with great delight: *"The entertainment has arrived!"*

The entertainment. Me. Trapped in a room with no view, stuck between two musicians who did not like me. What had I done? I was a little concerned. What a way to start.

"Sit down in that corner," says the photographer, neutral as always in these situations. "Are you asking me or telling me?" murmurs the musician, innocuously. "Which corner?" He looks around the room, eyes twinkling with amusement. "That corner! On the floor! Jesus, do you think I'll ever be able to get up again?"

He sighs good naturedly and plonks on to the floor underneath a lamp, spreading his legs out. "Hiyeeeaah," he waves, mildly embarrassed. "This is for what paper? *New Musical Express*? . . . Yeah, I remember. That's pretty amazing. I don't remember much. Memory is the first thing to go." What a thing to go.

Someone answered the phone for me. "It's a Mr Frish wanting you," I was told. Yeah? I picked up the phone, not too curious about this Mr Frish. Yeah? A mad dodgy Scotsman started screaming at me, something like Russ Abbott in a midi-kilt drowning in an acid-bath, something like a joke Scots soccer fan who'd lost his marbles, his bagpipes, his tartan can. This ranting Scotsman was pretty rude to me, and I quickly found out that his name was "fucking Fish".

Apparently I should have been

but never a TV interview goes by without it being referred to. And I say the same things!"

Could people get fed up with you?

"They could. But the public likes you to be predictable."

"BLIND WITH mascara and dumb with lipstick, I paraded the streets of Pimlico . . . I wore a fringe so deep that it completely obscured the way ahead. This hardly mattered. There were others to look where I was going."

Quentin Crisp is 73 and has lived in the room in Chelsea for 38 years. **"Mercifully I never made fun of old people when I was young, so I was never scared of growing old. My health is better than it might have been, there's just the rheumatism, and I also discovered when it's towards the end of the run, and I say this on stage, you can overact appallingly. This is actually put in a joke form, but it is true."**

Most old people do not exploit this.

"They don't exploit it, so if somebody says I feel I am growing old and I haven't got a style, I say to them being old is your style. Indulge the fact that nothing can be expected of you. When you are young you are always thinking, suppose I take the wrong path, in years to come I will end up fifty miles away from where I want to be. But now you only have a few yards to go you can do as you damn well please."

For 35 years he was an art school model, and for 50 years the object of hostility from scared moralists and irritated bullies. What he understates as his **"ambiguous appearance"** was not to annoy the world but **"to tell passers-by what they passionately wanted to know. If I were on a desert island I would merely have wanted to decorate myself. I was just being me. I've lived entirely by consent; however, being entirely individual is being selfish. Had I been born today I suppose I could have been less selfish because there is greater permissiveness."**

Writer Miles Chapman observed that "he spent 40 or 50 years in the subversive guise of a sociological leper, flouting the conventional canons of good taste, making his make-up, floppy fedora and other limp-wristed accessories into a cross between a strait-jacket and a suit of armour. He imprisoned, chastised and martyred some parts of himself so that other bits could blossom into the orchidacious creation that was impersonated so accurately on television by John Hurt."

Crisp took over from Hurt, playing the respectable and rhapsodic hallucination that the world began to adore. Crisp received the adulation, the wonder, with the same grace with which he absorbed the hostility and paranoid curiosity. Encouraged by an implausible fame, Crisp offered the world his gift.

"It was inevitable that I would be noticed. What was not inevitable was that I would be rewarded for making myself conspicuous. That is the remarkable thing."

He went on to the stages of the world to describe how 50 years of rejection and humiliation had contributed to his philosophy of style, how style was order. Style had been his sustenance, his insulation. Style is at the heart of his diplomacy.

"Fashion", says Quentin Crisp, **"is never having to decide who you are. Style is deciding who you are and being able to perpetuate it."**

This is, among other things, the greatest piece of rock criticism ever. It all falls into place. Sting is style; Steve Strange is fashion. David Bowie is style; Gary Numan is fashion. Bette Midler style; Hazel O'Connor fashion.

"When you look into your soul and find that you are vulgar then vulgar you must be! Nothing can be worse than cultivating a certain refinement to present yourself to people of refinement when really your natural medium is to be your horrible self. Style is not to me elegance, style is not to me stylishness, it is simply setting it all together, arranging it all so that it tells the world what you have to say. It is a constant striving to unify utterly all aspects of your nature."

Crisp's style slices right through the notion of "taste".

"I don't like the idea of good music, or good books, or good anything. Taste is something that I deplore. When you hear the voice of Vincent Price you know exactly what he will look like. I don't know how he managed it. But he has! Vincent Price has a pronounced style and this is miles beyond whether he is a good actor or not."

It is his strategy of style, the quality of his survival and his conversion of curiosity, the self control, the splendour of his venture, the complexity of his prosperity, the ingratiating candour of his narrative, the shameless manner with which he has melted into an allusive caricature of himself, that guarantees Crisp a certain kind of immunity and even perhaps a pale immorality. The voice is an inscription etched deep into his style.

AN IMPORTANT element of one's style is a conviction of self.

"I've said to audiences, if you were alone on a desert island you would need your life-style like never before if you were going to live. I'm sure there would be people who would die not of starvation, or of exposure, but because they would become lost. They wouldn't know who they were."

How do you explain what it is to know who you are?

"I think you have to go into the subject very thoroughly, and I think you have to abandon your parents' teaching – 'you shouldn't spend a lot of time thinking about yourself, try thinking about others'. I think you must spend a long time thinking about yourself, and you must not allow yourself to pass into a dream. Somebody said to me your view of life is narcissistic, and I replied Mr Narcissus fell in love with himself and when you're in love with someone you not only condone their faults, you idealise them. The faults become all *sweet*. This is what you must not do. You may have to embrace your weaknesses, but you must never *indulge* them. First of all your style is for yourself, but there is a relationship between the world and the stylist. I can only put it by saying that people are to the stylist what water is to a swimmer. They are the element in which he exercises his talent."

Anyone is capable of developing a style.

"Anyone can do it. It won't be the same as mine, nor is it my *faintest* wish that it be so. Oh yes, they've only got to think about it, which some people would rather *die* than do . . . I'm sure there are lots of other stylists, but they don't go on about it so. They just do it. I make it clear on stage that I'm not asking you to be like me, I'm only asking you to arrive at yourself in the way that I've arrived at it."

Do people put moral pressure on you because you reject so-called important things to worry about?

"When I was in Australia a man on tele-vision said, 'Tonight is cold and there are Aborigines or whatever they were out there and they are very cold and some will perhaps die from the cold. Do you really think that they should develop their style?" I said

immediately, I am dealing with problems which by world standards would be considered trivial. Of course, I know and everybody else knows there are people that just have so little in life that to get through the day is sufficient and so I would always accept that I am talking about something which everybody could get through their lives without. Yes, so that is a way of making a moral criticism.

"Half of the other people considered important I have to admit I genuinely don't consider important at all. Politics I consider a *total* waste of time, except for politicians. As soon as you realise that teaching is for teachers, preaching is for preachers and poli-tics is for politicians, then it all falls into place. So that, no, I would never vote, but then again I have to be wary because if I lived in a place where the two governments that will come without voting, fascism or commu-nism, existed, then I would be shot. So then I would vote. As I stood before the firing line I would say *hold everything*! I'll vote."

You've said that not only is politics a mistake, but also music. Is this merely an entertaining announcement or can you explain?

"Well, it's certainly what I believe. I can safely say that music is a mistake, which I think I can explain. In all other tribes music is a means of arousing and uniting the male population, usually to face a disaster, fre-quently a war. Now we have the male popu-lation aroused and excited and no war. So you have what is called soccer violence, because what are they to do with all this excitement that is aroused! Now, people don't listen to the world at all. They go around shut off from the world, and you can't help saying of what are you afraid? In the time of a woman called Miss Shapiro, which is before your time, as far as I know she sang two songs, and one of these was 'Walking Back To Happiness', and whatever you did or wherever you went you heard those words. So we all become one and we lose the feeling that we are in the world."

If the world went silent tomorrow the violence would cease.

"*Silence*!! And they would have to live in it. They would have to have *thoughts* and they would have to *speak*! There would be people in hospital suffering withdrawal symptoms – but they would recover and they wouldn't be drawing on this common nameless energy which they can't really use in any way.

"The movies are a means by which we think we shall rule the world. People try to extract from the movies, however absurdly, something that will put them in command of life, and this is good. Music does nothing. Music arouses the emotions and the emotions are a mistake. . . ."

Because they're not constant.

"Yes, because while you can still say I don't know what came over me, you're not really a complete person. 'And then I went really mad!' All these are confessions, they are not boasts."

What replaces emotion?

"You have reason. You know what you are doing. And better *still* you know what you're going to do and you do it."

What about outside forces?

"You can't ignore outside forces altogether, but you calculate that you arrive at most situations with your kit ready. If you are a burglar you have your lock openers with you all the time, you look through them and you open the door. If you're an emotional person, you arrive, you rattle the handles, nothing happens, you tear the handles off, you beat on the door, and you never get in. So I think you have to learn to survive your emotions, which you do by feigning not to have them and in the end you don't."

And you will be cold. . . .

"That's right. You will be cold and *splendid*!! The idea that the word warm and all those phrases are things of praise is a mistake, because you have to arrive at that inside yourself which is permanent, which is beyond fashion, fad and if possible beyond even emotion. So that you are able to say, come what may, including *death,* I now know what part of myself I will call upon for comfort, strength, whatever it is. This you can only find by abandoning yourself from this reliance on being human, emotions! . . . to me this is the answer."

This is not to deny enthusiasm or exhilaration?

"No. They're not quite the same. In fact it is even possible to be hysterical but not emotional. I'm very easily excited by notions, ideas, and I can quite imagine someone saying don't get so worked up. But this is not quite what I would mean by emotion."

Presumably some discipline is important.

"You must be very disciplined about your-self and very indulgent with others, which you can afford to be. You can in an indulgent tone suggest that people discipline themselves. Yes, so you need to be self-disciplined. But thousands of people would say that I live the life of a self-confessed *slob.* I sit around, I can't do any of the things that other people think are absolutely necessary, but the discipline takes the form of trying to make myself accountable all the time."

What was the force behind your accumulation of knowledge, wisdom, logic whatever?

"The need for self-preservation, I should think. I was always the one among many. If you are an object of ridicule, or notice, you will in the end ask yourself, what is it that I am doing? Who am I? – And am I willing to pay the price of being whatever it is that I am? So then you have to find the words to justify or at least explain, and then later you find the words to make entertaining what people started to find irritating.

"The real key is that everybody has to learn to do deliberately what they used to do by mistake. This is *forced* upon you. If you don't move along with all the boys at school because you feel, well I'm doing this just because we're all doing it, and you go in the opposite direction, everyone else asks why are you going over there, and you think to yourself I *want* to answer. Something which will either *appal* them or *amuse* them. So I think it began when I was born and became codified as the years went by."

Do you think that The Decision you talk about, the understanding of yourself, is in your case so startling and penetrating because there was such a need for justification?

"Yes, I *do.* I haven't thought of it – but that exactly explains it. Other people don't have to explain. If your parents are forever saying you look *marvellous* you don't really have to do anything. But if they say to you 'If you keep going on like this I don't know what's going to happen to you', then you think, well am I going on like this? And what will happen? And do I *care*? And then you have to think about your relationship with the world, and you very quickly realise the first thing is your relationship with yourself and when you've got that straight then you'll be all prepared for the world."

How do you expect people to use your overall performances?

"I offer them a glimpse of how I became

happy *in spite of everything*. In a way I am Miss Lonelyhearts. I know that I do help some people come to a decision. In some mysterious way *The Naked Civil Servant* was seen as a *message of hope* to America. A man just getting off a bus leant back to touch my arm and said 'I was just about to kill myself and then I read your book.' I don't suppose he was going to kill himself, but I expect he was deeply unhappy until he read the book. So in that book, which is a catalogue of *disasters*, he thought, well if he lived through it, with nothing, without talent, without money, without anything, so can I."

As the years have gone by since the showings of *The Naked Civil Servant* your homosexuality has all but been discarded.

"Yes. My sins have been washed away. I am a virgin. It's not referred to in most interviews now. I don't mind. It's the redemptive value of TV."

This is one of your "standard" answers.

"Ha ha ha ha . . . I can't think of anything else! Well, no, I can think of other shades of answers. Now, all sin is less – except to deeply religious people. 'Ordinary' people had a much stricter morality than they do now. I'm sure religious people have their fixed views which will never change, and pagans have their fixed views which will never change, but the people in between will now be able to say well . . . he's *queer*. Which is an *awful* pity, but there you go. What can you do? At one time they wouldn't have said that. So there's been a change in morality. Of course there is my age and my now being beyond sex and this means that I'm no threat to the world. I don't think there could ever be a scandal other than the scandal of my entire existence."

If I can use the word "considering", you are very kind to the world. You are always offering.

"Every *hour* of every *day* I urge myself on to justify the . . . *money*! and certainly the *appreciation* that I've received. I ask myself what *more* can I do? Indeed, when I was a model another model came during the rest and sat beside me and said we must do something about our wages and I said I agree. The first thing we must do is find a way of *deserving* them. I meant it!

"I used to say to the students, *what can I do*? Because they can draw their mums and dads sitting around, and yet I am being paid.

"I always have the desire to be of service,

to be of good value, to justify . . . and over and over on stage I say the words 'Am I saying the words that you *wish* to hear?' I must never think of myself as a teacher, only an entertainer. Once you suggest you are a teacher you imply that you look at the world from *above*. I must never do that. Some people do say 'Who the hell do you think you are?' and then I explain that what I say I say as an offering. I do like being obliging."

WHEN CRISP is not motionless and magnificent in an armchair, when he is showing me into the room or painstakingly preparing a delicious cup of coffee or carefully treading the room, there is a noticeable and somehow misplaced fragility. In all ways but physically he is ageless.

In conversation he both flatters you and contains you.

There is a final obscure hint of the unobtainable. He will tell you everything, but it is from a great distance. Most of his phrases are well-worn, but they could never wear out.

Soon Quentin Crisp is to leave the room in Chelsea.

"I would like to live my last years living in a room in Manhattan with a telephone and plenty of people who will come and see me when I can no longer go to see them. But on the other hand I do not only expect but do *need* quite a lot of time on my own. Even when young it was the same.

"I can remember when I first got a room of my own and I thought, I don't have to do a thing! And it really was wonderful. I didn't want to do anything peculiar, I just thought that no one is going to question the fact that I'm sitting here, no one can say to me, you're not going to slop around like that all day are you? I don't have to answer for anything! I can remember that.

"Of course if I spent every evening in on my own for a week, when I was 25 I would have thought, this is getting dreary and I would have gone out. But I never thought, help, it's six o'clock and I've got nothing planned for this evening.

"You could say I've practised being old."

THE INTERVIEW finishes with fine formality. Quentin Crisp shows me out. As I'm walking up Beaufort Street towards the Kings Road I turn round and Mr Crisp is sending me an immaculate wave from the doorstep. I will of course remember it forever.

forward to?

To find out, to start with, I asked Steve Harley. It was in a hotel room in Manchester, and we're standing by an open fire one hour after a show he had performed with Cockney Rebel at the Manchester Palace. I can't remember anything about the show now, except that I had trouble getting in. It was my fourth or fifth concert review for *New Musical Express* and I was so excited it never occurred to me that there might be bother and I wouldn't be on the "guest list". The godalmighty *NME* had asked me to review the show, and that was that. No messing. I *wasn't* on the "guest list". Had I lost my job? I think I cried in front of the ladies behind the box office bars, and they slipped me a ticket. These are the details you can hide when you write criticism for a music paper, and thus pretend that you are completely in control of world events, and all the sorts of musical twists and turns. Writing for a music paper and cutting into the sound and reason of musical all-sorts gives you one of the great opportunities to play at God with no real feelings of responsibility. I cried to get my ticket to watch Steve Harley, but in the review I cut into his sound and his very being with absolute lack of guilt. When you're young and in love with pop music, this is the kind of thing you like to do. It helps make the world go round: along with asking things.

It was writing about Steve Harley in the autumn of 1977 that made me realise that if you wanted to cut into the flesh of a pop type personality it was more reasonable, in a beautifully unreasonable way, to ask them some things. Let them torture themselves, so to speak, with their own speech, their own *chatter*.

I found out it would be much

BOY GEORGE
May 1, 1982
. . . after-thoughts,
under-thoughts,
perfumes, sounds
and colours. . .

GEORGE ON . . . BITCHINESS

"I AM A bitch, yeah, but I'm not a bitch for the sake of being bitchy.

"I'm not nasty! I don't think so anyway. I know I'm not vindictive. I just have a laugh. . . .

"I'm sure people slag me off! They always do. I've caught people talking about me loads of times. When Bow Wow Wow played St Albans I heard a skinhead say to his mate, Oh, that queer guy's going to come on for an encore, he looks a real state. And when you talk to girls they try to be real clever, they say, Oh, yes duckie, and I just rip them to shreds. It's so obvious to do that.

"Y'know, I'm not a queer, not that sort of queer anyway. I'm as camp as you are, or as anyone is. I'm not camp in a gay sense. Do you think I am?"

GEORGE ON . . . HIS APPEARANCE

"OBVIOUSLY I'M into myself, but I'm not walking around just saying, Oh, everybody look at me, look at me! I wear make-up and dress this way because it makes me look better. I'm not doing it to get people to stare at me. If I wanted to do that I could just put a pot on my head, wear a wedding dress and scream down the High Street. It's easy just to get attention.

"That's what people think they're doing, just that, but that's a load of shit. People also think that if you look like this you're running away from something, and that's a load of rubbish as well. I'm not hiding. It's a long way from hiding. I really don't think that there's anything wrong with wanting to make yourself look as good as possible. I'm not just a person who wears make-up. There is a lot more that goes into it.

"I tell you, I really hate decadence. I hate risqué people who go around with their tits hanging out, or people who try to have sex in public. I hate people who really think they're risqué and daring."

GEORGE ON . . . STEVE STRANGE

"I THINK Steve Strange could have been a lot more successful and respected if he'd just been a bit human about it all. People look at Steve Strange and the general opinion is that he's a prat, and they look at me and see that I wear make-up so they think I'm a prat as well. When I'm interviewed I'm always asked, Do you see yourself in comparison to Steve Strange? What do you say? I don't want to be rude about him. As far as I'm concerned he's doing what he wants to do and he's enjoying it and it's just nothing to do with me. He's there. He exists. So what?! It doesn't matter what anyone says to him or about him."

GEORGE ON . . . LAUGHTER

"I BELIEVE you've got to have a sense of humour. So many people involved in, like, all of this don't have a sense of humour. I don't know how they can do what they do without laughing at themselves and saying it's a real joke. I do it all the time. I go home and look at myself in the mirror and laugh at myself. Sometimes I just go home and cry. I look at myself and think, you fucking wanker! When you're really pissed off it does yourself a lot of good to laugh at yourself. To think, what a prat. Pull all the shit off your face and just laugh. Sometimes I look at myself in the mirror and just talk to myself . . . 'should I compare you to a summer's day' . . . hahahahaha!"

"I'M JUST a peasant," The Boy George tells me, "I'm really quite ordinary, but I can also be quite exciting as well."

There is something lonely and unromantic about The Boy George; more than that there's a peculiar strength and excellence that sneaks up on you or into you, something arrogant and exasperating, and ultimately a beautiful, unconditional directness.

easier for me than always trying to cut these pop type lovelies in the back: let them chatter!

To get face to face with Steve Harley after the Palace show, I must have cried my way into the hotel suite where there was an after-performance party. It wasn't planned, but when you start working for *New Musical Express* you tend to presume anything goes. So it was that the first person I ever seriously interviewed for a music paper was the proud, embittered, crippled Steve Harley – falling backwards into obscurity in the autumn of 1977; from pop star to has-been, the horrendous exile. That week on the cover of *Melody Maker* was a photograph of Billy Idol or some such punkish minimal who has since twitched forwards from obscurity into a states-protected soap of stardom. Harley, who in the early '70s had lavishly enjoyed a short series of grand self-conscious hit singles and who fancied himself as a blessed rock poet and immortal escape artist, was frightened and aghast that "some spotty kid with a safety-pin up his nostril should be on the cover of *Melody Maker*. What has he ever done?" He acted as if he had been given six months to live: a safety-pin securely fastened his demise. I stood in front of this little man who I had just seen confidently control 2,000 people in performance and I quickly gained massive experience. I went into this hotel suite thinking that all rock successes, however much I loathed their music, were somehow invincible, untouchable, and knew their way around. Harley crumbled to dust, took it all out on me, and I suddenly understood that there were a few stories to tell. These people had a rough time, in a roundabout way. You only had to ask. You didn't have to stand miles away and wonder what the

George doesn't ramble, he doesn't soft soap, and he doesn't make excuses. George says that he's probably apologised for something that he's said or done just twice in his life. The Boy has no time for stagey politeness, he's incredibly impatient, and he's convinced that a lively blessed honesty is something of more than passing importance.

His fast and funny conversation bites into the backs of snivelling sycophants and bores. Every sentence The Boy George utters or whips at you is framed by a disgusted snort or a delighted titter, or both. If he doesn't like you – and he'll make up his mind straight away – you'll feel his snap. George is shamelessly *common*, yet he talks a rare formidable commonsense. If you want to get anything done you have to concentrate hard when you're talking with him. As soon as he spots the off-white lack of imagination of a fool he snaps.

I risk a snap.

What's your favourite sexual position, George?

The restless eyes react first, and then . . . **"Cuddling, with all my clothes on. Embracing, that's my favourite sexual position. What's yours?"**

I'm turning the spotlight on you, George.

"Well, come on then. Ask some questions."

How honest are you going to be in this interview?

"I don't know. I might say something completely different in two days' time; which is why it doesn't matter. I've got no illusions. I know that I haven't got a brilliant mind that needs to be poured on to the pages."

What did you want to be when you were a little boy?

"A little girl!!! That's a joke, by the way. I'm not a transvestite. Everyone thinks I am, but I'm not. I wear Y-fronts! I'm a man! I'm quite manly, actually. I don't think I'm as poofy as I'm made out to be. I'm not a gay or anything like that."

What do you feel about people who are hostile because of your appearance?

"I think it's really stupid. But people don't hassle me that much. People don't seem to want to hit me. I don't know why! They sort of look at me and say, is it a geezer or a woman? And then they don't bother hitting you, they're like mesmerised. And you can shut people down when you've got the gab like me. Unless they're really insane, and then you just run away. Don't stay where you're not wanted!"

THE RESTAURANT where we're sat taking afternoon tea is decorated with mirrors and plants: a bright sun streams through large windows. It all combines to enhance George's crisp, clean appearance. There is a thoughtful, delightfully unconventional practicality about the way Boy George compiles and measures his appearance: mingling and juxtaposing and layering to create an innocent, informative quality. Dramatically plucked eyebrows supply the only hard lines.

We meet to celebrate and consider Boy George's liberating new "legitimacy".

After smirking and lurking on the inside and outside of this, that and the other for the past few years – making a name for himself if only because the face didn't suit the name – George has ended up in a position where he will be smart, smack at the centre of a lot of attention.

He's going to be a pop singer; and for a number of valid reasons he's very capable of being very good.

With his customary cheerfulness he recalls a brief time he spent as guest singer with Bow Wow Wow.

"The first gig I did was at the Rainbow in front of loads of people and it was brilliant. I'd never been on stage in my life before then and I really got turned on by it. Malcolm just gave me a hunger for it all. He made me really desperate to do it. I hadn't done anything ever apart from dress up and walk around getting pissed. I'd had my pictures in the paper but I was getting bored with the whole thing. I mean Malcolm only used me to keep Annabella. I didn't realise that at the beginning. . . . But I don't suppose I'd have got my band together if it hadn't have been for Malcolm.

"I'd started the band before I met Malcolm but after a while I just couldn't be bothered.

Once they threw me out of Bow Wow Wow I got really pissed off and first of all I just wanted revenge, and to be exactly like them but better, just rip them off. Then I decided I had to do something of my own. Because I'm a good singer!"

George grins happily and serves up gallons of seedy, sordid Bow Wow Wow gossip. He's in his element. Yap, snap, titter, snort.

GEORGE ON ... SCANDAL

"I'M NOT A scandalous person. I would never ever sell my sex life to the papers. Everyone I've ever loved I'll love till I die! The people that I love, I wouldn't talk about them explicitly because there's no need. And most of the people I've been out with would be really embarrassed if it became known because they're considered to be really straight. Nobody's perfectly straight, you know. What a boring way to be if you're perfectly straight!"

GEORGE ON ... BOREDOM

"IT'S BOREDOM that makes me still want to go out to clubs. Who wants to stay in? I go to bed sometimes and then get up to go out. I go to bed and I lie there and I think, hell I can't stand it, I'll get up and go out. I'll get drunk. I'm not going to get drunk to relieve myself in some way; I'm going out to get drunk so I'll fall asleep when I get back home. I lead a really silly life!

GEORGE ON ... MONEY

"WITH THE PUNK thing everyone was making impractical attacks on being rich or having money, y'know, but they all wanted to be rich. You have to be. I've got plenty of money, well, quite a lot. I'm not a millionaire or a thousandaire or anything. But I've got enough. And I worked for it, really hard, with the shop and modelling and everything. You can't just take things. I just want money so that I can be really irresponsible."

GEORGE ON ... DAVID BOWIE

"HE CAME down to Blitz, to get people for the 'Ashes' video, and he sent this girl down to get people who looked 'weird' and I was one of them y'know, and she said DB wants to see you upstairs! And I said, Who's that? And she whispered in my ear, David Bowie. And I just went, oh yeah. . . .

"I went upstairs and there was this table full of people just grinning blankly surrounded by stupid girls looking dead uncool. I don't know how he can stand it. He must think they're all a load of wankers . . . he must. It must really frighten him, he must have to treat the whole thing like a game of chess.

"A lot of people want to be like David Bowie, they want to be David Bowie. I don't. I think he's had it really. I think he's great, brilliant, but he's just THERE like Harrods or Frank Sinatra. I wasn't asked to do the video. I'm pleased. I wouldn't have done it anyway."

"I'M STILL really childish", The Boy George tells me. "I've never really grown up. I think that's a good thing. I don't make things a problem for me."

Boy George's completely up-to-date group Culture Club release their first Virgin single next week; "White Boy" is already causing a stir. . . .

The Boy and his boys John Moss (drums-percussion), Roy Hay (guitars-keyboards-piano), Michael Craig (bass) have the best look of a pop group since Japan or The Fire Engines or D.À.F. or Stimulin, and their sweetly spiced, correctly sexed sound spins new shades and tints and blues out into the current colourmotion.

fuck they were up to, who the hell did they think they were. You could walk right up to them and wipe the dust from your eyes. . . .

"Memory is the first thing to go," chuckles Jerry Garcia, trying to win me over with un-sour flower-power charm. I wasn't having any of this. I ask him, cruelly, whether he could stop existing now and not mind too much. "Yeah, I think so," he generously replies. "I'm not crazy about life. I wouldn't want to live here for hundreds of years. There isn't that much I'm interested in. There isn't much that I think I'm going to see that I haven't seen already."

So what sort of things concern you?

"Music. Music and drugs."

Does that limited concern manifest itself as the gross indulgence I see in Grateful Dead music?

"Weeeealll now, I don't know what you see. . . ."

I see gross indulgence. Perhaps because you're only concerned with music and drugs. He laughs. "No, actually, I'm concerned with a few other things. But in terms of what is actually compelling me to stay on this earth, there's really not a whole lot there. I'm interested to see what it's all about. It seems as though an awful lot has happened in a very short time. More has happened in the last 150 years than happened in all the time before that . . . trillions of years. It seems we're zipping up towards a moment. I don't know what's coming. But having come this far I'm determined to be around for the turn of the millenium. If nothing else. Just 'cos it's so close. Shit, it's only twenty years away."

He raises his eyes a little cheekily. So I would presume then that with this sort of attitude political force and the like is

Culture Club are a breeze; their advances are welcome, their caresses not vulgar. "White Boy" sounds best when the sun is shining: it's a surprise to hear Boy George sound so lyrical.

George has not thought once about the general "rock" barriers; he's not even reacting against them, like some of his predecessors. The natural extension of the post-rock events is a . . . naturalness.

"We want to work at what we do, not analyse it, just get better. Culture Club are real amateurs and that's it for now. . . . The whole idea of the group is to work at it and get better. There are things we want to learn . . . oh, fuck the music, I don't want to talk about music anyway."

Is it a career, so to speak?

"Well, that remains to be seen. It is a career in the sense that I've signed up for five years."

No!!!

"I have! But I'm happy about it."

It's ludicrous!

"I'm capable!"

What were you doing five years ago?

"I was living in suburbia. Look at me now!"

So where will you be in five years' time? Back in suburbia?

"I won't. I've got a lot of go ahead. I have! I mean, listen, we didn't get a record deal just by sending photographs to Virgin. We actually did gigs and got shouted at and called queers. I think it's good how we've done it. We haven't said expect this, expect that, we've not claimed to be anything. So you get what you want out of it in the end. If you like it, you like it. My little sister loves the record and that's all I'm interested in."

George titters, and looks for something else to talk about.

GEORGE ON . . . LOVE AND SEX

"I FALL IN love all the time. 24 hours a day. I fall in love with people for really silly reasons. I think people should fall in love a lot. It's great. Wonderful. I think it's good and healthy to be in love with people. I always go out with very nice people and I really love all of them. Not mentioning any names. . . ."

What's the type of person you're likely to fall in love with?

"The lorry driver's mate . . . 'cos they're oppressed. I don't go out with people just for the sake of having sex. It's too messy to have people like that in your life. They always hang around you and never go away. People never go at 3 a.m. after you've had sex with them. They just won't go away, will they? I used to do all that years ago. I thought I was fulfilling some need in me but I wasn't. Now, I just can't be bothered."

Did you lose your virginity to a boy?

"No, I did not! I went off with loads of girls at school. I used to be THE person to go out with at school, because I was such a puff. I did think I was David Bowie then. I had big hairy eyebrows. . . ."

GEORGE ON . . . ANDY WARHOL, ALBERT EINSTEIN AND MARILYN MONROE

"I HATE ANDY Warhol. I really hate him. Malcolm's much funnier. Andy Warhol really takes himself seriously. It's just terrible. He's an idiot. Like a big cheesecake on legs. I just think he's so awful."

Do you like Albert Einstein?

"I've never heard of him. . . ."

He was a scientist. . . .

"Oh, he's on the cover of that M single, isn't he?"

He thought that the physical body was something of a handicap.

"He probably couldn't get what he wanted. People always make these big ideas up about things if they can't get what they want."

He had Monroe.

"So what? Marilyn Monroe was just a glorified transvestite."

"I'VE STOPPED wearing as much make-up

lately," The Boy George tells me. "You probably haven't noticed. I'm cutting down. It's my natural look."

The Boy George may be painted and powdered and intolerant and cleverly unsettling, but he talks like a comedian.

"Do I? That's great! Maybe that's my true vocation in life. . . . Actually you print that and I'll kill you; I'll bomb your house."

George, beneath the banter and the bitching – or because of it – represents as much as anyone the new acceptance that the massive cultural pressures, and complications, mustn't be allowed to confuse and compromise.

Culture Club are up-to-date because they simply get on with establishing a quality, a procedure, a pattern that is unique to themselves, but which loosely corresponds with other actions and activities. It is an attempt to recreate or recover a purity that can develop into something unknown and delicious. There is at the heart of Culture Club a necessary, indefinable *hardness*.

And The Boy George, amidst all the cursing and complaining, cares deeply about people.

"I do like people, but they upset me so much. So I just pretend that I don't like them. Of course, I like everyone, I'm sure I'm in love with the whole world, but I just get pissed off with people because they let themselves down so much. And it depresses me that so many people are just like exactly the same.

"My brothers are boxers, my dad runs a boxing club. My little brother is a South London ABA champion. He's a really good boxer. My dad's really proud of him, but he's also proud of me because he sees that I'm achieving something. He sees that I've got a good product, that I've got something. . . .

"He knows me, he knows what I'm about. He knows that I'm not suddenly going to turn up at the house in a big Cadillac wearing a pink fur coat saying, Oh hello. I'm rich. He knows I'm not going to go off my head; he knows I'm not that sort of person. And I've no wish to be like that, I've no wish to impress anyone.

"I don't give a shit. I don't want to be a boring pop star, I don't want to be a rock star, and I never will be. How could I? What the hell have I got to do with rock'n'roll? I

take this seriously enough to want to do it, to want to be a success, but if it fails I'm not going to fold away and not be able to go out. I'm not going to hide. Who gives a damn? I'm just not desperate."

The Boy George looks around warily to see if anyone overheard him: and then he laughs at himself.

entirely abstract?

"Oh, I think all that shit is bullshit. I think the doings of people is really like small potato. Really! It's like playground!"

What about the individual stress that pressurises people?

"Even that."

What about murder?'

"Well, murder may have some kharmic implications. I think the idea of death . . . I mean, everyone dies."

Except The Grateful Dead, I drily interrupt.

"Well, there it is!"

As if to say, what are *you* going to do about it.

"The entertainment has arrived!" That's me. Killing Joke have a first floor flat in a large old house in Notting Hill Gate. We walk, through an echoey hall, up bare wooden stairs, into a small den, dense with a peculiar, scruffy kind of cosiness. There's an unmistakable sense of anticipation.

"So, who's Paul Morley?" questions Jaz, who reminds me of an evil-shafted Punch. He looks me and the uninvolved photographer up and down, licking his lips maliciously. I have to own up, and stick out a trembling hand for further shaking.

"You really don't like us, do you?" he growls, slumping into a shapeless cushion by the lop-sided door.

No, I answer flatly.

The bedraggled Youth appears, more Menace than Vicious, still in pyjamas, but not something to cuddle. He sits down on the other side of the door, leaning against the wall. He turns his nose up against me. The door is shut, purposefully. I am surrounded. Soft reggae forms some incongruous easy listening. The den is small and airless. And shut off from anywhere.

The entertainment shivers

MARILYN

December 24, 1983
. . . live life to the hilt,
but file it away for
later reference. . .

"If I worked in a chip shop I would make sure that I was the best fucking chip fryer in the world."

– –

MARILYN ON WHAT HE IS

"Who's to say?"

You could go far.

"I could go nowhere . . . as long as I go out for dinner with Diana Ross then I'll be happy."

What do you mind?

"People buying me grapes when I want bananas."

– –

THE MALE'S being photographed, and he's happily collapsing over soft furnishings, rubbing his body into his big baggy cushions, cheaply wetting his finger on his tongue, flinging his mane around his face, acting out his borrowed name to a quick perfection, pretending with his sparkling eyes to a special, rising bliss.

He giggles indulgently, rolls over, pulls the mane over one side of his face, peeps out, hugs himself; an animal, a baby, clown. . . .

What a tart.

"I like people thinking I'm sexy . . . doesn't everyone?"

The female's being interviewed, and he's telling big, small and awful lies, spinning out aphorisms that glisten with blatant contradiction – resisting, challenging, whining, losing, fluttering his eyelashes, giggling, winning, snapping, rolling back into the soft sofa, sinking into the cushions, wrapping a big red

scarf around his head and splicing the holy with the unholy. . . .

Such insincere, skilful seduction.

"What I'm saying to people is . . . look at me, if you want to look, but you don't have to look. Know what I mean?"

No, Marilyn.

"Oh, go on. Have another drink, girl!"

– –

I'M TWO hours late for the interview. Male Marilyn, in an awfully affronted snap-song voice, disapproves.

"I do not appreciate being kept waiting for two hours."

Who are you to act so royal?

He cracks his whip. **"Who are you to keep me waiting!"**

Ouch! But Maid Marilyn is the kind of girl you never want to say sorry to.

I get out of my bag of equipment a quarter bottle of Bells whisky. Marilyn giggles dreamily. **"Oooh, alcoholic."** *I can't do interviews without being intoxicated – aren't you the same? Marilyn tells some cream lies.* **"I don't drink. . . ."**

Don't you ever get intoxicated?

"Never. I rely on my sharpness . . . that makes me blurred, it blurs the edges. . . ."

Of reality?

"What's reality?"

I've been wondering that about you.

"What? Whether I'm a fantasy or a reality?"

Something like that.

"So," *says Marilyn, beginning his wicked tease, sorting me out before we begin to play our snappy, baity word games,* **"you're the one who's so *nasty* to everyone. . . ."**

He looks me in the eyes and there's a suggestion that I talk dirty. I spill my seed . . . at least, I drop my tape recorder. Batteries roll over the floor and under the soft furnishings. Marilyn giggles, his pleased giggle. I put my equipment back in order. We haven't much time.

"I'm sorry darling . . . I've got to go to Germany in a little while."

slightly. The musicians ease in for a kill. No joke. After my deeply unimpressed review of their first album, Killing Joke felt deeply that I undermined their virtue and value, and they wanted to meet me. Just to talk! I couldn't say no. After stabbing anyone in the back, I always like to meet face to face. It only seems fair, in an unfair kind of way. And you like to think that you can prove you were right, through intelligent, flexible discussion. The joke is, fists might be deployed in this hidden den.

"It was Paul and Geordie (the two members not present) that really wanted to meet you," smoulders Jaz. "Me and Youth really aren't that bothered." His shining eyes show that's a lie. His body seems primed and alert. Jaz starts chattering feverishly, so I crouch on a dirty two-seater sofa and switch on my equipment to emphasize the . . . business aspect of this Saturday afternoon sport.

Was I scared? Yes. Keeping your distance is much easier when you're a writer for a music paper, if you just want to pick up a penny and appear super-human. If you require fair play, you're mucking yourself up a mite. Rock music wasn't built to allow honesty a comfortable home. I remember that the last time I'd dismissed an l.p. in few and disgusted words, the group in question came so close to leaving fingerprint marks on my neck, it's not worth thinking about. Jaz and Youth, nicknamed like public school boys but glaring at me like street fighting brats, make to say – what are *you* going to do about it? I wipe the dust from my eyes.

What was I supposed to do about it? Harley was taking out something on me, something like his death, a fist fight in the kitchen with his wife last year, his pop irrelevance. He was

So should we play interviews?

"Oh, I hate doing interviews. . . . I don't see why I should sit here and put myself across to someone I don't even know and read all their criticisms of me afterwards. . . . Why should I have to do it?

"I am *me, me, me,* but I don't have to force it on other people all the time do I? Still, I'm told that it helps."

Marilyn pulls his knees up to his chest. "Oh . . . it's so cold. . . ."

He shivers, suddenly thirsty for love and affection.

This boy is trouble; and deliciously untroubled. I'll have to be careful.

"So what am I . . . you tell me . . . you're the analyst . . . *daddy.* . . ."

During this sentence he slips effortlessly from challenging big boy to wishy whispering little girl. I will have to be careful.

He giggles, indecently.

MARILYN ON BEING NICE

Have you got a grudge against the world?

"I don't think so. The world's a big place and there's a lot of people in it. Everyone's free to do exactly what they want, as long as they don't hurt anyone. . . . When you hurt other people . . . oh, like that guy who wrote that thing about me in the *Sunday People*: well, it didn't hurt me, but it was just so . . . twisted."

Don't you relish that kind of attention?

"I just think it's sad because it makes me realise that there are freaks in the world and I don't want there to be freaks in the world. I want everyone to be nice and to give flowers to each other."

Some people would say you haven't been nice releasing such a record. Oh Marilyn, you're so nasty for making us listen to that record.

"Switch off the radio."

Oh Marilyn, you're so nasty for making us look at your photographs.

"Turn over the page."

Maybe some people don't think you're nice because you're so secondhand.

"I've never seen anyone like me before. I've never met anyone like me before."

MARILYN ON BOY GEORGE

"First schmirst. . . ."

MARILYN ON HIS MEMORIES

"There are so many values and opinions and everything, and if I see something that I admire I keep it. If someone says something that I like or agree with I remember it . . . I'm an amalgamation of everything that I like.

"The individuality of a person is his or her different concoction of all the things around you. . . . There's no such thing as a person who's completely brand new and fresh. . . . Your wisdom is everything that has gone before you and everything that people have told you and taught you . . . and all your experiences. And I've experienced a lot and I always try to experience more things.

"I've tried all the drugs there are, I've been to all the different nightclubs, and discos, and through all the scenes, all the different aspects of music, and I've come up with my own version, the version that suits me. And it is a new thing, because it's a new blend, it's my blend. . . .

"It's like a food mixer: depending on what

you put in the drink what comes out will always be different. It always depends what you put in and what you take out . . . and tha's what I am. A food mixer.

Kind of."

-- -- -- -- -- -- -- -- -- -- -- -- -- -- --

MARILYN ON THE BITCH

"I try not to be bitchy about anyone."

Oh Marilyn!

"I don't . . . not at the moment. It's quite funny in situations like where you crack jokes, and I can lay into people verbally, especially when they try to force me to be something that I'm not or that I don't want to be, I can shut them up very quickly. But there's no satisfaction from doing that.

"I can bring people to tears by saying things to them, because I've got this horrible gift, or hindrance or whatever it is I don't know, to be able to zero in on people's minds and work out exactly what will annoy them 100% the most . . . and I say it to them. I used to do that all the time. I don't do it anymore. But I know that it's still there. I can still do it."

Do you hide behind masks?

"I used to. I suppose I still do in a way. At first, around the time I did the Riverside interview, when I'd dropped the masks, it was the first TV I'd done, and I was like waiting for the knives, and it was very painful. But once you get past that stage it gets better . . . and then the fact that you haven't got any masks becomes a mask. So you always have a shield.

"Everyone has their own barriers against the world. I try not to take mine too seriously."

Do you take anything about Marilyn too seriously?

"Not really. . . ."

MARILYN ON COMPLICATION

"It's very fashionable at the moment to hate Marilyn."

Can you understand why?

"Yeah . . . because when you don't understand something new, and you're frightened of it. . . . It's like AIDS, for instance. People do not want to discuss AIDS; they just completely don't want to know about it. But it's there, it's getting bigger, and sooner or later it's going to be shoved down people's throats, and people are just going to go mental."

You're as contagious as AIDS?

"I don't think of myself as a disease. I'm just a person who sings a few records now and then."

And who irritates people. . . .

"Probably. Because I've got the gall to do exactly what I want, and most people are frightened of doing exactly what they want. I adore it in people when they want to stick green hair on their head and wear black eyeliner. I think that's good. Do it! Who cares? But people who are desperate to put green hair on their head or wear black eyeliner and that kind of thing, they just won't or can't, and they just hate anyone who's prepared to do that kind of thing. It's quite funny really. . . ."

Do you imagine that you're so complicated that it's a case of people not understanding you?

"Sure . . . It's very difficult to assimilate someone after three interviews and a few photographs. It's very difficult to know someone and dismiss them through that. People think they can, though. It's going to take time and more interviews for people to get used to what I am."

Isn't the irritation simply that you're seen as one more unacceptable frivolity who's exploiting pop music purely for personal gain at a time when it's at its most soft-headed and weak-bodied?

"That's crap. I just think that if you take

taking from me my innocence. At the time, what Harley chucked out as "spotty and safety-pinned", something you could read about in the illogical, inconsistent, compelling columns of Caroline Coon, Jon Savage, Jonh Ingham, seemed almost life saving, certainly a rash smash in the face of the new-fangled etiquette of rock established in the early '70s, and I was somehow hurt that someone who exalted himself as an eccentric could be so pathetically resistant. Was Harley urging me in some odd way to save his life? Was he asking me my name? Was he really interested in my view of rock, pop, and the ultimate in paranoia? He was gripping on to me and taking it all out around me not because he saw a kid who fancied himself as a complex cross between Richard Hell and Charles Baudelaire who was never going to sleep in his search for sensation but because I was the *NME*. Meeting Harley was also a sharp lesson in the way rock musicians saw their relationship with these weird youths who called themselves journalists because their giant enthusiasms and cheek had got them jobs on music papers. Musicians can't help being fascinated by these makeshift, ragged critics, because all the words loaded over their shifting egos are bound to be entirely flattering when they're not flattening. Harley, who exaggerated the weight and menace of music papers more than anyone I met bar Geldof – and that's saying more than something – saw the *NME* as the vessel of some wicked, buckled wisdom, every writer shackled by the same hatreds and hubris, almost in complete control over the singers' destinies. I *was* the *NME* for Harley, even though to me I was someone out and about at the beginning of an

yourself too seriously you're in a sorry state."

But as a perfectionist, you surely reject the type of superficiality and vacuity that you seem to celebrate?

"I don't think it's at all superficial to really do what you want to and believe in. I believe in doing what you feel like doing whenever you want to do it. As long as it doesn't hurt anyone else. As long as you don't go out and rape people.

"It's so stupid. Everyone gets worked up over me wearing a sequined suit while there are people going out and murdering other people. It's all just so twisted. I mean, there's no one person who is normal, because there's no such thing as normal; there's no model human being who does all the right things and says all the right things, because there is no such thing as the right things. And once you realise that then it's fucking tough cookie for them.

"I think that to care about other people and to be genuinely interested in things around you and to forge ahead and to make everything all right for you is much more important than sitting around and criticising other people all the time and interfering in other people's business. . . .

"All the time, I do what's best for me. And through that I would like people to realise that I'm doing what's right for me in my way and hopefully they can get inspired by that and do what's right for them. I'm trying to make myself into what my dream of me is. . . . I don't think that's wrong."

— — — — — — — — — — — — — — — — — — — —

MARILYN ON THE TRUTH

"Of course I care what people think about me, but I have to believe that I don't care."

You've been telling me lies.

"No!! I believe in everything I say. I believe every single thing I say."

Even when it's a lie.

"What's a lie? What's the truth? Tell me what my truth is. . . ."

PETER ROBINSON was always shut away in a shadowy corner at school. The freak in the playground.

"All the boys were bashing people and smashing windows, he thought, and he was having to go home, and he was always bursting into tears. He wanted to enjoy himself, he wanted to be happy, but he was continually frustrated. *They* wouldn't let him be in the football team. *They* just didn't want him.

"If anyone knows that feeling then they know what I mean when I say that it just was not pretty."

The revenge was Marilyn: it's beginning to get pretty dramatic, as show business stories go.

Marilyn went from the Borehamwood school into the celebrated Blitz pool of fools, where a dainty, sweety decadence was dutifully practised and punk's black comedy was turned into fancy farce.

Marilyn was a party piece in the jumbled shrieking Blitz crowd, an errant angel in that pinky silvery crowd – this is how the show business story goes, and I don't mind. A complete Monroe replica: a big smile, a wonderful walk, and a crazy smell. The way he wore those tight skirts: it was a masterpiece.

And now, he's the last star of that breed to emerge publicly from that shaky sub-myth; the last one to try out on the sensation-seeking showbusy world his parcel of conniving, cunning, contrivance and comedy. Maybe, after all that, he's the best, the bravest, the sneakiest, the sexiest . . . bringing to pop entertainment a little bit more, and less, than one light, slight teenybop record suggests – more like a mouth that can melt all attempts to be sensible and reasonable and analytical.

What Marilyn understands is that unbeatable, unbreakable ambition that has made the million for the former London village idiots Boy George and Steve Strange; ambition that is never justified or considered, but that is some grand narcissistic design to grow larger than life.

— —

MAN ALIVE, moving girl, nothing can stop it. . . .

"No one created me. I created myself. I do exactly what I believe in. I'm moving towards what I want and people are bashing me from all sides. But it's no good, I'm still moving on, I'm still going in the right direction, and I know it's right, and I know I'm right, so everyone might as well just let me get on with it."

Has there been a plan?

"I don't make plans. I just live from day to day."

That's how you've ended up here?

"Well, I knew about two years ago that I was going to do a record: that was the only thing I knew. And so everything from then was like a time filler. I knew I was going to make a record, but I didn't know how, why, what, when, who . . . I knew it was the goal. And when I reached that there would be other things on the horizon. It's like steps up a ladder, you have to get on the first step before you can get on any of the others. Making a record is like starting at the bottom. Modelling is like below making a record. And I'd been through all that, and then it's like singing, acting de di da dum, up and up and up and up. . . ."

To where? To happiness. To be as happy as Barbra Streisand or Diana Ross: this is the burning red fire in Marilyn's free heart. That simple, devastating, perfect dream. To be beyond the bland naggings, the tedious snags of the grey-to-middling world that most have to share: to glow with fame, to verge on immortality. Marilyn wants to be happy, like the true (beauty) queen, and then some more, and so on.

Tell him: oh, he's so silly.

"Maybe. That's not my decision to make. I don't think I'm silly. I am happy so far, so I must be doing something right."

Tell him: oh, he's so naïve.

"Oh, that's nice . . . so refreshing . . . I'd hate to think I knew everything . . . I never want to be static. I must always be on the move."

Marilyn: she has an answer for everything.

"Oh, I'm getting a headache. . . ."

What, with all these questions . . . too much thinking, is it destroying your soul?

"I thought a sole was something that swam in the sea."

I'll beat you at word games. . . .

"Cat!" *he says, and tease-flashes his eyes at me, signalling something with his lashes. Oh, I wish I could have got that on tape, and been able to write it down. In that flash of the eyes, that split-up second, was all the Marilyn cunning.*

And he just will not keep still. The body is constant.

— —

MARILYN ON SHOW BUSINESS

"I want to get an Emmy, and Grammy and a Tony . . . that's my new goal . . . I'll probably fail miserably, but at least I will have tried."

You're just an old-fashioned girl, aren't you? You just want to be part of the blazing twentieth century superstar tradition.

"I don't know . . . I don't know what I'm part of. I don't like to be part of any movement or organisation because I think that is frightening."

I'm not being so concrete – it's like you just want to lead the classic show-business life.

"Do I?"

Emmy, Tony . . . they're quite conventional aims, aren't they?

"Are they? Who on earth would dream of having those things?"

Isn't it the usual type of fantasy?

argumentative trip through the more or less real pits and peaks of pop who didn't yet deserve to be seen as the *NME*. [In 1977, and for a year or two more, being the *NME* was no real shame.] But I *was* the *NME* for Harley, and it was my fault that punk was the hardest chunk for him to swallow, that he was busy dying, that he was fearful and crying. He saw himself as an old-fashioned scrapped comic, and couldn't dare admit it. At first I didn't ask any questions, as it somehow didn't seem my place. I still had my innocence. I didn't really know what an interview was. I didn't even really know why I was in this room by the fireplace. Harley, a galloping Geldof at talking, ranted so much, white spittle gamely peeked through his lips. And then, I just had to ask a question. I was obviously going to write an aloof, crashing review of the Harley show, as instinct told me this was the only way, but up to a point I would still have walked away feeling that Harley was a better person than me. I suppose I felt that you couldn't knock achievement, even in the face of mediocrity. And, then, I had to ask something. I'd got a hard-on.

"I've been looking forward to this for two years, you know?"

So tell me something, Fishy.

"I really like eyes . . . y'know . . . oh, no, that's the kind of wanky quote that's always taken out and put in a separate box. There's just something that floors me completely. I never look at myself as a form of intellectual at all. Just a Scotsman with a mouth. There's too many about these days. Are you listening?"

Try me.

"I met a beautiful girl at a party once. I had no sexual attraction to her at all . . . she looked like a ballet dancer, and she talked like a severe poet, and then she

"How strange that you should think so. I've never met anyone who wanted those things. How weird."

What do you think most people dream of?

"Washing machine ... new car.... The thing about England, it's so different from America.

"In England, you get your job in the chip shop and that's it. As soon as something positive happens to you, you think, that's it. You don't want to own the chip shop or anything, or get a chain of chip shops.

"You're just content to work there. That's the attitude of most British people I think.

"I feel that there must always be more beyond, so that you're always constantly striving for better and better and more and more. I don't think you should be stationary. I'd hate to be known as just 'a singer'. I never feel that what I am at the moment is the end."

— — — — — — — — — — — — — — — — — —

MARILYN ON COMEDY

"You're desperate for me to be full of contradictions, for me to admit that I'm conning people, that I'm some fictitious pop character, aren't you? I don't want you to be satisfied that you've made me admit I'm the person you think I am ... I'm the way I am and if you don't like it, then you can write any old shit about me.

Actually, I just think you're a comedian.

"Oh yeah, I am ... I like making people laugh. I like funny people. One of my closest friends said to me when I first started doing the record, you shouldn't be a singer, you should be a comedian. I said, but Blanche, what I don't want to be is a singer or a comedian, I want to be a person who does everything....

"It's like a rough-cut diamond, there's many facets to it. I don't want to be like your smooth one-surface person. . . . There's a lot of different sides to me. Hopefully."

— — — — — — — — — — — — — — — — — —

MARILYN ON MARILYN MONROE

"I get really upset when I think about her sometimes. . . ."

— — — — — — — — — — — — — — — — — —

MARILYN ON THE MIND AND BODY

What have you done with your body?

"I've been through a lot of different stages ... I sort of cared about it for a long time ... then I didn't care about it, then I did, then I didn't ... lots of different trips...."

What have you let people do to your body?

"I've let it be loved, I've let it be abused. Your mind is part of your body and if you let your mind be abused then you're letting your body be abused too. I've let people do that and it's like a knife. Sometimes when you let people in they want to leave you damaged. . . ."

Can you not separate your mind and your body?

"No ... I think it's all one thing ... when I meet someone I don't judge them on the outer shell because that's just superficial. What goes on in their mind, what they think and say, that is the most interesting, the most difficult thing."

Do many people get to your mind?

"A few. . . ."

Through sex?

"Sex is like the full stop after a sentence. The sentence is the mind. Having sex is rejoicing in the two minds being connected.

That's when it's exciting. If your mind is detached from your body, then you're thinking of other things while you're having sex, which is completely boring. You might as well be having sex with your hand."

— —

MARILYN ON THE FLOOR

Are you telling me more lies?

"Oh, no, it's probably just another contradiction . . . life's full of them you know!"

Oh, fuck you, Marilyn!

"Oh, I wish you would. . . ."

MARILYN'S CERTAINTY, the trick of his wit, the invincibility of his optimism soon wears down the questioning. Marilyn has the knack of making every question seem irrelevant. He wrecks the conceit of the interviewer splendidly – lesser writers than me must have real trouble puzzling out the crossfire, coping with the intolerance.

He slips and slides, races away, directly challenges the interviewer's right to ask such questions. The questions are beneath him. Or above him. He couldn't care less.

What are you doing in 1984?

"Album, tour, movie."

The old things.

"They're new to me."

Are you capable of doing a tour?

"Are you?"

Yes.

"Are you? I'd like to see you try."

He charmed the pants off me. And so once he's made his points – the determination, the energy – he loses interest, finds a new game to play, rolls around, rolls his tongue, blinks his eyes, curls up into the sofa, dangles his bait, plays around with his big red scarf. . . .

"Actually, I'm wondering if Paul Morley's gay. . . ."

I signal for the photographer to leave the room. And you said, Marilyn, that I was the nasty one.

"We all have our weaknesses."

Wet kisses?

"W-E-A-K-N-E-S-S-E-S . . . Your hair's really nice."

So's yours. So this is your technique: discover the interviewer's weak spot, in this case, pick up the interviewer. . . .

"Is that what I'm doing? You're certainly one of the most interesting interviewers I've ever been with."

The photographer leaves the room. Was I careful? Who's to say.

Full stop.

said that her ambition in life was to drive a truck on a Dire Straits tour! I live for things like that. You can see Niagara Falls or the fucking Eiffel Tower but you cannot beat talking to a drunk in the Grass Market in Edinburgh about what it was like to work with the Horse Artillery in World War One . . . and then sit down and write about it. . . . It's Kerouac! I've never lived in the '70s. Always an hour ago. . . . My capsule's got thin walls you know. . . . Pain . . . let's call it reality . . . it filters through the walls of a capsule to the point where it reaches the individual within, but by the time it gets through a thick capsule it becomes relatively harmless. . . . Subject: the two satellites that were lost from the Shuttle. Did you sit back and think how much they cost? How many people sat back and thought about that! If you did then you've got a thin capsule. . . . You see, I just want to be a window cleaner, cleaning the windows that we look through to see reality. . . ."

Are you a prat?

"Course I'm fucking not a prat. Are you questioning me? Do you think I'm a prat? Who the fuck's going to say, oh yeah, I'm a prat . . . I mean what I write . . . I've become an unqualified semi-expert on relationship technique."

Very clever.

Just who the hell do you think you are, Mr Fry?

"Never what it seems."

Smartarse.

"Sticks and bones. . . ."

And words?

"Can change our minds."

Just who do you think you are, Midge?

"You tell me."

I think you're a pop tart: a bit of everything. . . .

"A bit of a tart . . . uh, yeah, that's right. That's quite a good

GARY GLITTER

March 7, 1981
. . . and when he
sits down
the chair
collapses.

AT A PARTY sometime in the pre-cynical '60s, a group of people tucked in the centre of the mythical hurricane Swing were getting drunk and intimate and watching a showing of *Rock Around The Clock* on the black and white television.

There was Paul Raven, an aide on the rhapsodised TV programme *Ready Steady Go*, Michael Aldrin, a co-presenter of the show along with Cathy McGowan (ooh-ooh), Dusty Springfield, a whole crowd of gay and crazy people.

For some reason, they began to smirk over the names of those early '60s croon-boys: Vince Eager, Marty Wilde, Billy Fury. And then they started to predict suitable names for the '70s. Michael Aldrin announced, in an accent that John Inman would have gagged on, that he wanted to be Terry Tinsel. The group fell into each other's arms, giggling uncontrollably. Other names conjured up were Vicky Vomit, Horace Hydrogen . . . everyone wilted in hysterics.

Paul Raven said he wished to be known as Gary Glitter. It became his nickname.

Years later Mike Leander, a musical associate of Raven's — Raven had co-operated with Leander as a frontman on a number of flawed projects during the '60s — told Raven that he had written a song that was certain to succeed. Raven had been performing and recording for 12 years; the only time he stopped entertaining was while he worked on *Ready Steady Go*. He'd had no notable commercial success.

Leander suggested he should record the song, but to avoid the kind of prejudice the public show to known losers, Raven should also change his name.

In 1971 Paul Raven recorded the song as Gary Glitter, and craftily adopted an extravagant theatrical presentation to complement the name. 'Rock and Roll Parts 1 And 2'.

"The kids made 'Part 2' a hit," Glitter recalls, chest swelling almost enough to equal his girth.

A DECADE later pop music has flipped through a few new somersaults. Gary Glitter is watching The Human League at Hammersmith Odeon, confused by the drummerless tape-supported primitivism, amused by the lack of movement, impressed by the undeniable showiness. He loves the slides Adrian Wright projects on to a series of screens, especially the *Psycho* sequence with Tony Perkins and that victim.

Suddenly the League move into their 'Rock And Roll Part I' and a huge glowing picture of Glitter captured in The Act is presented. The song together with the picture receive the biggest cheer of the night. A boy in the audience leans over and asks Glitter what it's like to be a cult.

"I was absolutely flabbergasted. I couldn't

think what to say except, Well, it feels much the same as being a legend."

MONTHS LATER and I'm finding my way to Gary Glitter's maisonette set in a pretty mews in Earl's Court. I knock on the door and no one answers, so I push it open and find myself in Glitter's front room, getting ribbed for being late.

Chunky and cheery, in padded flying jacket and creased leather trousers he looks less a legend, more a weather-beaten market stallholder. His son Paul, a 17-year-old would-be billy-boy, wanders around preparing for the drive north for that night's show at Salford University.

It's just gone one. We clamber into a battered, once-proud automatic estate. One window has been smashed in, and patched up with lots of black tape.

Inside the car a cheap radio is badly fitted into place with more of that black tape. The power steering is said to be faulty. A few items of stage equipment and Glitter's costumes are packed into the back. Glitter slides into the passenger seat. Alan is driving.

The day before Glitter had been banned from driving, only a few months after he'd got back his licence after another incident. He jokes good-naturedly about the annoyance of not being able to drive for two or three years, accentuates the irony of how he was arrested this time. I think he's one of the happiest people I've ever met.

"I'm a happy person generally. I'm particularly happy now because I've got through the downs. I found myself going to court yesterday in a good frame of mind. I remember the first time I went to court I was shaking, but I managed to lose my licence then and exist for two years not driving, and so having that knowledge I just went in there for a laugh. I knew what was going to happen. I didn't really want anyone to know about it."

FROM 1971 to 1974 Gary Glitter was a barnstorming teenybop star, creating a fantasy out of a character that had roots back in music hall and '50s R & R. He was a luxurious mix of Liberace, Edna Everage, Little Richard and Max Miller.

After the fuss and fashion faded, Gary Glitter became — like Diana Dors, Lorraine Chase, Rod Stewart, Fiona Richmond, Simon Dee and Tony Blackburn — the modern day Empty Celebrity. However low and lost he got, he was still public property. He became one of those trivial diversions for a dull news bulletin. A pop musical Dai Llewellyn. The clock that was timing his 15 minutes had stopped.

description actually.

"It does seem like I've done everything. But it all seems to make sense, some sort of sense. Doesn't it?"
You tell me.

I just had to ask a question. I think it was when Harley compared himself to Ornette Coleman or John Coltrane. Enough's enough. A few hit singles can make anyone seem important, and being photographed, and being interviewed. But just because you can sing in rhyme and splash yourself with Dylan you can't begin to compete with *the real*. Enough. I lost my innocence and asked. . . .

Just who do you think you are? What a way to start. We argued. He tried to control me through condescension, I bashed into him with the standard punked spite protestations. I was in an argument with a pop star at The Midland Hotel: 5 stars. What was to become of me?

"What is it?" Jaz is moaning, "that you've got that you think you can justify writing that sort of stuff? All you can say as a journalist, right, is that 'I personally don't like the album.' You can't shout out to the masses 'This is shit because I think so.' You can say I personally don't like it, right? Don't you think that's fair?"
As fair as enough might ever be. But what's supposed to be fair about this? And anyway, it's the old dilemma. Whenever I write anything it's my *opinion*, it's so obvious. It may reach lots of people through whatever and however, but it can never be sacred. It's going to be a few thoughts; there might be interrogation and a slab of investigation and we might move somewhere because of it, but it's never meant to be a statement on how

Glitter has to battle against his reputation being made trivial, against the general attitude that he's disappeared for ever, before he can even begin to hope to be taken seriously (or at least accepted) as a contemporary cabaret entertainer who deserves to be around at least as much as Steve Strange and perhaps as much as Richard Strange.

"I find myself being asked to do *Blankety Blank, Celebrity Squares* and things like that. I just don't want to do it. I'd love to think maybe I could bring a bit of balls to programmes like that, but it's just not how I see myself. I'm not going to be one of the eight people in those squares. I don't mind filling the screen myself, but I'm not sharing it."

Like Dick Emery, like Bob Geldof, like Roy Hudd, Glitter still realises that if he is accepted, it could be as a figure of fun.

"Sure! I don't mind, as long as it's full out there. I don't care if they come to jeer, shout, scream at me."

THE ESTATE moves off. Before we reach the motorway we have to take a detour. We drive to an army surplus store in Euston. Paul races out to the shop. Glitter cringes as his son pelts over a busy road with scant regard for speeding traffic. "You do worry when it's your own flesh and blood," he says.

Paul buys a stretchy white belt that will be used later that evening to wrap around a snowy white outfit and harness Glitter's wayward bulk. The red roses that will be chucked into the crowd at the end of the show have already been bought.

We reach the motorway and head determinedly north. The power steering's holding up well. Dave Lee Travis is soon heard fighting through the cheap radio's crackle.

"I like being on the road", Glitter admits, taking snaps of me in the back seat with Pennie Smith's camera. He's been on that hard brick road for most of 20 years: in the spirit of Max Wall rather than Sam Apple Pie.

"When you're young all you want to do is play music and get your leg over. It's the bit in between that's the complication."

We talk about women in today's groups. He surprises me with his desire to know what's going on; he knows he'll never add to new developments, but he still wants to find out about new things.

"I think you have to try and know about everything that's done. If you don't take notice, that's when you get old! That's when you say that's what I see and that must be all that's there.

"I can still identify and be identified with a youthful thing, I think."

I ask him about Adam.

"I've never met him, actually. I was due to have lunch with them next week, but they all got flu. Poor dears . . . ha ha ha! But I do feel an empathy with what he's doing. Maybe only because of the fans. A lot of my followers are followers of them as well. And The Human League. There's a closeness. But Adam particularly . . . and they openly admit where they got the sound from. I think Adam's going to be a wonderful entertainer!!!"

Does he appreciate what Adam's going through now: star-heat?

"Yuh. At the height of my fame I couldn't go out of the front door, I couldn't go out of the back door, any door . . . I was smuggled out in laundry baskets and God knows what else. None of that will happen again! The thing is, it's never really changed that much for me all the time I've been singing. It changed when I got hit records, and the fame became the added thing that I didn't have before. Before all that I earned enough to eat, playing pubs or whatever, and I've always given the same amount of energy, which is all I can.

"Now, I'm not even trying too hard. I've achieved that; I've got rid of most of that ego thing. I used to wear it all the time. Now I can take it off like a coat. Which is much healthier. Ego is like a maggot in an apple. It can eat away at you until it destroys you. I've lost all that intense business of I've got to make it, I've got to make it. Now, I'm very loose about it all. I'm easy."

Many people considered that star time the end, not part of the development.

"Yeah. But now is more of an achievement. Not many people are doing what I'm doing. I don't see myself number one in the charts. It'd be nice, but I don't have the ambition. That was years ago. Y'know, my background has always been lead singer. Up front. The guy who the girls would scream at and the guys would get uptight about. Then it changed over, and I started pulling as many guys – from the point of view of an audience – as chicks. During the Gary Glitter hit-run at the beginning it was very much a male following. Then the media slightly changed it. It became *Jackie* magazines and all that. Little girls were coming along and screaming."

Did he relish that?

"Yeah. I enjoyed it very much. It was lovely. It was exactly what I wanted, I think, except at the time I was 27, so it was a surprise. It was what I wanted probably when I was 16 or 17."

Was it like the dream he imagined?

"Yeah, yeah, yeah. What I enjoyed . . . was the adoration of a lot of people, of a lot of women. I really did. The only problem was I didn't get a chance to enjoy it, if you know what I mean."

Nudge and a wink.

"The strange part of it was they all became terribly young, 13, 14, 15 . . . maybe a few older. So you weren't allowed to be too naughty – right? – plus there was all this rushing about and a security that I couldn't work out was to keep them out or keep me in. I still really don't know."

Gary Glitter was declared bankrupt a few months ago.

"I just couldn't go on spending money like I was. There's an official five years, and then they wipe the debt out. I don't think I'll be able to pay it off unless I have three number one hits, and that's very unlikely. Ha! Ha! Ha! I talked them into letting me be Gary Glitter, doing my shows, because that was the logical way that I could pay back the money. And I want to pay it back. My biggest disappointment is that the tax people won't let me have the kind of clothes that I would like. I can't be very Glittery, I have to find alternatives.

"In a way the bankruptcy thing is good because it's like I'm starting all over again, and so it makes me care. I can't go out and spend the money I like to spend – on other people primarily. It enables me to turn round to people and say it's your turn. I was generous and extravagant with the money. . . ."

Perhaps that's why he landed in the mess in the first place.

"I don't do this for money. If you want a lot of money you have to work at making a lot of money. I don't work to have a lot of money, I work at what I do because I like to do it. It's a by-product that I get money from time to time. I still earn a lot of money, but it goes to paying off my debt. I think I'm very entertaining and I think I deserve all the money I get!

"I do think the bankruptcy is a good thing in many ways. It's made me a nicer person. When I had a lot of money I don't think I was a particularly nice person."

I find that hard to believe.

"I think I was an OK person. But I wasn't too nice to my ex-wife or my kids. I didn't really have a chance to be nice. I was wrapped up in cotton wool quite a lot. It's brought me down to earth, and rock'n'roll is about being down to earth as well as being a dream. As well as."

As we ease through the outskirts of Manchester into the small city of Salford, grey clouds seem to hover just yards above us – a total contrast to the cold sunshine we'd left behind in London. Glitter is getting keyed up about the night's show.

"I'm still young! Of course I am. I don't want to hear the words middle-aged or old. I've never bothered about age, thank God. It doesn't enter my vocabulary. I thrive on youth, youth ideas, on changes. . . ."

We pull up outside a ghostly Salford University.

"Really though, I'm just a bull in a china shop."

It's five o'clock.

A COUPLE of hours before Glitter unleashes himself into performance, we sit and talk about what he's doing and why. Two years ago he was battling away on a Lovelace Watkins cabaret circuit, wasting his specialist energies on lifeless audiences.

His original audience had grown up, formed post-punk and electro-pop groups extending and transforming Glitter/Leander propositions, and a demand sucked him back into the rock whirl. Here was a challenge – Glitter charged up.

He played rock venues and clubs to audiences soaking in memories, responding to a rare, ripe vitality. Glitter's primitivism, punk pantomime, unimpeachable naughtiness made sense all over again. There was something there that hadn't dated. What he's doing now though, with a scruffy rockist backing group and in those uncomfortable University venues can skid close to being called unsound revivalism.

He knows the dangers, and once the standard show of strength for the visiting writer has been dealt out, a certain honesty filters through.

"I could end up like Bill Haley or something. I know you've got to give people something new, all the time. I do know that. But I'm trying to re-establish myself, create a new market, basing it on the Gary Glitter everyone knows. And loves."

things definitely are. That's absurd simply because certainty is absurd. And good criticism, or commentary, should add to the breathtaking, unrelieving uncertainty of this, that and the other. But it just seems silly to write after every article "this is my opinion, it is not fact, it is not conclusion." It's one opinion. It goes without saying. And I have the right because I made the right, and I take it from there. I never accept that people are so stupid that this won't be clear to them.

"Yeah," begins Youth, not with me, "all we want is honesty. We don't demand anything but that, right? It's not the music you're criticising when you do your reviews, you're criticising the attitude, and if you don't know the people who made the music, how can you begin to criticise their attitude? You can only guess where those attitudes have come from and what they bloody are, right? And how the fuck do you know, cos you don't, right? It's one thing talking about the piece of plastic, but you don't do that. How do you justify that?"

I don't like your music. I said that.

"No. You didn't mention the music."

I did. I didn't like the sound.

"I wouldn't have minded that."

It just turned me off.

"I can understand that," Jaz replies, having calmed down a bit. "We'd be right fucking prats if we were journalists, I suppose."

I found time, stood close to the wreckage, to feel saddened that such hysterical surface scratching, this excremental idiocy, could be taken seriously as a unit of guidance, as an exceptional entertainment, or as blue blue glorious blue flashes of inspiration and illumination. Bauhaus plunder and blunder

"Those kids want to hear my hits. A lot of people have never ever seen me do those songs. The new material will come. I'm looking forward to it. There's definitely a place for me. And I do commit myself. I'm not ready to give up. I want to act, say the things I'm saying in different ways. I don't want it to be a nostalgia trip. I think if I felt that's what it is now, I would stop altogether. I don't know what I would do though. I haven't a clue."

GARY GLITTER has his first fit onstage, bursting through curtains wearing a farcical look of frenzied surprise, at just gone ten. A small audience gathered at the front totally abandons itself. Even on minimal budget, with a David Essex-type backing group, Gary Glitter The Show is a fantastic form of fiction, an excess of nonsense and conceit, fancy and insanity that is timeless through its openness, Glitter's plain elation, an insatiable amoral greed. It's pure force, desire, lure. It's bright and beseeching.

Glitter is in awe, exalting and exciting through a performance of audacious pomposity and unspoilt self-deprecation. "Rock And Roll", "Leader of the Gang", "Good To Be Back", "You're Beautiful" sensationally involve the audience, pull them deep into the drama. It's a celebration of impudence and sensation, comparable almost to Bette Midler: a delighted, delicious stimulation.

GG The Show is cartoon, circus, sham. Glitter avoids the senility of contemporaries like Rod Stewart and the whole thing is hilarious but still more relevant than most rockist action. By eleven o'clock the fits are finished; roses are dispersed.

Two hours later, Glitter has shed his stage skin, signed the autographs, and is sitting quietly in the back of the estate. We're driving back to London.

"Usually", he confides, "I just sit in the car, have a smoke and a drink, relax, reflect on the show and my performance . . . I've never had a member of the press in the same car as me. There are some things I don't like to mention. It'll spoil the mystery."

He makes a few reasonable excuses about the smallness of the University audience. I tell him I thought the show was hilarious. He's not sure how to take that.

"Yes it is, isn't it?" he eventually agrees. "It's very funny. It is hilarious."

Is it meant to be that funny?

"Yes. If that is the way that you want to take it. People take it in different ways."

The estate slices through Greater Manchester towards the Motorway. Glitter opens a bottle of wine and lights a cigarette.

So what happened when the Gary Glitter of legend, the Gary Glitter more influential on the burst of today's music than Stewart or Elton John or Yes, faded away?

"It was a combination of things. It got to a point where I had to withdraw for a while, because it was getting too big. To a saturation level. I thought it's no good being there all the time. I couldn't keep up the pace, and I didn't really want to. I was desperately in need of a break, a holiday and everything else, so we did the farewell tour, intending to be back.

"The music around us was changing, and I was aware that it was changing, and I was continually ploughing most of my money into what I was doing. I couldn't carry on with just the money I was earning in Europe. It all got so silly. So I did The Retirement. I intended to take off six months to a year depending. Drop out, let things change a bit, and see if I could maintain my popularity."

Were you relieved it was over?

"Yeah! I was in some ways, even though I didn't know it at the time. There is no way I could have carried on that high. People were changing, everything was changing. The beauty of it now is that if I'd have stayed at the top I wouldn't have the thing that is happening now. It would have got really desperate, trying to keep having the hits. Now I just don't need a hit record. It would be great to have one, but I know that there's a whole bunch of people out there who identify with me and we're a gang, we're a team of funny people if you like. Hilarious! Yeah, good, and that's what it's all about."

Have you wasted anything by committing yourself to pure entertainment?

"The year I was out I had a great time. I did everything I wanted to. Went to Thailand, got out of my box, meditated, got into Yoga. I did all those things which brought me closer to understanding myself. I think it's not a case of knowing what you want to do, it's a case of knowing what you don't want to do. And I don't want to be manipulated, particularly from the point of view of making money. I'm not so intense about wanting to be a superstar. I am a kind of star, and because I know that and can identify with that, it doesn't have to take over my very being. It just means I have to come up with the goods. And by coming up with the goods, if I do, it could be the most interesting period of my life. It could now be Rock and Roll Part 3."

———

WE STOP off for petrol. Glitter spots a couple of policewomen and his eyes light up.

"I had a really dirty policewoman in Oxford. Maybe those two are on their way to the *Two Ronnies.*"

It's 3 a.m. We'll reach London by six.

"What I've been doing I've done since 1959. I think stamina's always going to be an important part of how long I can go on. I'm being naughty at the moment because I'm not taking good care of myself, physically. I don't watch my weight and things like that. Everybody when they get to a certain age whether they like it or not finds themselves slowing up mentally and physically. I've abused my body. I'm fatter now than I've ever been at any one point, which again is quite funny because I'm still doing what I do and getting a reaction. In fact it's getting better because I'm getting fatter and so it's funnier.

"I have a motto – somebody up there likes me. I've been very lucky. I've only ever done what I've wanted to do, which is sing and entertain. I don't know how to do anything else. I just know how to get up there on the stage and do it. Please God."

like bullshitters in fine art shops; drag themselves backwards through the tangled thorny foliage of rock styles; join together a few of the dots of pop art with snidy smug baggy abandon. Bauhaus are one of the most confused groups I have ever crashed into; they are not even capable of being authentically disgusting, or even evocatively crude, or disconcertingly scatological, or even vaguely sinister, and their loose change act just poured out at me like a melted plastic substitute vomit.

Murphy: . . . "by intending to provoke us, maybe a reaction you will get will be one of absolute anger and hurt."
Jay: "You could have got your head kicked in if we were Killing Joke."
The days labourer: I've been through a similar situation with Killing Joke.
Jay: "The initial reaction when we read the review and then heard that you were going to interview us, we thought how were we going to approach it? We came up with two possibilities: A being physical violence, and B being a reasoned discussion. We decided to plump for the latter, but this doesn't mean that the former isn't in with a fighting chance."

Why are you so worked up?
"Naah, not worked up especially, that comes over as paranoid . . . but Marillion are a band that like to smash against the walls of categorisation and we've been fucked up too many times by people comparing us to Genesis. People who never liked Genesis will then not think that they can like us. It causes a lot of problems. And we're just musicians. We don't believe in the fashion thing, in the sheep thing, the categorisation mode that has precedence these days . . . we want to be treated

TED NUGENT
May 5, 1979
He could galvanise
the dead with his talk.

IT'S APPROACHING MIDNIGHT, and in an empty, echoey dressing room, so bright it seems to have no ceiling, deep in the lifeless body of an elevated sports hall on the outskirts of Stuttgart, South Germany, Ted Nugent is pensively getting changed.

He has just performed an inevitably effective two-hour set of highly professional hammering hurricane muzak for 3000 raving German teenagers, but it's more like he's casually swum a couple of lengths of a 50-metre pool. He sweatlessly roams about the room slowly taking off his corny self-mocking stage gear, the animal skin waistcoat, the white skin-tight Crimplene flared trews, the bone and tooth necklace and, most absurdly, the silver beaver tail that hangs down from his backside.

"**Paul, you can't begin to imagine,**" he drawls, emphasising every second word in a slightly different way, "**and I mean, I am not exaggerating, but there're chicks in America that are just BETTER than the ones you see in** Penthouse **and** Playboy, **phenomenal chicks. And all they want to do is suck your dick.**"

He pauses. "**It's nothing, nothing at all, to have a half dozen chicks in your room. There is only one thing that determines it, and that's how much energy you got after the gig. Really . . . I ain't talking male chauvinist here. It's healthy and I treat them well.**"

Do you think you are a good person, I ask.

"**AARM . . . Yeah, I am a good person. I don't take advantage of anyone . . . I take good care of my people.**"

Maybe selfish, I push.

"**Yeah . . . on uh personal principles I am selfish in that I will not allow other ideas to surface in my music. That's very selfish of me. But that's too bad. However, with the money that I make from my ideas I pay my men very well. Cliff Davies earns over a quarter of a million dollars a year out of me. . . . I care for the people in my band.**"

But, I insist, your gross egocentricity. . . .

"**Oh, outside my wild talk about chicks, about pussy, I have never abused anybody physically or emotionally. Everyone I have ever fucked I'm nice to – that's going to look** really weird in print. But . . . there are loads of sides to me that nobody has any idea about.**"

What comes across in the music is that Ted Nugent is an absolute idiot.

"**Those gonzoid things are applicable to rock and roll. The intensity, the aggression, the uninhibitedness, the audacity, the cockiness, the sex, those are the things. And if those things break the ice then you can start talking.**"

As if on cue, into the room burst six enthusiasts, a babble of awed lower-teen German males, grubby and drab, clutching ticket stubs, posters and ballpoints, to get precious signatures. Nugent is pleasantly amenable, half-heartedly greeting them with an expected, "**Whoah . . . where are the chicks. . . ?**"

The huddle is the typical awkward, immature, sexually repressed, boring type I've always associated with Nugent and that ilk. The kind that is easily sucked into Nugent's studiously outrageous parents-loathe-it noise, where all suppressed desires can be safely channelled.

Nugent scrawls, and converses as coherently as possible with the grinning, chatting Germans. "**Good show, no?**"

Nugent really wants to know.

"Ya," the six chorus. "Good show. Good show," they repeat, pushing their English vocabulary. "It . . . was . . . not . . . too . . . loud," cheerfully articulates a round-shouldered, snotty-nosed member of the group, "for that, thank you, thank you. . . ."

Nugent acts mock startled; "**Not loud enough, wow, don't say that.**"

The six don't leave once they've collected their autographs, boldly crowding Nugent and carefully explaining their adulation and the number of his records that they've managed to save up for. Nugent nods sincerely.

"**Well, for that, thank you very much.**" He proudly shows them the artwork for his next album, "State of Shock", that comes out in America at the end of May. On the front, Nugent playing guitar, sparks flying from his fingers; on the back, an idealised glamour picture of the recently unveiled stud Nugent; inside a couple of dozen snapshots of roadies, musicians, friends.

He coyly points out a picture to the mindlessly seriously or not at all, to be put in a proper place. . . ."

But there is no such thing as an enlivening inventive critical perspective these days – just minor, mingy bitchery. You fancy a fair, conscientious and rigorous critical approach towards Marillion that if carried out intelligently and emotionally would probably condemn you as right titheads.

"I think so . . . as long as what we do has been properly listened to, not just pre-criticised . . . I get really fed up reading another character assassination in a live review that completely ignores the music we played or the atmosphere of the show, that just dishes out the same old prejudice."

But isn't such bitching valid in the context – another week's "entertaining" reading about the mad, maddening pop show (off) business? Look at the berk, look at him squeal. Next! You're on parade – what do you want? Bernard Levin or Philip Larkin droning on about you or something? Maybe you're not important enough. Just who do you think you are?

"It all becomes the ego trip of the journalist, and they for the benefit of their own show off will prefer to take things at face value. It's like watching a Lenny Bruce show where there was a lot of depth, you actually had to think about the comedy if you wanted to get anything out of it. It's the same with Marillion, you have to think about the jokes between the songs, the lyrics and the actual delivery. If you just go into it thinking it's going to be a carbon copy of some '70s extreme, then you're going to get fuck-all out of it. You have to look into the music, and in there you will find a form of awareness. . . . If you haven't got the time then there's no point in talking about it."

None of this means it's going to

crowing Germans. **"There,"** he says, pride in his voice, **"my two little children."** It's a picture of two sheepish, blond-haired, pink-faced infants. The Germans go aah but they don't really understand. **"I love those children,"** says Nugent.

███████████████████████████

Car Journey Number One

Me and Pennie Smith have been waiting at the Holiday Inn, 15 miles outside Stuttgart, for an afternoon. Ted Nugent and aides arrive from England just before five. The day before Nugent has flown into England from America on Concorde, a flight the rich man in him will expertly detail the advantages of for interested parties.

He strides purposefully through the hotel doors leaving his aides scattered behind him, and with four steps is up at the reception desk checking in. Thick hair flows in waves down his back, light brown, glowing, no split ends. His face is lightly tanned and clean shaven, except for a few token hairs in the middle of his chin. He manically chews a thick cigar butt. He looks a lot younger and less rugged than I imagined. Small darting eyes are hidden for now behind expensive sun spectacles. A well-dressed, fit and healthy, rich young American.

We introduce ourselves. For Nugent it is perfectly natural that two Britishers should be waiting for him in The Holiday Inn, 15 miles outside Stuttgart. **"Yaah,"** he roars in approval, **"You got the questions, I got the answers. Start snapping, start snapping!"**

We are, you could say, rushed off our feet by a gross, noisy Groucho derivative.

"He wasn't like this before," whispers Pennie, who's met him previously.

I don't really have time to work out what this means. He's off, ranting to an aide, maybe trying to impress us.

"Last week we went to the Eric Clapton concert" – the words shoot out of his mouth – **"and I am here to tell you that I will not be that wounded until I am buried in the ground for two years! That guy is a neutral! I mean, like it's snooze rock. C'mon, Eric, wake up. . . . So anyway after the Clapton concert I went and saw Asleep At The Wheel, and they were good, a little sing-time, doo wop diddy, and that was cool, so then I went over to this club, and I got up on stage with Blackfoot – good band! – I couldn't believe the audience, they were great, and I stole the show."**

He lets out a piercing laugh.

"So I jammed all night man and then the next night we went to New York, and I jammed with Soft White Underbelly, alias, the Blue Oyster Cult, who were playing at The Bottom Line. And there's Buck Dharma there bumping into my kneecaps he's so huge . . . I get on stage and start jamming, and there I am jamming away and my amp packs up – is this a conspiracy, I think – so I have this fucked-up amp and up comes little Buck, sees what's happening and fuck if he doesn't plug me into his amp. Chivalry is not dead!"

He's to tell that story three times during the next six hours. **"Hey you guys coming to the soundcheck?"**

Nugent's been in the country 50 minutes. We pile into a dark Mercedes and a nervous local promoter drives us to another side of Stuttgart. **"We were in England Monday,"** Nugent tells us, **"and we went around . . . we saw that club in London . . . Dingwalls, pitiful. Just pitiful. That place would be bombed in Detroit. They would bomb it out of sheer pity! I met some guys from The Clash there . . . I don't think much of them, I don't know much. I never heard them. They were nice guys. Their hair was so silly I tried not to look at it. Hair like yours. I couldn't believe it. Why do you get it all cut off like that?"**

It's cheap. I do it myself.

"Cheap! I do mine myself too, and it's even cheaper 'cos I don't do nothing to it. So beat that one!"

Long hair in the rain, it plasters all around your face – it's uncomfortable.

"Tie the shit in a pony tail."

And get my ear cut off?

"You get your ear cut off? Well, I'm gonna

wear a pony tail in England just to see if anyone has the balls to cut my ear off. If they cut my ear off they die, and the first four members of their family die with 'em. They really went over the edge, didn't they, the punkerellas.''

Nugent stares out of the window with a smug look on his face. "Their self-appointed edge. The edge prior to the edge. Like the edge is way out at the distance, and they couldn't make it so they made their own edge and went over that." Another scraping laugh. "But I can get a kick out of it. I mean, they hide all the lepers and retards these days so you got to have some kind of laugh.''

By your standards The Clash make a wild noise.

"I honestly haven't heard them," he comes down to earth. "One band I do like . . . I don't know if they're of the same vernacular . . . is the band that does 'Roxanne'. The Police.''

The Police, I moan!

"Have you heard that song: fucking gorgeous! That song is great. One of the greatest songs I've heard in years.''

Maybe a little too polite. . . .

"Polite?" Nugent is 85 per cent deaf in his left ear. He's seated on my right, so he has to twist round to make out what I say. "I don't know about any connotations of that. I just think the song itself is ROCKING. Polite? What's polite about it?''

Oh, it holds back, takes its time . . . snoozes.

"Mmmm . . . I don't go by that. My ears are in charge of that area. That's a great song. The guy's voice! And that snare drum. CRACK! . . . CRACK! . . . CRACK! . . . I love it. I'm gonna hire that guy so that he can chop firewood for me this year. He'll earn a lot more money than he is now. A great little tune. In fact, I wrote a song called 'Ebony' last week that's kind of like that, only much better." Obviously.

"Not quite as *polite*.''

Theodore Nugent is 30 years old, has been playing rock 'n' roll for a living for 15 years, and has been married for nine years. At the moment,

as a career man, he has never been so successful, and his marriage is wrecked. That is no coincidence. The divorce procedures that he is currently stumbling through dominate his conversation, and the ramifications of those procedures dominate his life.

Deep down beneath the too-confident, ultra assured, wild man guitar hero is a confused, complex and oddly lonely man, who cares only for his two little children, Sasha, aged five, and Toby, aged two, their well-being, and his ability to maintain their well-being. The pain, bemusement and realism of his divorce from Sandy Jezowski, also 30, is something he can't quite get used to and doesn't really know what to do with. It interferes.

Nugent's job is to con people who want to be conned, to blow out raucous comedy, to blabber more and more about impossible feats, exaggerated achievements, his unequalled genius. His is the skill of outrage, irreverence and disrespect. He is a master of exploitation and manipulation, which is why he is so wealthy. But the current reality of an unwanted separation bites into this comfortable, self-made world, and throws him off balance.

Ted Nugent is invincible? Ted Nugent is in control?

It's taken Ted Nugent 14 years to build his world. He is one of America's established entertainers who's measured in unreal statistics and platinum discs. In Europe he is a raging cult figure. Both sides of the water he is a bona-fide love-to-hate personality. All this is something he has built carefully, shrewdly establishing and meticulously maintaining the standard crass 'n' bland heavy rock that western teenagers have an insatiable appetite for.

He calls the specialised science and objectivity that produces this highly sellable and universally appealing commodity 'rock 'n' roll' but although the list of ingredients, the main inputs, and the catalysts – his guitar playing and his aggresion – sound reasonably convincing and relevant, it's a rambling, superfluous and predictable "rock 'n' roll" that has little to do with what most think of as rock.

He cans his music, and plasters an outrageous, colourful, blatantly fictionalised label on the tins.

be of any use to interesting people.

"I just wish people would look deeper . . . maybe people are scared that just maybe a band influenced by the '70s could actually be the one true band of the '80s. . . .''

Scared? Surely it's just indifference.

"It's a matter of pride. . . .''

I'm indifferent towards Marillion – I've done my research! – and it isn't a matter of pride. It's just . . . indifference.

"You don't like the music. It happens.''

So why are you so pissed off with your critics?

"Because I cannot stand people who come to us with pre-thoughts. I cannot stand it when people treat us so lightly.''

A review of a show at the Glasgow Apollo that laughs at Big Fish is not a problem like spending a night in El Salvador.

"I quite agree with you.''

So what are you moaning about?

"The narrow mindedness of people who influence other people. I want my band to be reflected true to form. I want to be able to answer.''

Why is it so important that you answer?

"Because we're trying to break down the walls of prejudice and characterisation . . . because we get away with it . . . because we confront reality situations that people always want to ignore . . . because I pull back the curtains on painful situations that people don't want to know about and say, look, can you handle this. . . .''

I'm quite clever and I've done my research and I don't get any of that from Marillion. I get blurry blarney, honest endeavour, damp over-compensation, portentous demonstrations of concern, galloping gibberish. . . .

"Perhaps then you should

And makes more money in a year than you or I earn in a lifetime. Now, this is not rock 'n' roll. Or, it is.

Nugent broke through to "superstardom" in 1975 with "Ted Nugent", which followed three albums with the legendary Amboy Dukes and four snobbishly respected solo albums. Those early records defined the recipes and routines of the act, and Nugent has slid through four more platinum albums refining and perfecting those attitudes and systematically smoothing out the faintest hint of fundamental spontaneity.

Pre-1975 intense cult status was not half-way appealing enough for Nugent. Can you imagine an obscure John Wayne acting out bit parts in soap operas?

"The people who didn't dig me back then will tell you what a big-mouth asshole I was because I was always bragging and showing off about how big I was going to be. Yeah, I knew it all along. I told my mum and dad when I was watching the Nelsons, Rick Nelson, back in '59. That, yes, that is what I am going to do man. My dad used to make me write out what I would like to be when I grew up, when I was seven or eight, and there was no such thing as a rock 'n' roll star back then, so I used to write folk hero . . . or a guitarist back in Michigan . . . ."

That success took a long time coming didn't bother Nugent.

"Yeah, it took a few years coming before I became as successful as I knew I always would be. But that's all right, that's good, y'know. The house you spend ten years building will house you better than the house you spend two years building."

He married Sandy Jerowski in 1970, five years before his breakthrough. They split up at the end of 1977.

"It was her decision," he confesses, a dazed and hurt victim when the Nugent barriers have been thrown aside. **"It was the last thing on earth that I wanted. Because I loved my wife with an unequalled intensity, like everything else I do. I just lived for her."**

For Sasha and Toby, Nugent would sacrifice . . . **"whatever necessary. I would drop my career like THAT if I had to. What is more important than guiding the upbringing of your offspring? If anyone's got anything more important please step forward. I defy anyone."**

████████████████████████████

Car Journey Number Two

After a rushed soundcheck and half an hour's thudding jamming in the dressing room so that the Nugent band could familiarise themselves with each other after a long layoff (when's the last time you played together, I asked Nugent later. "Oh, two weeks ago." That's a long time! "I think so."), it's a drive back to the hotel. I sit next to him in front of the Mercedes – he's decided to drive – and in the back are Pennie and Nugent's drummer and co-producer, ex-If man Cliff Davis, a tidy, short haired and articulate colleague.

"You promised me that if I did the European tour I wouldn't have to drive with you," claims a grinning Davis. **"Bullfucker,"** retorts Nugent. **"You don't mind my driving!"**

You like to drive, Ted?

"Yeah, I love to drive. I guess you might say I am a driving fanatic. I love off-road racing, broken terrain, hills, gullies, deserts, rocky terrains. I have impeccable depths of perception and reflexes."

Davis and Nugent discuss the sound and sequence of "State of Shock", Nugent typically exaggerating every detail to unreasonably disproportionate levels. After they've run through certain aspects of this new product, I ask what would happen if the new album bombed, figuring to discover if Nugent would operate as automatically as he does now without the response and money involved, or function as he once did out of definite love.

He explodes. **"SHEETE!!! Then I will personally cut off my dick and eat it! I will cut my cock off on the Ed Sullivan Show and chew on it. That is what I'll do if the new album bombs. I will guarantee we'll outsell every** album we've ever done. Next question please."

Except the next one.

"That's right. I can only be beat by my next venture. What kind of question was that, Paul?" he laughs.

A probing one?

"It was a SHITTY one. HAHAHAHAHA. There is just no way that will happen. I am a rock 'n' roll fan and the rock 'n' roll fans amongst us will be buying it. I just happen to keep on producing that which my rock 'n' roll fandom ears demand."

Ted Nugent firmly believes all this.

I lean back in my seat and think maybe I won't ask any more questions.

Davis asks him how Dingwalls was.

"Dingwalls was disgusting!" he relishes as we charge down a quiet country lane and the speedo nips comfortably up to 120 kph. "The bands there would be drawn and quartered in Detroit. It was just disgusting. I had a real kick. I had a riot. Plus the painted hair! All the manifestations of these people's lowness! It's just HAHAHAHA ... ridiculous ... HAHAHAHA, you know what I mean. Fucking A! Oh! There was only one good-looking chick. I swear man, it was like a bad case of anaemia had struck.

"Until I met Pennie here just every chick I've ever met from London just is the biggest piece of wet shit I've ever seen. In my life. I mean, I realise that I am spoilt ... some of those Hawaiians and Detroit women, and those Californian phenomenons, but nevertheless, in England ... Jesus Christ!"

As Nugent thrusts the limousine down the autobahn at 150 kph conversation turns to a recent *Rolling Stone* interview where he was allowed to hint for the first time that he isn't the ruthless, arrogant madman his legend suggests.

"I don't live a careful life," he states, one hand on the wheel, the other brushing his locks out of his eyes. "If I do the cover story for *Rolling Stone* like I did, even though I am going through a dangerous and threatening, typically threatening for some people, divorce ... I wasn't careful what I said. I wasn't careful what I exposed to the inter-

viewer. If I have a feeling – and a lot of the time I have my foot in my mouth and I am the first to agree with that – but if I have an impulse statement to make, I am not going to sit there and go (in wimpy voice) maybe I'm not right, I'll just say it!

"Nothing is so important, conclusive, whether it's said or done, that it can haunt you for the rest of your life. Nothing is THAT important."

Despite the fact that people immediately around Nugent make it difficult for us to get close to him, he himself is ever ready to talk and make sure everything's OK.

"Is Pennie having a good time?" he asks me at one point, genuinely concerned. At the hotel he invites us up to his room. He pulls out a stack of pictures of Sasha and Toby for us to look through. Darling and dainty, they're caught in all sorts of poses and postures. Nugent makes to ring them at home in America.

"Aren't they beautiful?" he sighs.

It's difficult to disagree with him.

I ask about moral guidelines.

"I hope they will be responsive to my guidance. Um, morality at five and two is, er, rather distant. As far as my relating constantly to pussy, I just consider it a fantastic form of recreation and an honest, legitimate, proper and righteous form of communication and relationship to have with the opposite sex. AAH ... having 100 girls isn't any different from one girl, except I like it a whole lot better!

"Aah, as far as the guidance of my children goes I believe I have a fantastic and ultimately righteous concept of what is right and what is wrong and good and bad, with unlimited attitudes getting right down to never hurting anyone, never stealing anything, never misguiding anyone, never picking anyone's brains.

"As far as the application of morality to my children as regards sex itself, my son obviously will do just great, applying my attitude ... my son'll be just fine ... but my daughter will have to make her own

question yourself."

Very clever.

Do you believe in Adam Ant? The 27-year-old Ant trapped in a third-floor suite of Manchester's Portland Hotel is very believable. Dressed in comforting black, his hair pushed away from a beaten looking face, minus the miracle make up, this pre-prepared Adam appears as a primitive, shrunken version of the f/ant/asy – not yet drunk on the aches and pains of fame, the frictions and salvations of fortune, but noticeably tipsy. Wrinkles encircle his eyes; his cheeks are sinking.

Here is the fresh-faced Adam who has been nagged at for too long by the idle Eve, here's the fighter who's been through a lot of trouble and who wouldn't mind some ... applause: an embrace.

His mid-afternoon, unpainted physical presence is, for me, emphatically unnerving. There are not enough myths or associations tangled up in Adam for the unattached observer to feel subdued, to feel shock vibrations. Adam, alone, at this moment, away from the songs, is particularly ordinary: this is not to say that Adam will never find that *extra*.

"If Robert De Niro walked into this room now," Adam warns me, "you would bog yourself. I swear."

Downstairs in the hotel lobby a tiny representative of the outside world clamour – a 15-year-old girl – had just been allowed into Adam's suite to pick out with delicately painted nails fifteen minutes of the man's life. She hands him a rose. She has definitely felt something special, been near to the extraordinary. She can't explain. . . .

"He kissed me! I'm not going to wash for a month! He gave me this wristband. . . ."

She can't believe it. Her friends can't believe it wasn't them.

decisions and it won't be easy."

Nugent can't get through to his children, and is angry and troubled. But he doesn't take it out on anybody. Not once did I see him get angry. Is this man too nice to live?

Car Journey Number Three

Nugent climbs into the driving seat of the Mercedes again, and we take off for the actual gig. By now it's obvious he isn't the stubborn, condescending lunatic I'd expected; it's just that he believes faithfully and religiously in his self-created world, that he's somewhat shaky outside of that, and that no one attempts any serious, persistent disagreement.

My own occasional complaints are greeted with disbelieving bellows of amazement. Like I said, it's his world, how can I upset its rigorous logic.

Darkness has fallen, and Nugent skilfully speeds the car down unlit roads. I wonder if he ever thinks about influence or responsibility.

"I consider it, but I don't dwell on it," he softly decides, "and I don't think that I am inspiring anything detrimental. I realise the music's intensity and gross uninhibitedness does inspire some negative forms of uninhibitedness . . . be it liquor intake or in some instances manifestations of violence . . . but I surely don't want anyone to get hurt, I don't want anyone to cause damage and I don't think I inspire that.

"But I surely don't preach to them . . . I think that it's generally known about my attitude towards drugs and liquor, that I don't do them, but I don't impress that . . . that's because I gag on liquor, I can't stand the taste. I puke my guts out if I smell the cork out of a bottle of wine. And, er, as far as drugs go I've seen too many assholes bite the dust in various forms to want to be involved.

"I always want my level of awareness to be optimum, y'know whether it's playing guitar or driving like this."

We ease around a sharp corner, Nugent perfectly in control.

"I've seen so many good people just nosedive into the gutter because of drugs."

"Did you ever get drafted?" I ask on impulse.

"If I'd have made the army we wouldn't have had all that trouble in Vietnam", Nugent shoots back, " 'cos I would have won it in a year. I had a serious and fantastic career and I wasn't gonna go and play soldiers and waste my incredible talents. So I got out. It was easy. Look what those people were dealing with. I am an intelligent person. I analysed the situation," Nugent cryptically reveals. "I went in and I did it. I got out."

None of this "intelligence" comes through in your music.

"I doubt if you can tell my intelligence from my music. I seriously doubt that my intelligence has ever surfaced. Except for acknowledgement of certain worldly facts. I keep my intelligence for sustaining what I do. Intelligence coupled with sheer audacity."

Are you surprised at what you get away with?

"No. I'm amazed, but it doesn't surprise me. I expect it. A lot of people are real quick to point the finger at me and call me bigheaded, conceited, loud-mouthed. Who does he think he is? To them I say EAT MUCHO FUCK! Because . . . HAHAHAHA . . . because I have unquestionably got a grip on things. I have just got a grip on things period. The Nuge is under control. It's as simple as that."

Do you get complacent?

"SHIT!! DO I GET COMPLACENT!!! My dick is so hard it hurts my navel constantly. I am ready." Nugent shakes his mane, and there's a fire in his eyes. "Complacency was scratched out of my Webster's long ago. I am . . . I get relaxed. Complacent? Sorry, unavailable to me. No way. Fucking A. Ever tried fucking with a soft one? Can't do it, Paul. Since I have become single my intensity has multiplied. . . .

"I took a breath at the end of '78 because

I was in such pain. I was running on auxiliary power in '78. I was only able to rock ass in '78 because it is inherent to my nature, my belief and my attitude.

"Every night I cried before I went on stage but I still kicked ass when I got out there. 'Cos I was really in the pits in '78. I have never experienced that. I just remember crying every night. But once I got out on that stage, the sanctuary of rock 'n' roll. Phew! Put that dick up in the air, boy. Whereas now I am inspired by my relationships with all the different girls. There's nothing like a good piece of ass to inspire rock 'n' roll."

After the show I stroll into the tuning-up room searching for a drink. And Nugent is there, sat upright, politely talking with two young German females and a bearded local teacher – who has brought along a coach load of teenagers to the concert and now has them safely tucked up in bed in a nearby hostel.

Nugent is attempting to learn some German words, not to get the girls into bed. The trio soon leave, and he quietly, but not wearily, asks me what I thought of the gig. I think of more numbing guitar solos than I ever thought possible, leaping over amps, appalling melodrama, posing, posing, pummelling, pummelling . . . with much effort I manage to make a circle out of my thumb and index finger and shake it his way.

He hums.

"It was a typical first night," he reflects.

It was a nightmare, I think.

So what does he want people walking away from a Ted Nugent concert to feel?

"I want them to feel that there was the greatest rock 'n' roll that they've ever felt in their lives."

There's an unusual commitment in what he says.

"That's what I want them to go away feeling. And that I'm the best mother of a guitarist on earth. And that it's more fun to go to a Ted Nugent concert than anything else in the world. That's what I want them to think."

The way Nugent boasts about the critical

elements in his music he should make a rock 'n' roll that at the very least falls somewhere between Mott The Hoople and The Angelic Upstarts. Unprofound, simplistic, but chaotic and dynamic, music that starts at the very top and hurtles.

He talks convincingly about thrust, uninhibitedness, spontaneity, drive, but to me his music is an excruciating, streamlined and gleaming hangover of banal heavy metal bluster, blotted of all edge by the years and whatever else.

I don't want to talk about Ted Nugent as a musician. He has perfected his science as neatly as Fleetwood Mac, Wings, Supertramp, and is as far as Neil Sedaka from the ethics of even the traditional rock 'n' roll he enthusiastically expounds.

This is both sad and disgraceful. But for Ted Nugent, in his world, what he does is the real rock 'n' roll. And people love it. Is it me? No. I am right. I live in the real world.

Sometimes, so does Ted Nugent.

Just after midnight the six German fans are herded with difficulty out of the bright dressing room.

"Bring some girls next time," Nugent shouts after them.

"Ya! Ya!" come back nervous affirmations. Nugent is now dressed in street clothes: jeans, shirt, strong boots. He's sat cross-legged next to me on a wooden bench, vigorously chewing gum. There's silence for a while.

"What time is it?"

Midnight.

"That makes it six in Detroit. I could still call the kids."

I ask Nugent if he still loves his wife.

"No. Not at all. I'm sure that it's a defence mechanism. I'm sure it's almost fake. And I really don't want to dig down deep enough to find out if I do or not. Because I have gone through so much painful agony. I don't even want to think about it. She treated me so horribly I can honestly say that I hate her ass . . . y'know . . . I don't know if I do but it's what comes out."

For the next ten minutes Nugent desperately

Does it disappoint you that after sixteen years of The Grateful Dead and what you've struggled and soared through, people like me can be so disrespectful of you: think you are rusty, crusty, dusty and musty?

"No! I don't give a damn . . . I would be afraid if everyone in this world liked us. The responsibility! I don't want to be responsible for leading the march to wherever. Fuck that. It's already been done and the world hates it. Humans hate it."

Wasn't that leading the march thing a '60s attitude?

"Fuck no. Hell! For me the whole combination of music and the psychedelic experience taught me to fear power. I mean fear it and hate it. In those times there were lunatics that were constantly trying to nail The Grateful Dead up as being the vanguard of some power trip. It was always the same thing. It was basically Hitler . . . y'know?"

Does David Sylvian worry what other people think about him?

"Only on a day when I'm feeling incredibly superficial. That's to do with the physical being. How people see you, how they represent you, all that is irrelevant in the face of any proper development. This body is the equipment that you have to carry with you through this space. I feel troubled by it, in a way, I think that when I no longer have a body, what trouble will I have. I find it clumsy. That's why I always wear baggy clothes, because the more shapeless it becomes the less I worry. When I'm performing I'm at the height of my awareness of how inhibited I am by my physical appearance."

I want to ask you about your sex life.

"So?"

So your "detachment" is from the body that is people's

attempts to impartially discuss and discover the cause of his wife's disillusionment with him; naïvely, bravely, with chronic disbelief, he relates how well he treated her, throws up numerous motivations as to why she left him but perhaps missing out on the true reasons.

After a gritty discourse on the impossibility of monogamy I observe that the feelings surfacing in the conversation are totally distinct from the clumsy and coarse reputation.

He allows himself a wry smile. **"Oh yeah. But that's because the press wants to flash on my biting people's tits off and stuff like that, which I do relish in saying, sure. Those who are close to me can get off on it but they know it's nonsense."**

That's what sells the music.

"OK . . . I don't think so . . . I think the music sells the music. But it's fun to read about, y'know, taking a nail and hammer and nailing people's dogs to doors.

"I am out to live the spectrum of feelings . . . I don't know if it was good for me or not to experience the pain I felt last year, but overall I think it was better for me to have experienced it than for me not to.

"Because I always figured I was strong just to have kept going as long as I did without the success, with some of the bullshit I had to wade through. But if I thought I was strong before last year, now I know I'm strong. Because what I have just gone through makes everything else look silly.

"I had nights when I would just cry ALL NIGHT. No sleep, nothing. It was RIDICULOUS. Then I got to a point when I was going, what are you doing, asshole. It's over! That is it. So what's next, y'know. . . .

"I had one cocked one night, and I was ready to blow my brains out, and I looked at it and I thought, you stupid fucker. What about Sasha and Toby? I laughed, cried, laughed, and I just thought, Nugent, you're a prick. Who do you think you are! Especially with my regard for firearms. What an INSIPID gesture."

Despite the fact that you're obviously sensitive and complex, your albums have all made similar blunt and irreverent statements.

"Absolutely. Absolutely."

Don't you feel inhibited by that?

"Not at all. Because that's rock 'n' roll. I certainly have no intentions to expose my innermost soul to people. If in the practice of my normal pursuits my inner soul is exposed, then that's fine – but it's hardly a major reason for concern."

But as a musician surely it is a concern to expose your soul, share experience.

Nugent chews his gum more rapidly. **"Yeah, but I'm an individual involved with things immediately around me and with people immediately around me. I think that it's insane to think that any purpose is to be served by exposing my soul to the world, my beliefs, my principles, my troubles. It would be basically inconsequential to the world. It is of no consequence."**

But what you do now is of even less consequence.

"No it's not. The intensity of music cannot really be discussed in the same breath as my personal attitudes.

"I think that without rock 'n' roll the crime rate would soar. There's a lot of quote rock 'n' roll unquote that people have probably humped on and learned things from. I don't think people are going to learn anything from my rock 'n' roll.

"Maybe some people will listen to 'Great White Buffalo' and realise that you can't market animals and expect them to be around for ever, but I don't think so. I think they listen to 'Great White Buffalo' and they listen to the guitar riff. I don't think a whole lot of people sit down and contemplate my lyrics. 'Oh, I don't know where they come from/But they sure do come/I hope they're coming for me/Cat Scratch Fever' . . . I don't think that it is of too much consequence! *'Wang dang what a sweet poolin' tang/You shakin' my thang like a wang dang a dang.* **HAHAHAHAHA. . . . That's great if you want to screw a lot, which everybody should, but I don't really think it's a major force in the moulding of the consciousness of the young people of America!"**

As we get ready to drive back to the hotel, I ask Nugent if he believes in reincarnation and what he would like to come back as. He shakes his head in disgust.

"I refuse to answer that, it's just stupid. If there's one thing that I don't believe in then it's that. But if we were working for Walt Disney and I had that opportunity I'd rather come back as myself, 'cos this is as cool as shit. There can't be anything better than this."

Even after the last year?

"The last year is only one year, man. I have a hundred to choose from. The way I look at it is this. With the incredible positives that I have experienced in my life, who am I to bitch about one negative. I mean, come on Nuge, keep the chin up! The great things that I am able to experience in this life ... and someone says I shouldn't have a little pain. Fuck me! Live it up."

immediate point of reference, of contact?

"Yes. There's an amusing section in a film called The Tenant. There someone tells the story of someone who had his arm amputated. He wanted it buried, but he was told that he wasn't allowed to have it buried. He said, why not? If my head was chopped off, which would you choose to bury? They said the head, not the rest of the body! And it's true, you relate everything to the head. I would say that my arms and legs belong to another because I relate everything to up here. The head. Is it I am *in* my body, or I *am* my body?'

"Do you really want to do this interview?"

Try stopping me asking Paul Weller a few things.

"Fair enough, you've got to earn your bread and butter, but I just cannot see the point of someone doing this just to pile up his amount of words for the week."

Do you not like being asked questions because you feel the person asking is not really interested?

"Sometimes. I don't feel comfortable. I don't want to make rash statements. I tend to hold back . . . I wouldn't say I was dishonest though. It's just I don't want to say something that two hours later I will completely disagree with. I haven't got the answers, any answers, and I never like to pretend that I have. I have to be cautious."

By the time I got to Mick Jagger of The Rolling Stones I was obviously enormously excited, but somehow I wasn't sure whether I should admit this. The morning of the interview I assumed an appearance of steady satisfaction, convincing those around me that it was all under control. As usual I hadn't

MEATLOAF
December 19, 1981
Peace be with you.

IN THE BEGINNING there was The Silence. And then there was . . . CRASH!

MEATLOAF'S real name is Simple Simon. His first memories are of falling off a high wall – CRASH! – and of having his photograph taken – FLASH!

The bump on his head and that first shocking flash have been considerable influences on the young character's life – the monster, see, is never calm, and anything outside its immediate control is snatched at and watched over with deep suspicion and free scorn.

One night in Manhattan we try and tempt the flushed beast into having his photograph taken. It has just twitched, farted and fumbled its way through a 90-minute interview with yours truly the English explorer, but it doesn't take seriously the comfortable custom of matching new photographs with interviews.

"Still photographs; they drive me up the fucking wall," *the beast had confided to me.* **"But I'll work damned hard for these photographers. Most people having their photo taken just stand there. Not me, kid. I sweat. It's like being on stage for me."**

Anton Corbijn waits patiently for Meatloaf to walk on stage. He's been waiting four days.

"There's hundreds of photographs of me," *Meatloaf hisses at his publicist immediately after the interview flounders to its end around Meatloaf's virginity.*

Aides try to chain the beast, but it sees only flashing lights and startling visions. It becomes as agile as a baby monkey escaping the chains of common sense. His aides huddle together and pretend there's nothing wrong – it's all in the work's daze – while the beast spitefully unwraps a bite-size tantrum. Anton and I selfishly wonder why they let this untamed beast out into the big colliding world.

Meatloaf's publicist, wife and record company representative – all shadows in the background as I subject their monster to the tortures of conversation – all describe the beast as a "big superstar".

Big superstars are gods amongst men – or men amongst gods. Big superstars, the charming American way of life forces us to have it, are protected species. English explorers and Dutch photographers are rarely allowed close. Meatloaf, the beast, the big superstar,

is looked after with religious tautness. Innocence and nearness could upset the beastly system.

In many respects – respectful or otherwise – he is pampered with defensive intensity as if he alone holds our civilisation, our future, together. For his handlers, his keepers, his aides, perhaps subconsciously his followers, the smooth-cheeked beast represents Rock and Roll, America, the Heavens, the dark depths and the Holy Ghost . . . his heart beats money, his soul stamps down on curiosity and sentimentality.

America 1982! Rock and Roll forever more! You want to believe it?

THE BEAST is wrapped up in cotton wool, as cosy as Presley in his coffin, and limousined to another location. Along the way the helpless hero is coached into believing that having his photograph taken is not going to trouble his balanced divinity. For this beast, though, vigilance and willpower maintain civilisation: self-sacrifice is for the devil-dogs. His extravagances, he believes, are more beneficial than "truth". At a publicist's office filled with carpets, paintings, toys, and antiques I could sell and live off for five lifetimes, Meatloaf, a member of a protesting species, is brooding. His brooding causes a mist to descend over Manhattan. Anton unpacks his cameras. The monster snarls at the first glimpse of a Nikon.

"So let's get these damn things over with," *he growls, stampeding his way through the office.*

Anton positions the cry baby bunting in front of some artwork from the two Meatloaf albums. Meatloaf stands there like a huge lump of unwanted meatloaf: unsweating meatloaf. Anton takes some preliminary snaps, then suggests that Meatloaf act up a little. The beast shrugs his shoulder violently and pulls a spoilt face: he's wet his pants.

"This is all you're getting, take it or leave it," *he grumbles.*

His arms hang limply, his face stiffens and reddens. The beast is touched with fire. Photographs are for the birds, or something.

Anton asks the big superstar if he'll flex his muscles, maybe an alternative to the Meatloaf clenched fist, clenched face cliché. The beast gobs on reason.

"I'm not going for any of that American strongman shit," *he spits, spraying the room with uncunning spittle.*

He pulls his fingers up to his nose, to scratch its redness. Anton accidentally snaps this dreadfully off guard moment. CRASH!

"I'm not having that silly photograph printed," *snarls the beast, pushing Anton out of the*

worked out what I was going to ask – what I preferred to do when asking the questions was begin with something casual but provocative that would push out the interview into the strange, revealing areas I was always despairing towards. The despair was growing. With Jagger it didn't occur to me what this first question should be right up until I sat opposite him in his office. "How've you been then?" I asked, hoping this would be interpreted as an enquiry about the last twenty years of Jagger's life and lead into an hour's monologue of classic insight and revelation. Jagger, always very self-conscious of appearing "ordinary", like a middle-class MP drinking tea out of a brown mug, nonchalantly replied, "All right."

Panic set in. It can in interviews, where you need desperately to find out inside an hour or two more about a person than they might easily tell their best friend. Then it became a matter of determining Jagger's sanity, but he would have none of that.

I had decided I would act out the spiteful mistrusting punk, absolutely unconcerned at the prospect of interviewing Jagger. There was maybe slight truth in that I could take Jagger or leave him, he wasn't a major block in my thoughts at the time. But my mother's advice upon hearing of the meeting, that I should not take any heroin from him, was a suggestion that interviewing Jagger was a bit more taxing and intriguing than I pretended, as I presented myself at the Rolling Stones' office, drunk from early afternoon lager. My decision to assault Jagger for a kind of betrayal of some vague class and cultural forces that no-one had ever properly worked out anyway was not aided by my journey to a toilet seven times during the first half hour I waited for him. For Jagger had worked out his

way and skulking out of sight.

His wife rushes off to retrieve him. His publicist, the man from the record company, the band member who'd tried to cheer him up by singing "There's No Business Like Show Business", hang around helplessly. Anton and I just want to go home and leave these silly people to their games.

I wander off into a side room, find a broken acoustic guitar and strum some broken blues – smooth the savage beast away, some hope, suddenly CRASH! the bomb has dropped/the heavens have opened/my time has come/is this the way I go?/Meatloaf has flung a chair to the floor and is surging towards me obviously to sit on me. My bones turn to rubber in anticipation.

"Is it true that if this guy doesn't get his photographs then the interview won't be printed after I worked real hard and gave you the best interview I could?"

I'm speechless. The monster turns ever-decreasing circles, foaming at the mouth. Eventually he draws me and Anton to his bosom and explains his situation.

"Look, this hasn't been the best of days. The management I had yesterday I haven't got today," *he bleats breathlessly.* **"Do you understand what I'm saying? You got an interview, maybe next time we'll get the photographs done, OK. . . ."**

We nod silently, cautiously eyeing the beast's claws. The pitiless monster's little wife pitifully signals to us – "We all have our bad days."

The monster turns and storms out of the building, dragging his wife in his wake. He disappears from view like a bat out of hell – or a big superstar out of a rich publicist's office – and returns to his perch on top of the Empire State Building.

Silence.

MEATLOAF'S REAL name is Freddie Parfitt. The fat tramp sits in the bar gulping a drink the gullible Englishman had bought him. To pay the Englishman back he just has to speak into that little tape recorder – recall a few things about his life, let go some opinions. Easy. Make it all up. Be a better story anyway.

"When did I lose my virginity? 14, 15 . . . God, I don't remember. I remember it, doing it. Did it set me up for life? Naah . . . ain't no big thing . . . means much more to girls, I think. Women . . . What?

"Am I proud to be an American? . . . Shit I'm proud to be in the world . . . I don't huh let me think . . . uh I don't . . . God . . . They're gonna call me treasonous here . . . I don't think of it that way.

"Does being an American mean anything to me? Mmmm . . . no . . . I can't say it does. History, tradition, values, it doesn't mean a damn thing to me, to tell you the truth.

"Hum . . . all right, America, it means all-night television . . . I think it's the generation of Vietnam . . . because that's where I was, right at that point, in the '60s, the age of going to Vietnam and all that . . . oh God . . . see, I don't feel . . . Aw, I dunno, the Star Spangled Banner is a hard melody to sing and most people can't do it. I don't think I would want to live in Russia, I can tell you that. They're almost . . . I don't think they're smart, no . . . they're almost Neanderthal, their bone structures and faces, they look Neanderthal. I don't think they're bright people at all. They're scary, they're frightening for sure. . . .

"So I'd want America over Russia? Hey, shit, if it comes to that, I'll be in Nova Scotia. Are you kidding! Look, I'm happy here. I don't consider myself unpatriotic. I wouldn't cheat on my country. If everyone stands for the National Anthem, then I stand as well. Shit, people are going to call me treasonous and Charlie Daniels won't invite me down to the Volunteer Jam no more . . . but, like, I'm as glad to be an American as I'm glad to be alive . . . I wouldn't like to be somewhere where I couldn't do what I wanted to do, that's where I wouldn't want to be.

"Do I think we have a future? Sure! Look, people, they'll see us through, people will make us survive, all the people in the world. Even the Russians? Well I don't know about that. They're people as well? I'm not prejudiced, I said they were Neanderthal, I didn't say I hated them . . . sure I'm optimistic. Look, even a Neanderthal man knew to run away when he saw a club coming. Even he knew to run away from a dinosaur.

"Everybody's worried about nuclear this that and the other but I just think that what's going to happen is something'll scare us all half to death and that'll be the story . . . I do not think the world is going to blow itself up! There! If everyone thinks the world is going to blow itself up then it's damn well going to.

"I mean, it's like there's a baseball game and Reggie Jackson is at bat and you could sense it that everyone everywhere in the stadium knew that Reggie Jackson was

going to hit a home run for the Yankees and the first pitch he hit a home run . . . and everyone was going Yeah, I knew he was going to hit it, y'know . . . I'm telling you, it's the power of positive thinking; and I'm telling you that enough people thought Reggie Jackson was going to hit a home run over the centre field wall and the son of a bitch did. . . .

"I believe in the power of positive thinking, sure I do. Is there a religion that goes with that? I don't know . . . arm, thanks for the drink. . . ."

The big bum had paid the price. He waddled back into obscurity.

MEATLOAF'S REAL name is Meatloaf. The man's publicist and the wit from CBS International are truly or dutifully amazed that I get 90 minutes of soft to hard talk out of the big superstar. Usually – they flatter me – give him an hour at the most before he loses interest.

Heck, people of the free world, I talked to him like anyone I'd meet in a New York bar, whereas he usually gets interviewed by rock and roll journalists. I'll talk to anyone, even big superstars or bar bums, even flustered simple simons like Meatloaf. Some people are a lot harder to talk to than others. Some people don't want to listen. Some can't see that listening really matters.

The only time Meatloaf appears to hear anything I say to him is when I introduce something into the play that's usually left outside such a talk – like faith, death and charity. Then he'll stop abruptly.

"What?!" *he'll shake his head.*

I said, what could kill off rock and roll?

"Oh . . . er . . . nothing can kill it off! Guns! Bombs and guns! That's all. It'll be there forever. Shit, are you kidding?. . . ."

Do you love yourself?

"What!? Do I love myself as a person? I don't hate myself. I'm not madly in love with myself."

Are you beautiful?

"Me? Yeah! I think that I am the Nureyev of rock and roll, if you want to know my opinion of myself . . . Y'know, probably Jagger is the Nureyev of rock and roll, but you know I ain't gonna tell him that. . . ."

There's a tiny laugh. A Meatloaf laugh is truly a nervous reaction.

Most of the time Meat the giant steam-stammers on, celebrating the "timeless" glory of his craft, claiming a little too jealously that nothing upsets him, making the expected assumptions/distinctions about rock and roll and its place in his world and maybe a far corner of mine.

He lashes out bitterly – "Bitter? Nah I ain't bitter" *– at all that presumes to dislike him. He fidgets with an address book, knocks the table a lot, sips Perrier water, shifts restlessly in his chair, sometimes knocks me on the elbow to emphasise a point and talks at quite a pace. His hands flutter and his eyes bulge when he thinks I'm perhaps humouring him, or misunderstanding him.*

"I'm not hip," *he gloats,* "and I'm glad. Because I hate hip. Hip doesn't last. I was never hip. It's not my style."

To Meatloaf hip equals The Go Go's or, for peace's sake, REO Speedwagon.

The big superstar and I are foreigners. There are some words and phrases we use that we both recognise. . . . For him, though, there is no doubt; for me doubt doesn't just hover over the interview, it moves with no manners at all right the way through. Maybe doubt is my definition of (aah!) rock and roll: doubt transformed, contained, conquered, revolutionised. At another extreme my definition of rock and roll is "delusions that shrink to the size of a women's glove". For the beast the definition is . . . "Heart and soul, man."

Of course: words that come to mean nothing except what they're meanly forced to mean.

"Heart and soul, that's what rock and roll is. That's why they don't like me here . . . I'm an alive person. I don't want to be sterile and my opinion of American radio, American critics, everything to do with American music, is that it's sterile."

This from a man who likes the new Foreigner LP.

"Hey, 'Juke Box Hero' is a great tune."

I'M SURPRISED, given full in the face the monster's temperament, that he agrees to talk with me. I'm pitched right in the middle of some turbulent changes in Meatloaf's attitude towards his entertainment and environment and towards the control he has over it. His confusion about, and simplification of, the wealth and worth of his music – its influence or purpose or conditions – is the estranged equivalent of much tough pop music contemplation in this country. Not even Meatloaf is immune from the complications introduced by rock and roll's age or the terrors of metaphysical acceleration – not even mass success can preparation for the interview far better than me. He was an hour and a half late. Lager sped through me. I went to the toilet twenty times. The fact I waited so long for someone I was going to aggressively reveal as a dying sham made my spiteful motives seem a bit daft. But an interview's an interview. You can even get addicted to the process. Jagger arrived looking fit and fast and as I followed him upstairs I heard the receptionist whisper to a friend "he might as well do the interview in the toilet. He's been there enough times."

Have you ever felt that you were losing your sanity?
"Yeah. Sometimes. But I don't think so at the moment."
Have you ever lost it?
"No (guarded). Not completely. I try to hang on."
What keeps you hanging on?
"I dunno . . . (shrugs) really . . . it's easier to ask what drives people around the bend, what kind of people have really gone to the edge, what about them. I mean, if you stay together I think it's just because you have a really stable bottom part to you. Something underneath. It's difficult to say when it doesn't happen to you what it would be like. I've seen people go through it. But I don't know what it actually is that sends them there. That's the thing, it's difficult to bridge the gap. . . . People have either gone temporarily or permanently over the edge because you cannot really see it from their point of view. So you can't do nothing to help them. You don't know where they are. It's really hard."
Do you ever think that there are people looking towards you for some sort of sign?
"Yeah, but there's fewer of them . . . I never waited on anyone's word. I can't ever remember that. I suppose there are people who do. Pretty stupid,

supply that immunity.

He gurgles with defensive panic about the purifying potential of his art and the irrelevance of "politics" in its methodology. All his actions and decisions are irrevocably framed within the traditional, American notion of rock and roll. Rolling on because of its weight and the ferocity of its bodyguards. No doubt about it.

Meatloaf's management troubles seem due to the relatively slow sales of "Deadringer", the follow-up to the classic "Bat Out of Hell" (three years in the British LP charts). For Meatloaf reality is selling millions of records and that not being enough. This is American rock and roll reality and it means that Meatloaf can take on the role of hurt, ignored artist whilst selling uncontrollable amounts of records.

Everyone knows really that "Deadringer" will end up selling as much as "Bat Out of Hell", but you've got to act the part. American rock and roll reality is defined using lots of noughts, lots of nothing. American rock and roll means that Meatloaf devours myths and lets myths devour him without considering the resultant energies or effects in any provocative, presentable way.

American rock and roll is exertion, safety, religion, dread handling, absent wishes, escape. Now we're talking. . . .

"I'm giving people the chance to escape. I believe that entertainment is escapism. I don't believe that politics has any goddamn business in rock and roll. I just don't think that's what it's about."

What drives you?

"Everything drives me, man. To be better. To make the records and the shows better than they've ever been. I just want to be better; it's always been inside me."

Would you like to change the world?

"No, because I don't have that need. The only way I want to change the world is in the three hours that an audience is mine."

Into what?

"Into whatever I feel like changing it into. I have that power."

To create fantasies?

"That's what it is."

As a conscious strategy?

"No, no . . . it's a gift . . . a gift from the heavens, from the gods."

What pisses you off about yourself?

"What!? Oh, I'm a perfectionist. Well, I am and I'm not. On stage the band can drop a beat or come in wrong or something but that doesn't bother me, though it drives some people crazy. The only thing I get mad about on stage is if someone is too drunk or stoned to perform. That's the only thing that will make me go absolutely be-serk."

Do you drink?

"No . . . and I don't do drugs . . . I drink when I perform. It's the only time I ever drink. Before I go on I have about four shots of tequila and about four litre beers and on stage I drink wine, but I never get drunk."

It helps bring out the primitive in you?

"Yeah, I think that's what I do it for . . . it just lets me go. Phew! . . . I just go!"

Is it frightening?

"It doesn't frighten me at all, are you kidding? I love it. But I wish I could do it everywhere. I'd like to throw these crackers all over the room, but you don't do that in the Gramercy Park Hotel . . . but if I was on stage or doing a film and my character felt like throwing those crackers around the room then I'll be doing it."

So this gives you a chance to re-shape reality? To throw off the shackles?

"Yeah . . . and it's a great feeling and . . . well, there you go, you hit a nail on the head . . . it gives you the listener, the audience, a feeling, if you're watching me . . . well, it lets you realise at the same time through what I do. There you have it. That's what I do. It's better than preaching politics."

Have the rules of "entertainment" been ignored as rock and roll gets on with its big business?

"Oh yeah and it drives me crazy . . . I mean, when you see my show, it's like a three ring circus. Hey! I'm doing *Saturday Night Live* this Saturday and the first song I'm doing is Chuck Berry's "Promised Land" and it's not on either album, but it's going to give people an idea of what I'm about. I keep adding guitars and eventually there'll be nine guitars on stage. We'll end "Promised Land" with nine fucking guitars on the stage."

MEATLOAF IS AS much a joker inside American rock and roll reality as Jagger. Come and get me, for no good reason. Is the joke on Meatloaf? Is he a caricature?

"No, I'm not. It's real."

Oh yes? Isn't Meatloaf an admission that all rock and roll is acting?

"It's an admission that when Chuck Berry and when Little Richard get up and sing 'Rip it Up' and 'Long Tall Sally, she's real sweet'

... I see Long Tall Sally. That's acting? That's putting it across and that's what acting is. . . . You putting what you have here (heart) across to who you're putting it across to."

Is he, through the scandal of his work, (sympathetically) taking the piss out of the rock and roll practice?

"I did that and nobody understood it. In one show at New York I got shot as Billy in 'Stagger Lee' and I flew back as an angel in 'Swing Low Sweet Chariot' and I was making total fun and they didn't understand it. You gotta understand, you're dealing with New York . . . not the comic place of the world . . . they did not understand that I was making fun of myself, of them, of everything.

"There's a lot of tongue in cheek in what I do."

Do people take their rock and roll too seriously?

"Oh, God almighty, yes they do . . . I mean like Bruce Springsteen, and I know him personally, but all of a sudden they made him some sort of saviour. They did it to Bob Dylan and it drove him crazy. If the guy farted everyone wondered what the heck it meant. . . . Right now Bruce Springsteen is the god of the American people."

What has he actually done for those people?

"Nothing really . . . but the thing is, these people, they start to believe their own press, they start to believe that they are God and that they can do anything. That's not true, man. I don't care how big you are in this entertainment business. It's there, it's over, it comes and it goes."

Can people still be receptive to a truly uplifting power that might be inherent in rock and roll?

"Are you kidding? When you give them rock and roll, you bet. . . ."

On that simple unadorned release level?

"Fucking A, man . . . I'll tell you what . . . the radio people in America may stop my records being played, but they can't stop the promoters from booking me into a place and from people coming to see me and they can't stop the kids going crazy over it. . . ."

Do radio people in America consider Meatloaf to be dangerous?

"To their credibility. Y'see, it's dangerous to their egos, because they have said the American people only want to hear *this* and if all of a sudden the American people decide they want to hear this and that and that and this . . . that's what it is in England.

"In America the radio's dead, no one listens to it anymore. But there's going to be changes. Radio will beat itself. I don't have to worry about them. I mean, I laugh. It doesn't make any difference to me."

Yeah?

"Sure. . . ."

But don't you want to do something to change the situation?

"Yeah . . . well, I can't stand it. I can't stand those people who run the radio business. It's sickening. Sickening. They're power mad. I'm dealing with Hitler."

Conditioning that is surely political.

"Yeah . . . in that sense. But I'm not going to write songs about it . . . I'm not going to bring it to attention through my entertainment. It's a separate world. In other words I'm not going to scream to the audience go call your radio station and tell them to play my records. I'm not going to do that. That's hitting below the belt. That's not playing fair to me."

They play unfairly.

"I don't care. What goes around comes around. What you put into the lives of others comes back into your own. I believe that."

MEATLOAF'S REAL name is Humpty Dumpty. HD the artless, paced out, swelling beast spinning through the clutching, cluttered, wrecked space of American rock and roll reality. He smashes into the troublesome cosmic obstacles that must accompany the egos who sing rock and roll songs for the trained expectant youth of the world. CRASH. He breaks down, he breaks up. The simple man is not involved in a simple world.

All the King's men, all their horses, all his fans, all his critics, all the politicians and all the beggarmen can't put Humpty together again. But his family can.

I go to America with my head pricking and crackling with the pop of Japan, ABC, Human League (prickling and cracking me as much as, oh, Rauschenberg, Tom Lehrer, Steve Lacey and Dennis Potter). I come back with my head loaded with the rolling rocks of Tom Petty, Bruce Springsteen, Foreigner, Styx and Meatloaf. The bubbly pop tickles noses, colours tongues, shifts values and values shift: the rolling rocks literally demolish or dictate people's lives. Rock and roll American reality has reached hysteria. All it's faced with is the CRASH! It is an iceberg, a black hole, impossibly vast so as to block people's views. American rock and roll reality — now we're

I think."

Do you feel a rebel – if you ever did?

"I don't think I ever did. Not since I was fourteen. Well, I ran out of rebelliousness when I was sixteen."

You must have felt idealistic after that?

"(unemphatic) Yeah. . . ."

And felt from those early days that you could carry it forwards in some way?

"Yeah, you did. . . ."

And felt that you had the power?

"Well, you certainly didn't have the power. You hoped you did. You felt you might have, if you had the chance. By the time you get anywhere and get anything you know that the power is absolutely useless, and you couldn't do anything with it even if you had it. It's all imagination, a load of old bollocks. That's being self-centred. Thinking that you have something that no one else has got."

People put you in a position where you almost did have something.

"Yeah, almost. Almost is the key word."

Are you saying that idealism is irresponsible?

"No, not at all. But I don't think that The Rolling Stones were idealistic. . . . They may have been slightly nihilistic maybe. But they were only idealistic as far as making records goes. We really just wanted to make records or do what we wanted to do. Instead of being told what to do, which is more or less the position people find themselves in now."

Were those the complete boundaries you set yourselves – playing gigs, making records? You must have had other ones?

"There were others, but those were the most immediate ones. That was what we were kicking against. People didn't want you to play in their town halls, people didn't want you to play in their

talking – is a fuck of a mind control. But who is to say that the release, the individual "stimulation", of Meatloaf or Styx or the Rolling Stones exemplifies the problem, the tragedy, of entertainment much more than the value, the gift, of entertainment/pleasure?

American rock and roll reality is just one exaggeration of all the problems we face.

Perhaps the problem with it is the lack of exchange, the hopeless expectations, the huge collection of separate blocks of hugeness. . . . Of course there are other places to look. As far as it goes – and who can explain that *– American rock and roll reality doesn't crack open the world or spur people on; it smooths over the cracks and drops people in it. Right down there at the bottom, American rock and roll reality is MONEY. And it is a reality that can reduce a strong beast like Meatloaf into a quivering messy mass.*

Does money mean much to him?

"No, it really doesn't. I was screaming down the phone yesterday – I don't give a shit about the money!

"What means something to me is that I have two kids. That means something to me. Those kids. One's six, the other's ten months old. If it's money we're talking about, if I have to deal with money, I can give those kids what they should have and put them in the world in the right place and give them what they must have. If they have to make it on their own, then they have to make it on their own. I'm not looking to make them rich, but I'm saying they can't do anything for themselves now and I want to make sure they're clothed, they're fed, they go to school. You know what I'm saying?"

Did you feel cautious about bringing a child into "this" world? Did you feel they had no future?

"No, no, I didn't feel that. We may be blown up by a bomb, but there is a future. I mean, I feel that every day is a future, you gotta understand that. Every day that my daughter lives she's proud of something and that's great. So if tomorrow we all blow up she's had the thrill of some great days . . . I don't believe that we will go . . . I go moment by moment . . . Yeah, I get depressed. My wife just had a nervous breakdown, but y'know she's better now. . . .

"Heck! There are things to feel passion for . . . my wife, the kids, the challenge . . . Hey! Looks like I've been given a challenge here. Right here in America there's challenges constantly. I love it. I love to fight!"

What kind of future does he want for his kids?

"Just to . . . be brought up with the ideas that they have the right of their choice over their lives. They should have the right to be who they are. That's what I want for my kids. Too many people in this country have not been brought up with the right to be who they are. . . ."

What stops it?

"All kinds of things . . . government bureaucracy, lack of education, not having their rights as a human being, parents who don't care about them. . . . Oh, I think a lot of it is parental responsibility. That's the first responsibility."

How is he as a parent?

"I don't dislike it. It doesn't scare me. Doesn't bother me. Yeah, it's fun. My kids and my wife are probably the most important things in my life. But when it's time for business, it's time for business. Y'know, but if I wasn't a parent it wouldn't bother me, but I am so that's great. It's sort of like, I don't consider myself to be typical so you're not gonna get, Oh yeah, yeah, the kids' kind of answers. My beliefs are real different, my beliefs in how I do things are real different.

"There's a great phrase . . . I don't fit into a pigeonhole. Literally, physically or mentally."

MEATLOAF'S REAL name is not worth worrying about. Does he want to die calmly or sensationally?

"On the stage. Absolutely."

Halfway through the awesome "Bat Out Of Hell"?

"No . . . right at the end . . . I'd want to finish! The ultimate ending. I don't want to die halfway through, that would be a bore. Right at the end, he died!"

What would you miss most?

"I don't know, because I don't know what I would like about where I was going."

We're going somewhere, are we?

"Sure! I'm going somewhere, of course. Saturn! Saturn is like the transition place. You go to Saturn for a while."

Will they know you there?

"Of course. They'll know you too."

How would you like to be remembered on Earth?

"As a beached whale! Ha ha ha . . . I don't know . . . somebody who tried. . . . Somebody who stood there and took the punches. As Rocky! Huh huh I may have lost in the 15th round but hey I was a *fighter* . . ."

MEATLOAF CLINGS on to the Empire State Building, grumpily irrational, powerfully in love with the promised land, lashing out at all the attackers. . . . He's wounded, he falls off, hurtling to the ground. CRASH! Who will clear up the mess? And then there was The Silence.

clubs, so your energy was unfortunately focused against that, rather than anything more interesting.''

Did you feel that reflecting young people's unrest was important?

''Yeah, that was a good period that. But it can't go on forever, with a group of individuals or a generation. And it was all over so quickly, really. After that, it's all bullshit.

My mother warned me not to take any heroin from you.

''You're lucky you have a mother that cares for you!''

America is a big land full of lost people, many of whom like rock music. That's something that you could say. The Clash would like to hear that. They're out and about in America taking on this huge new challenge. The Clash continue, with all the cares in the world. Why give up? No submission. It's their way. Their way is to go after your minds, after your hearts; their way is as distrustful as it is gullible as it is committed.

What do you want to achieve?

(Strummer) ''I want things to be different here. I want things to be different in England. I want stupid things like people being happy . . . and real music . . . and an end to all the shit. . . . I just feel that to be able to contribute, that's an achievement in itself. Little things do change, but it takes a bloody lot longer than people would want . . . in a way, that's what I mean when I say there's too many smiles, you know what I mean . . . because, although I enjoy the playing, I can't stand it when people just want it to be all boogie . . . 'cos that's no challenge, that's exactly what people are expecting. People are always getting what they expect. Well, I want to give them something that they're not expecting. I do want people to have a good time

ALICE COOPER
February 20, 1982
Consider me!

LOU REED
April 21, 1979
Condemn me!

IGGY POP
February 2, 1980
Convince me!

IN THE EARLY HOURS OF A SATURDAY EVENING IGGY POP, THE AMERICAN SINGER, OPENS THE DOOR OF HIS TINY HOTEL ROOM, AND I ENTER. THE ROOM IS PROFOUNDLY BEIGE. IGGY IS WONDER-FULLY CASUAL. A FEW PERSONAL POSSESSIONS ARE ARRANGED FOR COMFORT: A RUG, A GUITAR AND PRAC-TICE AMP, ALFRED JARRY'S NOVEL *SUPER-MALE.* AS WE TALK HE WILL EITHER GRIN WITH GREAT GOOF OR APPEAR INCRED-IBLY EARNEST. HE IS NOT AVERSE EITHER TO A SLY PRETENCE OF INNOCENCE.

I START THE INTERVIEW BY ASKING: WHEN YOU STARTED SINGING AND YOU SMEARED YOUR BODY WITH PEANUT BUTTER ON STAGE, KNOCKED YOURSELF OUT WITH MIKE STANDS, SPILLED BLOOD ON THE STACKS, WALKED ON THE AUDI-ENCE, DROOLED IN THEIR MOUTHS, BROKE YOUR BONES, DRUGGED YOUR BODY – WERE YOU NICE TO YOUR FAMILY AND FRIENDS OFF STAGE?

– –

I interview Alice Cooper, the American singer, in his modest French hotel room. Resembling a Harryhausen hybrid of a prune, a crow and a well-Becketted Billie Whitelaw, his liquorice thin frame is bent awkwardly into a chair and he's blowing Q-tips through a straw at pictures torn from a soft-porn magazine and pinned to the door. He grins the sort of grin you associate with a vampire in Scooby Doo meeting Dracula. "Want to play whoresniping?"

Who would want to blow Q-tips at photo-graphs of naked young girls at ten in the morning? Perhaps someone who lives in a black castle in Beverly Hills and chews live chickens for brunch. "Want to play whoresniping?"

No. I start the interview by asking: are you not just some coarse old devil, some minor eccentric, the real regular guy faking wildness?

– –

It is a Sunday morning, and I talk to Lou Reed, the American singer, in a Düsseldorf hotel bar. Reed does not like journalists: not one little bit. To achieve an interview I have had to endure a slightly ridiculous ritual involving a form of security check and two days of self-consciously absurd harassment from the singer himself. Finally he allows me exactly one half-hour for an interview, placing a watch on the table between us in order to time the conversation. Of course, he doesn't allow me half a minute over-time. We seriously play the game.

I start the interview by asking: do you ever feel people regard you as a hero? The name "Lou Reed" and the things it supposedly stands for?

– –

"THAT'S NOT REALLY FAIR ON ME! YES AND NO! I FELT THAT IT WOULD BE BEST TO CONFINE MY OUTBURSTS, THAT IT WOULD BE BAD MANNERS OFF-STAGE. LIKE I SAY, YES AND NO. I BASICALLY GO BY RULE OF THUMB. I'LL GENERALLY PUSH MY FREEDOM TO THE LIMIT, IN ANY SITUATION, GIVEN HOW FAR I CAN GET AWAY WITH IT. SO, YEAH, OF COURSE I WAS NICE TO MY FAMILY AND FRIENDS, BUT SOMETIMES I WAS A BASTARD TO SOMEONE ELSE. THE PEOPLE I WAS WORKING FOR WERE NO FRIENDS OF MINE! AND REALLY IT WAS JUST A THING THAT THOSE AUDIENCES DESERVED. THEY REALLY DESERVED IT."

HAS THAT CHANGED?

"OH, I THINK IT'S CHANGED A GREAT DEAL."

YOU MAY HAVE BECOME MORE, ER, REFINED BUT YOU STILL TOY AROUND A LOT.

"BEHIND THAT I GIVE THEM ALL I'VE GOT. SEE, I'M INVOLVED IN ROCK 'N' ROLL. IT'S NOT AS IF I WAS AN ARTS MAJOR OR SOMETHING."

SO YOU SNEER A LOT?

"ROCK'N'ROLL INVOLVES SNEERING AS PART OF A DAILY LIFE. AND Y'KNOW, THERE'S A LOT TO SNEER ABOUT. I LIKE TO SNEER!"

– –

"There's nothing original in this world. Except tupperware. Now tupperware is original."

Are you an immoralist?

"No. In fact there are dirty words that I don't even say. I have him (points at an assistant) swear for me. I just think that swearing shows up a complete lack of vocabulary."

Dali tits to you, mate.

and enjoy themselves and I think that's what it's all about really as far as a concert is concerned. But somehow I cannot feel good unless I feel that the audience has gone away and thought about what's going on. . . . The after effect, the after taste is what I'm really after."

Why?

"I think if you don't push for these things . . . if you don't push all the time for something . . . you're letting people down. You've got to do something."

Hang on! "We play what we want to hear."

The Fire Engines have glamour, and have soul, and are in such a state! How can we get depressed when there is such a noise and such a new-vision CLAMOURING at the solid doors of all the dead dulled rock folk still clinging whilst there's stuff to be shot out. The Fire Engines are CLAIMING. . . . "We don't think very far ahead. . . ." The Fire Engines are FASHIONING. . . . "We're against plans and solutions and ambitions and making a career out of this. . . ." The Fire Engines are famous. . . . "We wouldn't mind some money." The Fire Engines have it in them. What's the point in getting bored? "We'll change. It's only natural. We might last. We might not. For now, this is it." What are you up to? "You never go for a perfect sound, you just generate excitement . . . you have to push yourself . . . it should be a raw-boned wham bam dance music. . . ." Why do your sets only last for 15 minutes? "What we don't want to do when we play is get bored, for a start, 'cos there's no point. The intention is to do 7 songs a night." That's value? "That's it for sure. What's the point in getting bored. What's the value there? The amount of excitement you get out of something is more

"I like Dali a lot, you know. He is organised confusion; like me he reacts against everything and there's no story or anything . . . and the only thing I ever remember Dali saying that made kind of normal sense was when he said once that the perfect communication is confusion. Now I understand that!"

Look at that sparrow by the umbrella!

"Remember Hellzapoppin? They knew! They were the first ones to look directly into the camera and say almost cruelly that NOTHING is as it seems."

So; some minor eccentric?

"Look, I'm an American. Being an American is about being in Beverly Hills. You work your way up to Beverly Hills, and then the fun game begins. There is no reason to leave."

What have you ever done in your life, Alice?

"Oh, millions of wonderful things."

— —

"Yeah."

Is that a kind of pressure?

"Is that a kind of pressure?"

Yes.

"Yes. You're getting a very straightforward interview, so relish it."

That pressure affects you?

"That pressure affects me?"

Yes.

"Yes. Everybody has pressures. And everybody has pressures that other people can only imagine. You have pressures that I can't imagine. Well, I can try and imagine them. It's just a matter of degrees I would suspect. There are some pressures I have which you can probably imagine . . . and my biggest pressure is to live up to my own expectations."

Your own?

"My own. Not anybody else's."

Not live up to your reputation?

"Oh no. Oh no. I mean, *that* I have to live down. I don't know if my expectations are that high, it's just that they're very hard. Very hard."

Expectations to do what?

"*TO BE THE GREATEST WRITER . . . THAT EVER LIVED ON GOD'S EARTH . . .* in other words, I'm talking about Dostoevsky . . . Shakespeare."

This great as what kind of writer?

"*A writer* . . . I want to do a rock and roll thing that's on the level of *The Brothers Kara-*mazov . . . a body of work . . . you know, I could come off sounding very pretentious about this, which is why I don't usually say anything . . . I prefer not to. . . ."

— —

"Oh, I've made rock and roll history. I'm not bothered about that."

In what way?

"Oh, you'll never understand."

Try me.

"Did you ever notice the way I manipulated. . . ."

Does anybody notice?

"This is a business. There are those that do and those that don't."

Does it matter?

"The dog told me to do it!"

— —

"IT'S IMPORTANT TO ME THAT I CAN ALWAYS LEAVE TOWN WHEN I LIKE . . . VITAL . . . I NEVER WANT TO BE STUCK WITH THE POTATOES AND PEAS, AND SOME HAG WITH GOOK FALLING OFF HER FACE, AND ME TAKING IT . . . THERE'S MOMENTS WHEN I CAN TAKE A LITTLE PEAS AND POTATOES FROM THE WORLD . . . AND I CAN FEEL THAT I ENJOY COMPROMISING . . . SOMETIMES THERE'S AN ART TO COMPROMISE. . . ."

YOU CAN MAKE THE CHOICE TO COMPROMISE MAYBE. FOR MOST PEOPLE THEY ARE FORCED TO TURN COMPROMISE INTO AN ART, THERE'S NO CHOICE.

"THAT'S INTERESTING. SOME OF THE PEOPLE I ENVY, SOME OF THE ARTISTS WHO CAN WRITE THINGS THAT I COULDN'T WRITE, I SENSE THAT THEY'RE THE TYPE WHO WORKED THE OTHER WAY ROUND FROM ME AND TURNED COMPROMISE INTO ART, HAD TO, Y'KNOW. I JUST STARTED OUT WITH A BIG WILD RESOLVE THAT NOTHING WOULD GET IN MY WAY, NOTHING WOULD BEND ME IN HALF, NOTHING WOULD TAKE IT FROM ME. WHEREAS I SAW A GUY LIKE JOE JACKSON ON THE SCREEN THE OTHER DAY AND HE SANG GOOD AND I LOVED HIS FACE . . . AND I THOUGHT THAT GUY IS LIKE SELLING SHIRTS OR SOMETHING, AND HIS ART IS VERY COMPROMISED. HE QUITE LITERALLY HAS TURNED A COMPROMISED ATTITUDE – NOT IN A BAD WAY – INTO A VERY CAREFUL ART. THE ENGLISH ARE VERY GOOD AT

THIS. WITH AMERICANS IT DOESN'T QUITE COME OFF AS GOOD. LOOK AT CHICAGO! THAT'S HARDLY COMPROMISE. THAT'S SUBMISSION. A GOOD ENGLISH COMPROMISE LIKE JOE JACKSON AT LEAST INVOLVES SOME ENERGY. BUT A GROUP LIKE CHICAGO, A SYMBOL OF AMERICAN ROCK, ALL THEY'VE EVER DONE IS LUXURIATE ON THEIR BACKS, AND THEY COULD ALWAYS GET MONEY FROM THEIR DADS, AND THEIR ONLY COMPROMISE WAS, WELL, AM I GOING TO SMOKE HASH OR SHOOT HEROIN? IT'S ALL THAT AND THAT'S ALL."

––––––––––––––––––––––––––

"My psychiatrist calls Alice 'him' . . . he says, what does 'he' think of this. I say, I can't tell you. Alice only lives on the stage. I cannot explain it. Don't know how I created it. All that I know is that the character lives. He stands different than I do; he has different manners. My wife says that it's a totally different person. It's something that I could never do without. I turned 34 yesterday and I've got more energy now than I've ever had before . . . and that's hard to explain. I created Alice as a vehicle in the late '60s, to get attention. Because I was competing with 200,000 bands in Los Angeles. I said – what the fuck have I got to lose . . . I'll try anything. And the hippies fucking hated us, nobody liked us. Which was great at the time, because it was all the peace and love shit. I just couldn't get into that peace and love con, it was such an illusion . . . it was awful, and a lot of the way Alice is came from hating that. And there were great rumours about Alice and I never deny them. People used to say did you kill live chickens on stage. And I say well I didn't but Alice might have. So now, what can I be called that I haven't already been called?"

Sad and misguided?

"I'm an American!"

Confused?

"I won't be! But when I started drinking heavily I forgot who I was. Who was what. People used to think Alice lived in a big black castle, and I figured, why not let them think that. . . . But then I lost control. I thought I had to be Alice all the time. That was the kind of thing that killed Jim Morrison. I went through this period of being truly sloshed and I was slipping away. I just didn't know who was who. When I stopped drinking I

thought that Alice was dead, it was his fuel, the drink. That's what I thought . . . then I realised that his fuel was anger. I realised that I didn't need to be Alice all the time . . . I can control him. I know where he lives . . . up on the stage . . . maybe I could call him up if I was in trouble. . . . All I would have to do is drop into that frame of mind and it just happens immediately. When that happens, my whole life changes. My whole brain changes. It's a strange kind of ecstasy. Everyone should have their Alice."

Are you all right?

"Does a tree make a noise when it falls in the forest and there's no bear around to hear it?"

––––––––––––––––––––––––––

During the last twelve years do you think you've come anywhere near to being "the greatest writer ever?"

"I'm on the right track. I think I haven't done badly. But I think I haven't really scratched the surface. I think I'm just starting."

You have recorded a tremendous body of work . . . (Reed interprets tremendous as meaning classic not extensive.)

"Well . . . I don't think that for a second . . . Every once in a while I'll hear one of those things on the radio, hear some of the old things, and I'll say, hey, you know that ain't half bad. I thought the show we did in Berlin was a kind of culmination of all this . . . like the band I have is incredible . . . I can't operate without a band for what I want to do . . . and part of what I want to do is have something that only takes place once . . . so as a consequence you can't point to it as an indication of anything. I mean what we did in Berlin, I just thought it doesn't happen every night . . . I mean you try . . . I think we can do better than that. But I was very happy. It was guitar symphony, guitar orchestra, I mean especially with the kind of guitars that we're using. It just gets awesome. You can conduct it. I always wish . . . well, in a way I'm glad that they don't take rock 'n' roll seriously, but in a way I think they should. . . ."

They?

"Oh! They is them, y'know, everybody thinks of a them, the them I'm thinking of, the them you're thinking of, give or take a person. Like the 'Sister Ray' we did went on for half an hour; it had just one vocal on it, and it was incredible. If we weren't rock and

important than the length of time involved. Look at that fucking Clash triple album . . . I'd rather pay £7.99 for a great fucking single than £1.99 for three albums of fucking shit. . . . It's just useless. What we want is just to be there with real excitement. How long can that last? I don't know . . . but while there's trillions and trillions of records released all the time and everyone is surrounded by this pop music thing the one thing we must do is never sound dulled and faded and cheap . . . what's the point? We have to be a group that's out and about for all the right reasons."

And they are?

"What's the point in getting bored?"

No point. It's only natural. I could see it clearly.

This is a mission for Fish, so there must be no compromise – whatever "compromise" means, it's as obscured as passion in this little context. He feels that he has to warn people. Like all the new rock romantics, hearty, head banded, lyrical, ingratiating, the feeble context allows them to feel important and inspired, to slap our faces with their wet sincerity. Fish MEANS WELL. Perhaps this is the definition of rock rebellion – to mean well. Are you a guilty boy, Fish? "Yeah, I feel guilty. I feel guilty about Ireland because I cannot do anything." Why are you guilty?

"Somebody's got to fucking tell somebody that they feel guilty to make somebody else feel guilty to make somebody else feel guilty to make somebody stand up and say, I can't handle this any more, let's try something. To talk about Vietnam, which you could say is a pet subject of mine, nobody really knew why Vietnam started, and with Vietnam you had a generation told by a nation since 1945 that killing was wrong, that the

roll, people might say isn't that marvellous . . . it really took you . . . it went past rhythm, it went past key . . . I hate talking about it actually. People make music to express a certain thing or they write lyrics to express a certain thing, and you can't really talk about it like this because that was you talking. That was your talking. That was it. Anything else is not going to be nearly as good. Because it's constructed and crafted . . . I hate the word crafted . . . to do, to be it, and if somebody says to me well what have you to say, I say, well THAT's what I have to say! To talk to me you know won't be anywhere near as good as listening to that. I've really worked on that."

"I could do the Johnny Carson Show! I could do Hollywood Squares! I thought this was a terrific joke. . . . The same guy who scared the shit out of middle America, the guy who almost got killed for having long hair and wearing make-up. Someone was winning a car out of me and they probably wouldn't let their kids go to an Alice Cooper concert. I sat there in Hollywood Squares and I thought that everybody would get the joke. . . . Here was Alice Cooper as an American symbol. That's really odd! And no one got the joke, because it didn't fit into the straight idea of rock rebellion, which never had much room for irony, I suppose. I lost nearly all my fans because they thought I was going soft. They like to see everybody staying on their side, no espionage, you know! No infiltration. . . . You see, I thought it was funny to have my photo taken playing golf with President Ford. There is something real wrong with that photo. And no one thought it was funny. It was really discouraging. They thought I was going soft. Selling out rather than really messing things up, that's what they thought."

Who's they?

"The ones who'll never understand. The bears who never think about whether a tree makes a noise when it falls in an isolated forest they've never even seen. But then what can you do. . . ."

— — — — — — — — — — — — — — — — — — — —

"CAMARADERIE, LOYALTY, GOOD FOOD, INTOXICATION, SEX, UM, SEX, AND . . . ESPECIALLY MENTAL EXERCISE, WHICH I LIKE A LOT. MENTAL EXERCISE LEADING TO HOPEFULLY ALWAYS BEING IN A SLIGHTLY BETTER POSITION TO PREDICT MY OWN FUTURE AND TO DIRECT IT. THOSE ARE SOME VALUES THAT I'M FINDING, NICE VALUES. GOOD VALUES. YOU DON'T PAY TOO MUCH FOR THEM."

FROM THE UNTUTORED OUTRAGE OF OLD, TO THE THINKER LOOKING FOR THE GOOD LIFE. SAVAGE TO CONNOISSEUR. . . .

"IT'S QUITE A DICHOTOMY!"

AND NOW YOU'RE SEARCHING FOR THESE VALUES, AND THEN THERE'S THE PROBLEMS OF IDENTITY, DESTINY, COMPROMISE, MOTIVATION. . . .

"THOSE ARE THE SORTS OF THINGS THAT I SHOULD ALWAYS HAVE HAD ON MY MIND . . . I HAD THEM ON MY MIND, BUT NOT EVER ENOUGH . . . BY THE TIME I GOT TO WHERE YOU'RE SUPPOSED TO GO IN ORDER TO TURN INTO SOME SORT OF MAN, I GOT CAUGHT UP IN THE DRUG THING THAT WAS GOING AROUND IN AMERICA. IT WAS LIKE WILDFIRE . . . I WASN'T THE ONLY ONE BY ANY MEANS, OR THE ONLY TEN, OR THE ONLY THOUSAND, OR THE ONLY MILLION. HALF THE COUNTRY! YOU SHOULD BE OVER THERE NOW, THEY'RE ALL ON VALIUM, EVERY DAMNED ONE OF THEM. IT'S WORSE THAN IT EVER WAS. IT'S JUST LEGAL NOW. IT'S A BIG PREOCCU-PATION, AND I JUST GOT CAUGHT UP IN THAT, AND ANY THOUGHTS I HAD ⤴ THEY JUST GOT SUPPRESSED. RATHER THAN BECOMING A PERSON SINGING ABOUT SUBJECTS, I SORT OF SUBLIMINATED THE PERSON AND I BECAME, IF YOU WILL, A HUMAN ELECTRONIC TOOL CREATING THIS SORT OF BUZZING, THROBBING MUSIC, WHICH WAS AT THE TIME VERY TIMELY, BUT ISN'T NOW. SO I'M GLAD THAT I'M NOT DOING IT ANYMORE. I STARTED LOSING MY MIND AT ABOUT AGE 18, 19 . . . THAT IS WHEN I STARTED TO LOSE THE ABILITY TO ARTICULATE TO MYSELF OR OTHERS IN ANY FORMAL FASHION AS A WRITER WHAT WAS REALLY ON MY MIND. PEOPLE WOULD SAY TO ME, HEY, YOU HAVE A FEW GOOD IDEAS JIM, WHY DON'T YOU DO THEM. I'D JUST SAY, YOU GOT ANY MONEY? YOU KNOW THE SORT OF THING."

DID YOU EVER THINK DURING THIS TIME THAT YOU'D SEE THE EIGHTIES?

"I HAD NO IDEA. I HADN'T A CLUE."

YOU SURVIVED. OTHERS DIDN'T.

"PROBABLY BECAUSE WHEN THEY SOBERED UP THEY DIDN'T HAVE IT."

Ten years ago, weren't you just diluting and softening for mass appeal other acts and entertainers?

"Like who?"

Iggy Pop?

"Oh you're kidding! I grew up with Iggy. He used to come and see me in Detroit. Iggy and I were best friends back then. We did nothing that was alike. I went for the trapping of the thing, the big show, and Iggy, of course, was street. Ha! I thought you were going to say Ray Coniff or something."

How many times can you perform "Schools Out" on stage?

"Over seven and a half million, thank you."

"I DID. I KEEP GETTING THIS TEMPTATION OVER THE LAST YEAR TO BECOME LIKE NURSE NIGHTINGALE FOR ALL THE JUNKIES IN THE WORLD. BUT I FIND THEY'RE NOT WORTH IT. BECAUSE THEY'RE NOT LIKE ME. THEY HAVE NOTHING TO OFFER. SO LET THEM STAY STONED."

How does performing a good show, as in Berlin, fit into your larger ambition!

"However good you can do it without an audience, with one it can be better. With an audience's energy there . . . like, I thought of the audience as one big YES. I mean, they were right there from the top . . . I really do not like talking about these things. The more people going in the right direction, the higher you can go with it, and the better it can be. It's just when you have a couple of thousand plus the band who are all pushing there's got to be something going on. . . . Things happen that are just extraordinary . . . that you can never forget unless you don't do them for a long while. It's hard to get things like that on records. Actually, come to think of it, it's hard to remember special occasions. Isn't that a beautiful line! It's really so true.

Have you known lots of special occasions?

"If I think about it, yeah, but I think that you want to extend the special occasion. Like there are moments – we all know what the moments are. A special occasion is like a whole lot of those moments . . . a special occasion could also be one monster moment. Like a week-long guitar symphony! I'd like to think, why stop there. A long time ago I said, like, wouldn't it be great if you had a thousand guitars in the Grand Canyon all tuned to E . . . everyone just hits it like that . . . and a pre-amp guitar equals the saxophone section, and two pre-amp guitars and a guitar synthesizer all just droning in E, which happened in Berlin, in fact, and a soprano sax, which sounded like a violin, that's really soothing, very relaxing . . . a guitar orchestral. Again, I know this sounds very pretentious, but I mean what I say when I say you can conduct it. The whole idea in rock and roll of swelling in music, of peaks, of valleys, of going up, of going down, dynamics seems to be ailing . . . why they don't have that much anymore is beyond me."

Do you listen to other rock 'n' roll?

"I like Roxy Music, Bryan Ferry. I like David Bowie. That's it. I like disco as well. I think Ferry and Bowie are very clever."

On what level are you talking? Traditional?

"Well, as my friend Don Cherry would say, on a traditional level and a little bit more."

WHERE DOES GREED ENTER INTO YOUR WORLD?

"I WANT TO BE PART OF IT. I WANT TO KNOW ABOUT *IT*. I WANT TO LIVE AS FAST AS POSSIBLE, WHICH DOESN'T MEAN GRINDING THROUGH FOUR GEARS BEFORE BURNING UP AT TEN MILES PER HOUR. I WANT TO GO AS FAST AS I CAN IN A GOOD DIRECTION. I'VE BEEN AROUND AND IT'S A BIG KICK. I WANT TO LOOK. I'M VERY MENTAL. I WANT TO THINK. AND THE MORE I THINK THE MORE I NEED. WHAT EXCITES ME IS AN IDEA IN A BOOK OR SOMETHING I'M GOING TO DO THAT I'VE NEVER DONE BEFORE OR A PLACE THAT I'M GOING TO THAT I'VE NEVER SEEN BEFORE. WILL I REALLY GET IN THERE AND BELONG? SO THAT I CAN LOOK AT, SAY, ITALY ON THE MAP AND SAY, YEAH, THAT'S WHERE I COME FROM, OR THERE, THAT'S MY PLACE, I'M IN THERE. I FEEL VERY MENTAL, ALERT. AND ALSO EXTREMELY LIMITED. EXTREMELY LIMITED. I'M IN ROCK AND ROLL, WHICH IS LIMITED."

Second World War was a disaster, but sorry you have to go and fight in a country that is armed with faith, a country that pleaded for American help, a country that only wanted identity, individuality. And they took guys and they dressed them up in uniforms and they took them from the streets and from the colleges and totally fucked their heads up. 1,750,000 soldiers and two thirds of them are qualified as being in need of psychiatric help . . . it's a total head-fuck syndrome. . . ."

Yeah?

"Yeah! But the generation that the nation had taught had the education to turn round as a unit and say, no, and it was through music that it happened, people like Dylan . . . a generation stopped the war through awareness. Musicians making a youth culture out of the whole fucking reality situation, the whole fuck-up within the Pentagon and within Washington. . . . And I think today you could probably see the seeds of a rock renaissance within certain bands that could bring about an equivalent kind of awareness leading to change. . . ."

Are the bands clever enough to assume such responsibility?

"Of course! These bands are talking about real life situations in a way that you have to think about it. The key word in music nowadays must be passion, because passion will always outlive commercialism. . . ."

Passion has come to mean nothing in rock: it's just a buzz word.

"You can always tell if passion is there."

As an indication of meek sincerity?

"If you think that, that's your problem."

Very clever.

Have you heard of The Fire

Do you feel you have the experience or whatever to achieve your ambition to be a great writer?

"I could not answer that. I think it's very very pretentious of me to even think of it. On the *other* hand I think I have it in my pocket, that there's no end to how incredible it can be. Just amazing in a contemporary sense . . . just amazing. But I keep things like that to myself. So . . . so! I'll give you a good line. I'm very good at things like this, it might not be true, but . . . to keep from being shot down you have to fly higher than people can shoot, y'know."

Why do you work within rock and roll?

"Aah . . . because I'm one of those kamikaze pilots and I like to be shot down once in a while. I like to start out where everybody else is and take them with me."

Can you see yourself becoming a great writer in the terms you talk about within rock music?

"I have, in my darker moments, thought that the form couldn't hold the content. I think that it is possible to . . . do something . . . it is just that it goes unrecognised by most people. They don't know where to look, or why to look, or how to look. Who is there to show them these days?"

Do you think your best writing ever will be "properly" recognised?

"No. I rather think that it won't. It's just that *I* know."

That's all right?

"It's the only thing that really matters. Everyone else can say it's wonderful, but what's it matter if it's a piece of shit as far as I'm concerned. I'm not kidding anybody unless I'm kidding myself. I've had things out that I thought were trash and people said they were great . . . and you're going to say oh what? and I'm not going to say. The thing is, I've always tried to do my best to my standards. That's it. That will do. Who should get in the way of that, when they don't know what I want with my work, what I'm after. . . ."

— — — — — — — — — — — — — — — — — — — —

"IT'S THE WAY PEOPLE LOOK AT ROCK AND ROLL THAT MAKES IT SO LIMITING. THEY DON'T SEE HOW IT CAN BE PUSHED OUT AND BEYOND, HOW IT CAN INVOLVE EVERYTHING AND MORE . . . THEY ALWAYS WANT TO BRING IT DOWN TO THE SAME BITS AND PIECES."

WHO'S THEY?

"OH, YOU KNOW, THE ONES AROUND THE CORNER, THE ONES WHO WON'T LET YOU GO, THE ONES WHO JUST WON'T LET GO. WHEN I STARTED I WAS ALWAYS PLAYING MY MUSIC TO THIS FUCKING ROCK AND ROLL AUDIENCE WHO HAD BUT ONE IDEA OF WHAT ROCK AND ROLL SHOULD BE. THE IDEA THAT ENDED UP WITH CHICAGO, Y'KNOW. I WAS PLAYING LIKE SECOND BILL TO TEN YEARS AFTER, YOU KNOW, AND PEOPLE WOULD JUST SIT THERE AND GRUMBLE AND COMPLAIN ABOUT IT NOT BEING ROCK AND ROLL – WAS I TAKING THE PISS OUT OF THEM, THEY WANTED TO KNOW, WAS I A JOKE OR WHAT? THEY'D JUST SIT THERE AND GET MAD WHICH I WOULDN'T ALLOW BECAUSE I HAD TO GET MY BAND TOGETHER. SO I HAD TO THROW THINGS AT THEM AND THAT STARTED THE WHOLE THING AND AWAY WE GO. I JUST COULDN'T ALLOW THEM TO SIT THERE BECAUSE IT WAS ALL TOO CRUCIAL. YOU KNOW?"

— — — — — — — — — — — — — — — — — — — —

If you read any English text book it says that when anyone says "y'know" it means that they don't.

— — — — — — — — — — — — — — — — — — — —

"Did you have fun at the show?"
No.
"Well, that's too bad. A lot of people did."
So.
"What are you after? I'm not going for the ultra-intellectual, you know. I don't really want that kind of person. And if they were really intellectual, they'd see things in my show that are just on another level. I see it as being funny. Things that I do realise the audience aren't getting. But what do you do?"

Not pander to a dulled idea of rebellion and shock?

"You mean a rebellion that's still based on growing your hair . . . you're talking of something diabolical, I suppose . . . Well, I have those thoughts. You could make an entire audience come at the same time! If you wanted to . . . attack every sense . . . attack smell, have a shocker in the seats, bring the lights up to white heat, you bring up the sound, everything at the same time, then hit them with a flash . . . and suggest something.

You could say anything at that point and knock them out. Just one word.''

Why don't you do that now?

"Well, I can't think of the word to say! And if I did know the word, then I'd be preaching, wouldn't I? But you have to hold back in this game, you have to. No one would be there, no one would care if you went all the way. Why should they? Going all the way is as bad as not moving at all really. I know what you're after, I know how you feel I limit myself, but I have to hold back . . . I have to always realise that I am working in a world amongst people who think that a photo of Brooke Shields in a tight pair of blue jeans is disgusting."

Aren't you being complacent?

"No, no, no . . . I work through *people's* complacency and apathy. Can't you see that? *No.*
"I hate you.''

So why were you so rude to me – writers never get it right, never ask the smart questions?

"Well, look at your predecessors. I'm going on track record. You know, the corny old line . . . the audience is like a member of the band, and the journalist is the roadie. It's just that my experience of journalists has always been negative."

Do you think that any form of criticism is generally irrelevant?

"Well, it doesn't have anything to do with anything. It gives people something to talk about I suppose. But if people want to know anything about me, there it is, in the songs, on the records, and if they want to know what the records are like, they should hear them. Or not. But not read about it through someone else's interpretations. . . . I like playing in a band and I like making records. But I hate talking about them, especially to idiots. I mean, I've mastered the really funny, insulting interview and all that, so that we don't go near anything of great concern to anybody since that's not what they're interested in anyway. . . ."

A lot of your interviews are simply one-sided comic repartee?

(Snigger) "What else . . . How else can one deal with the absurd! The questions that I've been asked, and the people who've asked them, have always struck me as comic. It's

like I've always thought of it as something out of a very bad soap opera on TV. It's like kids imitating journalists. I mean, Hemingway was a journalist, Dorothy Parker was a critic. Delmore Shwartz was a critic. . . .

''No, I don't hate you Paul . . . I quite enjoy something like this, it's like a work-out for the mind. I thought you were just going to come along and ask how I got my name, you know.''

That would upset you?

"Of course."

Don't you deserve it?

"I hate you."

Do you ever think of your audience when you make a record? An audience?

"I don't care what my audience does. I don't want my audience to do anything. That's up to them. They can do whatever they want. I'm just happy I make rock and roll records."

Is it a privilege?

"It's a privilege to hear the records. I think I deserve it . . . this privilege. I know I'm no slouch. I just like to keep track of myself. As for the people who get to listen, how do I know what they think, feel or want to do? As far as what I do goes, I'm the judge. How can I use anybody else as a judge – they have their own thing to do. If something goes out there and everybody hates it I go through some changes, but at least I liked it. You know?''

"IF SOMEONE IS NOT SEEING THE FULL PERSPECTIVE OF ME, IT'S MY JOB AS A PERFORMER, ENTERTAINER OR WHAT-EVER YOU WANT TO SAY – AS THE ONE PRESENT – TO MAKE IT POSSIBLE, BECAUSE YOU'RE A BETTER ARTIST IF YOU CAN PUT IT OVER BETTER THAN SOME GUY WHO'S JUST AS GOOD BUT CANNOT PUT IT OVER. LET THE WORLD BE YOUR MOUSE-TRAP. HUH! TO UNCOIN A FAMOUS PHRASE. WE GONNA TALK ABOUT FAME SOME MORE?''

I'M NOT TALKING ABOUT FAME.

"YEAH, I KNOW, BUT IT COMES WITH FAME – THE ATTENTION AND UNDER-STANDING THAT I MIGHT WANT TO DEMAND

Engines? I ask, a little ambitiously.
"What?''
Well, they played fifteen minute sets.
"Fifteen! Phew!''
As long as one of your songs. It's an injection of sheer tonic; I think they must define boredom differently to you.
"Yup,'' grins Garcia, tight lipped.
They're violent, terse, joyous, an uplifting celebration, and the point is – what's the point in being bored? All the things you say are in your music that I can't get out. Garcia pours carefully articulated reason on to my glorious fury. "For me music is a full range of experience. In music there is room for space, there's room for quietness, room for sorrow, room for anger, hate, passion, violence.''
I do agree. We still seem to be talking about different things though.
"It is not my desire to say there is only this or that. For me it's a full range of experiences, and within that it includes a thing like boredom. Sometimes boredom is what is happening in life. That's what it's about sometimes. Sometimes the tension between boredom and discovery is like an interesting thing. The idea of noodling around aimlessly, and we're notorious for that, but then hitting on some rich vein of something that we may not have got to any other way. I want it to be the full range. Fifteen minutes? We've been going sixteen years and we're just beginning. We are just starting to get it together.''
I gasp. Garcia continues.

Being of the Bauhaus protective sacking means being prepared to do a lot of pretending, defending, disguising, and exaggerating. Bauhaus find an idea, dust it off, lick it dearly, stretch it, tear it, drench it in dank perfume, burn

FROM AN AUDIENCE. LOOK, IF THEY LIKE A RIFF THEY CAN LISTEN TO THAT – THAT'S GOOD ENOUGH FOR ME, AS LONG AS THEY LIKE SOMETHING. I'M ONLY BOTHERED IF THERE'S NOTHING THEY DON'T LIKE, NOTHING THAT GETS THEM. THEN I WORRY AND START TO KICK DOWN DOORS AND GET CRAZY AND FURIOUS, AND JUST GO NUTS. BUT AS LONG AS THERE'S, ONE THING THAT THEY LIKE. . . ."

SO THIS RECOGNITION OR WHATEVER IT IS – IT WILL HAPPEN?

"NO, BUT I'VE SPENT ENOUGH TIME AROUND AND ABOUT TO FIND DIFFERENT THINGS. . . . SOME PEOPLE WILL JUST NEVER GET IT, AND MAYBE THAT'S A SIGN OF LIFE OR SOMETHING. ONCE, LONG AGO, I WAS CONCERNED WITH MAKING IT ALL HAPPEN AT ONCE AND NOTHING ENDED UP HAPPENING. SO I TRY AND WORK WITHIN MY LIMITATIONS."

LIMITATIONS. YOU ONCE SAID THAT YOU WON'T GROW ANY MORE AND DON'T WANT TO. THERE'S A CHILDISHNESS YOU SEEM TO WANT TO KEEP.

"EXACTLY. AN INFANTILE: 'NO I DON'T WANT TO GROW UP ANYMORE. FUCK YOU! KISS MY ASS!' YEAH, I FIND THAT. WHAT ABOUT IT!"

WHEN YOU'RE TALKING ABOUT LIMITATIONS ARE YOU SAYING THAT YOU'VE STEPPED AS FAR AS YOU CAN?

"NO, IT'S THE OPPOSITE. THE LIMITATION IS IN HOW DAMNED ADULT YOU HAVE TO BE! I LIKE TO RUN AROUND LIKE A LITTLE MONSTER. BUT I SORT OF BECAME ADULT."

WHAT'S IT LIKE BEING AN ADULT?

"IT'S EXCITING. YEAH, IT'S GOT ITS POINT. DOORS OPEN, DESTINATIONS BECKON, WOMEN INVITE ME IN, MEN LAUGH AT MY JOKES. IT'S NOT BAD. AND NOW, IT'S MY BIG KICK TAKING CARE OF MYSELF."

– –

Isn't the way you do rock and roll a drudgery – the touring boringness?

"*Yeah . . . but I get to do this (throws Q-tip at the picture on the door).*"

What do you mean?

"*I've never met anyone who is not absurd.*"

What do you mean?

"*There is nothing funny about Idi Amin. There is nothing funny about only having a spoonful of cabbage to eat every week. Then*

I can go and make a noise and be a millionaire."

What do you mean?

"*I will be around a lot longer than John Denver.*"

Well done.

"*I'm an American!*"

– –

How do you get on with the business side of it all?

"**I don't. I've been through a lot. Musicians are probably at the bottom of the ladder. They're the people who get stiffed the first and paid the last. I don't relate to the business. I don't think I ever will. I've never really gone into it in any way. I tried at some point, but I just couldn't. My experiences with business have been worse than those with journalists, and I have the law suits to prove it. It's . . . it's . . . unspeakable . . . I mean, people like to go out and play and that should be enough without having to deal with all the business.**"

So how have you survived to still make records?

"**I've been very lucky. I'm also very good. I'm also very stubborn. What keeps me going is that I really love making rock and roll records. I love playing in a band. Why does anybody do anything! Here it is. I will be very depressed if you do a hatchet job on me . . . not depressed . . . because I'll expect it . . . It's just that at this stage of the game I don't need to be maligned anymore. That's why we'll keep the interview to half an hour. Not that I needed to be maligned before, it's just that I didn't realise I didn't need to be maligned. Finish.**"

– –

"FUCK DEFINITIONS! I FEEL VERY CONSERVATIVE. I FEEL IT. IT'S SOMETHING YOU FEEL. I AM A CONSERVATIVE. I AM! EVEN THOUGH IT'S OBVIOUS THAT I'M NOT THE WAY MOST PEOPLE THINK OF THE WORD. BUT I AM. I'M A FANATIC. AN ENTRENCHED CONSERVATIVE FANATIC."

FOR AN AMERICAN-BORN 60's ROCK INDIVIDUAL YOUR APPROACH AND PERSPECTIVE IS VERY UNUSUAL AND UNSETTLED.

"YEAH . . . I DON'T THINK I SHOULD HAVE BEEN BORN THERE. I NEVER DID FEEL RIGHT THERE. I NEVER KNEW IT EITHER. I DIDN'T EVER WANT TO BE BLAND. I

WANTED TO KEEP GETTING GOOD, AND YOU DON'T KEEP GETTING GOOD WHEN THE GOOD AMERICAN LIFE GETS YOU. I LIKE TO KEEP OUT OF THE WAY, YOU KNOW ... WHEN I GOT MY FIRST BAND I MADE SURE THEY WERE STARVING AND STONED AND IT WOULD MAKE THEM PLAY BETTER. I'D SLEEP ON THE FLOOR AND ALL THAT GARBAGE AND IT SOUNDS SILLY NOW, BUT WHEN YOU'RE TWENTY AND A PROVINCIAL AND TRYING TO GET YOUR FIRST RECORD CONTRACT, IT'S A GOOD TECHNIQUE. A SOUL VERSION OF THE ARTIST IN THE GARRET. BUT IT WORKED. I'VE ALWAYS BEEN ANTI THAT PLUSH GARBAGE; PLUSH FOR ME IS IN MY BRAINS."

BUT YOU LIKE YOUR RUGS THOUGH?

"I DO LIKE MY LITTLE RUGS. I LIKE OBJECTS FOR WHAT THEY CAN DO TO MY BRAIN. A HOTEL ROOM IS NEVER GOING TO BE THE SAME WITHOUT MY LITTLE GREY RUG ON THE FLOOR, WITH THE FUNNY RAIN GOD ON IT OR WHATEVER IT IS. AND I LOOK AT HIM AND THE FUNNY BLUE SHAPES ... THESE ARE NICE OBJECTS, THEY'RE PRETTY. I LIKE PRETTY OBJECTS. AND FOOD THAT SMELLS PRETTY. THAT MAKES ME FEEL PRETTY! AND I PLAY PRETTIER. BUT I'VE NEVER STUMBLED ACROSS ANYTHING OR ANYONE IN ANY MODE OF LIFE THAT I FELT I HAD TO DEPEND ON EXCEPT FOR ... I STILL SEEM TO BE HOOKED ON THIS SINGING SONGS BUSINESS ... I JUST WANT TO GET BETTER AT SINGING SONGS. AS OPPOSED TO ... I COULD ENTERTAIN THE THOUGHTS OF GOING TO WRITE A BOOK OR ACTING. BUT I'M HOOKED ON ROCK 'N' ROLL! I DON'T WANT TO DO THIS OR THAT, I WANNA MAKE MUSIC!"

— — — — — — — — — — — — — — — — — —

"Only Tupperware."

it, colour it darkly, splatter it with luminous green dots, take it for a walk through a tatty waxworks of horrors, lead it into safe temptation, feed it diluted hallucinogenic drugs, paint a crazed face on it and then – only then – consider it fit and pretty for the public airing. Sometimes they do all this without having an idea in the first place. . . . Their bass player is weedy and could be an all purpose Stiff session musician. The drummer is plain Ron. The guitarist mocks up an accident victim sweet chop look. The singer has an outrageous pout and the pout's name is Thomas Mann. Bauhaus are staining the Old Vic stage, opening wide their cheap and greasy macs to belligerently flash their dismembered pretensions. Bela Lugosi is pronounced dead, the Bauhaus members are mildly intoxicated by their own assumed audacity, the man with the Thomas Mann stalks the stage refining his own insignificant arrogance, the whole show drowns slowly and piteously in the "muck" and "sick" and "shit" of the group's carefully rehearsed melodramatic and sentimental vileness.

I say this: Depeche Mode and their particular MIRACLE OF SIMPLICITY is enough on its own to fill me with some kind of enfolding radiance – let that be known! Anyone who could sulk all the way through Depeche Mode's kissing, tingling, IMMEDIATE killing show at the Hammersmith Odeon must be very ill indeed and of course their sulks don't make a damned difference to the life inside Depeche Mode, to the new waves of energy Depeche Mode are contributing to. There is no absence of wit when Depeche Mode are on stage. "Life", they imply, "is neither good nor bad: it is original." Based on this premise, their songs are pre-

IRON MAIDEN

May 8, 1981
Some take to brandy,
others to lies. And we?
Why, we took to
fairy tales.

THE UNSMILING, but unthreatening, Iron Maiden are being photographed in the bright white tiled shower room of a compact sports stadium in Offenbach, near Frankfurt, Germany. They stand close to each other, shoulders touching: limp and patient, quiet and thoughtful.

The session is taking some time: the group are obviously used to snappy photo-sessions and they look slightly bemused by the care that's going into the photography. The docile Maiden are painstakingly placed into position. I try to ingratiate myself into the friendly, but private, Iron unit . . . it's all very arty isn't it? I chuckle.

"Well," says the group's singer, gravely, "**it's a lot better than sitting on a car bonnet and shaking our fists at the camera.**"

This strikes me as being very poignant.

IRON MAIDEN finish their soundcheck and prepare to travel back to their Offenbach Novotel for pre-match food and drink. Their luxury touring coach is jammed close to the stadium's backstage door, but there's still a gap of a few yards between the door and the coach. Hanging around hours before the show are scores of German boys: stringy hair covers their ears, their pale faces are streaked with light fluff and red blotches, blue denim is saturated with patches and badges, each single one of them assumes a plaintive toughness, a metal "fearlessness".

The Maidens and their minders force their way through the scrum to the sanctuary of the coach. The hopeful eyes of boy fans clutching posters, albums, magazines, picture discs, try to peer through the drawn curtains of the coach: what do their heroes get up to inside this monstrous mystery-mobile? Read comics, drink lager, watch *Mean Machine* on the video, suffer colds and flu. . . .

A young fan bravely bangs on an uncovered window, catching the attention of the group's bass player. The bass player gives a coy thumbs up, then notices I'm looking at him. The German fan – who looks as if he could come from Sheffield or Kansas or Lille or Glasgow – probably thinks he's been given a sign from heaven, or hell. The bass player shrugs his shoulders at me, seemingly a bit embarrassed.

I think to myself: it's quite touching.

BASS PLAYER Steve Harris comes from London's East End, where his dad is a lorry driver. At 15 he wanted to be a footballer, had a

trial at West Ham, and he used to laugh at what he saw as old hippies sitting around smoking dope and freaking out to Jimi Hendrix. His mates gradually turned him on, while they were playing chess, to King Crimson, Jethro Tull, Genesis.

"**I fahnd fings goin' on in there that I'd never fort abaht before.**"

He describes his background as not particulaly tough, he liked school for the sports and the mates. Other jobs apart from Iron Maiden have been an architectural draughtsman, packer, labourer, road sweeper and, for three days, dustbinman. "**I had to give that up 'cos I was right fed up with the maggots crawling dahn me neck.**"

Singer Bruce Dickinson lived with his grandparents in Worksop until he was 7, then with his parents in their Sheffield hotel. They sent him away to boarding school hoping he'd become a doctor or a lawyer.

"**But at boarding school I discovered rock and roll, which was, like, not planned. Ha ha ha ha ha!**"

He went to Queen Mary College in London having scraped three E-grade 'A' levels. He spent his three years at college singing in bands. "**I was no student.**"

Before Iron Maiden he sang in Samson, and he's also spent time in the army, been a traffic surveyor and compiled the Kelly's Directory for Hackney. At school he liked to fence, but he recalls that he was thrown out of the boarding school for "**pissing on the headmaster's dinner**".

IRON MAIDEN, groups like them, and their fans, have marked out and withdrawn into a very specific territory; they occupy it with a very special pride, a self-referring knowledge. They are quite prepared to let people (enemies) into the territory to look around, even comment; they receive the standard hostility with a mixture of good humour, sad confusion and ingenuous defensiveness. A bridge leading out of this territory links it with very little but: Cream, Hendrix, Zeppelin, Purple, Sabbath, Free, Cooper, Genesis, Zappa.

The territory is a place to dream of adventures: running free through the hills, forever getting girls on their knees, scrapping with Satan, battling with vermin and swimming through space. What goes on inside this territory is: simple, friendly "good fun", nice, uncomplicated devotion, a heroic isolation. Monsters, tanks, reptiles, rapists, maniacs, murderers, thugs roam the territory, but it's never *for real*, they're all harmless – IM is an extremely soft land, the monsters and the maniacs are really just teddy bears and dolls. . . .

occupied with unpredictability, surprise and discovery and underpinned with an almost comic jauntiness. The songs have young bodies and an intense vivacity. Depeche Mode have defined as well as anyone the pop choreography of transience. For the moment: only a moment. What was that? It. For the moment. Be bored with that, brats, and be bored with life. The fleeting moment; the kaleidoscopic light of changing environment and circumstance and perception and . . . what was that? Depeche Mode are absolutely on the brink of "a" – rather than the – next moment. So absolute, so arbitrary. Depeche Mode left the air mild but spinning with colour and sensation. They wrecked the cliché that an electronic group can only be bland and wistful on stage, or that a synthesiser group empties life of spiritual content, through the sheer suggestive consistency of their transmission and the energetic business of their presentation. They did Gerry and The Pacemakers' "I like It" as a third encore, and everything fell into place.

They are the boys who want tomorrow, with the best will in the world.

Bauhaus are recording some new music at a North London studio. The group are sat close together when I arrive, collected around a small mixing desk. They're almost holding hands. I am completely ignored. I am the dirt the wind's blown in. They don't care for me. Is it something that I said?

"When you came in," their singer Peter Murphy shudders later, "it was a real sick feeling . . . it was horrible. . . ."

Who would have thought that a collection of words, a pile of images, teased together, cut and dried, and presented in such a trivialised context could cause

BRUCE AND Steve don't see how heavy rock can harm; they see no problems. They listen politely while I list some problems:

The crudest manifestation of a spiritual yearning within all of us; the clumsiest adoption of trance techniques; the silliest handling of the unknown; a desperate pursuit of adventure; a loveless, pathetic attempt to introduce excitement into dull lives.

Safety in numbers, safety in what you know, safety in just staying inside the territory.

A lame promise, under the dirty surface, of sex, power, knowledge. . . .

They shake their heads. Heavy metal fans are just out for a good time; they don't consider that a bruised, beaten up, bloodied set of images and a badly broken language is being served up, that there's a lack of coherence or quality in the communication, that the whole enterprise is a badly garbled and scarred version of the type of exhilaration young people deserve. For Bruce and Steve it's a case of: if people enjoy it then it must be "good". A battered case?

Iron Maiden recently reached number one in the UK LP charts. Their Offenbach show is part of a huge world tour that visits 18 countries, including France, Japan, Belgium, Germany, Sweden, where their LPs easily reach the Top Ten, and America, where their latest LP "The Number Of The Beast" is moving into the Top 50.

By the end of the year Iron Maiden will be one of the most successful rock groups in the world – through reducing life to a series of grunts and scratches.

After the Offenbach show Steve, Bruce and I talk into the early hours of the morning in the Novotel bar: German, British, French fans hang around waiting for autographs. Steve talks in a sanded-down East End voice: Bruce is comparatively well-spoken. A certain sense in their conversation is drowned by a stubborn IM perspective. They are extraordinarily tolerant. At one point, whilst I'm calling Bruce corny and grotesque on stage, his elbow catches my knee. "Don't hit me," I plead. He apologises profusely. **"Sorry, sorry, I'm not like that at all!"**

We start by talking about Eddie: Maiden's teddy bear. Eddie is the exaggerated horror-headbanger featured in all Maiden artwork: a nine-foot Eddie muppet model dances on stage during their final number, flanked by two red, agile devil-imps.

I say to Bruce that in some ways Eddie symbolises the Maiden-Metal appeal. There's the gimmickry, the ugliness, the cheering supposed other-worldliness, the sweetened and lightened black magic, something easy to identify with, something that is larger than life "but that hasn't a life of its own".

As Bruce begins to answer Steve leans over and says: **"If you don't mind me asking, could you tell me where the khazi is?"**

Well, yes and no. . . .

BRUCE: YEAH, I think you could be right. I think there is more to the actual music side than that. As far as the overall image goes, the way Eddie is related to Iron Maiden, there may be a lot of truth in what you say. Oh sure, he's definitely larger than life, but in other ways he's very much tongue-in-cheek. He's not to be taken deadly serious. People can find some fucking serious grief about Eddie, saying that he's real horrible, but it's no way that it's anything other than a good laugh.

There's a conscious humour within heavy metal?

B: There's a lot of humour about us, put it that way. We try and debunk a lot of your standard heavy rock poses. We do a bit of it ourselves, but at the same time we take the piss out of it.

As with most heavy metal groups it appears that Iron Maiden are a parody of the excesses involved.

B: Maybe we fucking are! But that's because we're human beings and we don't take the whole of life completely, stupidly seriously and all we want to get over is that we're just normal guys out for a good time. I think that the music stands up, like, on its own, but there is no reason why you shouldn't give a show that is a good laugh.

On what grounds do heavy metal fans base their discrimination of the music?

B: I don't really know, to be honest with you. I remember what I wanted . . . I suppose they want to see people who can play, they respect certain values like professionalism, and they don't want to be treated like shit. They pay good money and they look forward to seeing some good music being played by decent musicians who really put their soul into it. If a pile of shit walks on, well, they'll soon let you know if they don't like it. You can't get away with just farting.

Y'know, you'll find that a lot of heavy rock fans are into jazz-rock music as well, they have a wide taste in music. I think heavy metal fans are more open-minded than people give them credit for.

They all look the same, they wear dowdy clothes, it's almost as if they've swapped "life" for just "heavy rock". . . .

B: No, no, it's not like that at all. They have a great time with the music and what's important about someone is not what clothes they wear or what their haircut's like; what's important is what's inside their head. All this thing about the denim being a uniform and all that, I don't think the fans see it that way. They don't see it as a uniform but as a way to identify with other people that like heavy rock. It's like saying I like heavy metal and I'm friendly.

STEVE: It's true, a lot of them wear their patches and everyfink to show other people that they're proud of what they're into and they don't give a shit what people fink. You know what I mean? The fans are, like, fed up with the slagging, the music and the clothes and everyfink else and it makes it even more a closed shop because they fink, fuck it, we're into what we're into, we have a great time at the concerts, and fuck everybody. . . .

B: I mean, what's so bad about it all? It's not as if people go away from our shows punching other people's heads in or chopping people up with axes because of our songs. We loathe and despise violence. . . .

Do your fans feel more alive after an Iron Maiden show?

B: I hope so, because that's what music used to do for me.

S: I hope when they go home they're so fucking wasted they can't fight anyone, you know what I mean?

B: It's like when I used to clock "Deep Purple In Rock", the first one like, and I'd whack it on and it was just like plugging in. You felt great, you were right there with them, you felt what they felt. You look for the shiver that goes up the spine and if it's there, it's fucking great.

But don't you feel that the music you play encourages an intellectual and moral complacency?

B: "Moral, intellectual complacency" . . . Well, the only way I can answer that is by saying that we place a great deal of thought into what we play and I think a lot of people place a great deal of thought into listening to what we play. I don't know in what sense you talk of intellectual complacency.

It appears that the type of people who like your music, all their experiences and attitudes, come from and move back into heavy metal. There's

this obsessive identification with a music that, let's say, doesn't do much to add to vocabularies.

B: I don't think that's true at all. There's bound to be exceptions, there's going to be the odd maniac who doesn't think about anything but headbanging furiously against a brick wall. But most of the people keep it in perspective. It's not an obsession with most of them, if that's what you're saying. I mean, you get a few obsessives with all types of music.

S: We had some people follow us around for the whole of our last British tour and it's not somefink I would've done when I was like 15, 16, no matter how much I was into a band. Like I was really into early Genesis; it's somefink I can't really explain, it's just I fucking liked them. I went to see them three nights on the trot and I was pissed off I couldn't see them a fourth. But to travel around on a whole tour . . . that's incredible, they're so into the band, and really I'm not sure what to fink of that.

Does it frighten you that young people place so much faith in you as individuals?

S: Well, it frightens me in a way . . . there are some guys who have had Iron Maiden tattoos put on to their arms and that frightens me because it's so permanent. I said to 'em, I said, fuck they're for ever, what you going to do when you're 50 or 60, you probably won't be into us any more? They said, yeah but we're so fucking into it, the energy and we're enjoying it so much, we'll be able to remember the good times we had. That's the way they felt. It's total dedication which to me is a bit frightening. You know what I mean?

B: You have to be realistic; if people are going to do that, there's not a lot you can do to physically prevent it. What you have to do is keep saying that we're just normal geezers, we're not gods, we never will be, and if we met you we'll buy you a beer, or you can buy us a beer, or lend us a quid. . . .

How do you feel about any influence or power that you have; this music directs the attention of a considerable number of people.

S: I don't feel any difference to when I was playing at the Marquee two or three years ago.

What do you feel about an energy you create reaching more and more people?

S: I just want to play on stage and enjoy myself for as long as I can. Let's face it, we all get old, and I know that I won't be able to

such antipathy; but then, half a wink in the wrong place can cause a murder. And who's to say why you like one thing, and don't like another – in pop music of all places. Why fall for Depeche Mode but fall over Bauhaus? Can it all be due to boredom?

Separated by sinister black blocks of ice, the group and I move to the studio bar. I try to be friendly; they're content to stay blank. They make it very apparent that I have bruised them. I am the dirt that's dropped from the ceiling. I turn on my tape recorder. They turn on theirs. The conversation will be recorded on two cassettes. This is serious; it's surprising. This is desperate; it's terrific. I start to work. It's very cold. To Bauhaus I am just another hack who is going to extract some words from the group and scatter them carelessly over some dull, simplified and lazy quarter impression. For Bauhaus I am just another pop journalist who takes everything for granted. As you well know, I haven't that conceit.

I am just a day's labourer.

Garcia chuckles, shoves a leg underneath his body, and looks me in the eye with genial firmness. He's continuing. "I don't think of myself as an adult. An adult is someone who's made up their mind. When I go through airports, the people who have their thing together, who are clean, well groomed, who have tailored clothes, who have their whole material thing together, these people are adults. They've made the decision to follow those routines. Brush their teeth regularly and all that. If you get to that stage all you get is rock solid boredom. With no surprises, when you're pretty sure that your best years are behind you. I run into people who are 24, 25, who are into that bag and I feel tremendously

deliver this kind of performance forever . . . In ten years' time I won't be able to do this and I tell you I don't even want to think about that day. It's gonna be a sad day when that happens. It's like, all it is, I really get off on what I'm doing and I'm sure a lot of the younger fans would love to be in my position and maybe in a few years they will be.

DOESN'T HEAVY metal turn in ever-decreasing circles: each new generation attempting to recreate a feeling they knew about for the next generation without altering or developing the music, or enhancing the experiences and observations?

S: There's no way that we're a re-run of Deep Purple, for example. We're nothing like what's gone before. Obviously heavy rock is what we draw our influences from.

B: Basically we're talking about intensity. The intensity that people put into music has been the same since the year dot. There's no dilution of intensity in what we do. There's the same kind of intensity in what we do as there would have been in the music some medieval lute player did in the court of King Ned. He really gets into it and everyone goes, yeah! What a raving lute player! Y'know, and he smashes his lute up at the end of every gig or something.

That kind of intensity has always attracted people and galvanised them. It's an intensity that is there in heavy metal and yet it's always fucking clobbered. Nothing else is clobbered like heavy metal.

For all the shaking, aggression, volume, clenching, the music appears to be not so much intense as bland and superficial.

S: Bland!

B: Superficial!

S: It isn't superficial. Fans genuinely are into the music. It isn't treated in a superficial way by the fans.

B: Fuck, I would describe our music as being anything but bland. You put an Iron Maiden album on the turntables and watch your fucking mother-in-law drop the dishes or something. It's not bland at all. It sticks out like a sore thumb.

It's like you just take those things for granted; but it surely isn't the case, that it "sticks out".

B: People go, oh it all sounds the same but what does sound the same is a lot of the crap they play on Radio 1 that passes for pop music and all that sort of shit. I mean, that is bland! That stuff is designed so that people don't switch the radio off so the whole thing sounds totally the same from minute to minute to minute.

S: Yeah, it's just background music.

B: I hate background music! But you know. . . .

S: Hold on, this is a good point . . . we had a number seven single and they only played it on Radio 1 when they had to, like when they played the Top Forty. You would fink that as it was in the Top Ten they would play it more. But I mean, maybe they were worried that when it came on the radio people were going to say, oh get this shit off, what is it? So how can it be bland?

Because the tricks, the techniques or whatever of the music are so well known. I would have thought the style of music is very acceptable.

S: If it is acceptable why the fuck won't they play our singles on the radio? Perhaps cos mebbe it's gonna frighten the muvvers who're listening and doing their ironing and they'll have miscarriages or something. . . .

This seems to be what you want to hope: that your music is hard and unacceptable for "straights" . . . it seems that your music is comforting more than anything, and whilst this gives you success, you are too inarticulate and insensitive to merit the type of following that you have.

B: Erm . . . I don't think . . . basically you're saying that heavy metal musicians are too dumb to deserve an audience.

You don't deserve this size audience because you're dealing with experiences or emotions in a destructively enclosed way, a harmfully sensationalist way.

S: Well, we don't deal with all the experiences that we have in life; we don't sing about everything that we go frew. There's lots of different fings that I'm into that I don't particularly want to write about.

And why not?

S: I'm into football, but I don't want to write a song about it. I might one day if I get the inspiration to write about football, y'know, or about anyfink. A lot of it is a fantasy fing. Y'know what I mean? People get a bit fed up with having politics rammed down their froats . . . people have like said to us, y'know, you're a working class band, why don't you write about where you come from? And about politics and that, and how hard done by you were and all that business, but, y'know, we don't want to. . . .

B: What's the point of telling people who haven't got a lot of money that there are lots of people who haven't got a lot of money? What's that all about? Punk bands, like, tell people who are being shat on by other people that they, y'know, are being shat on by other people and did they know? What's happening?

Perhaps at an energy level your music can be accepted as quite reasonable – if not up-to-date – but as with a lot of heavy metal groups you graft on to this energy a very peculiar and deformed series of symbols – relating to a naïve horror thing, or a desperate projection of masculinity. The horror thing, this Beast/666 business, seems especially disturbing.

B: You're talking about the Gothic horror bit. . . .

Yes. You're delving into areas that are rich and intricate, in a sub-comic book way: trying vainly to be mysterious where no mystery exists at all.

S: But hold on here, I mean, a lot of it is a fascination wiv the fings that are unknown . . . like all the films that are successful at the moment are like talking of the unknown fings that people don't quite know about. Like 666 and all that, that's just one song, there are other songs that deal with reincarnation and things, y'know.

It seems sad to me that there should be lots of young people turning to heavy rock groups for the mysticism in their lives.

B: The lyrics have a lot to do with melodrama and things like that. I mean, they really play up on situations. I really don't know, I can't give you an accurate description of just why I love to watch, say, the old original Bela Lugosi Dracula movies. . . .

S: You watch a film like that and it's just great. . . .

B: . . . and there is something there on a deeper level. It's not just a case of look mum he's sank his fangs into her neck. Y'know, there is something on a deeper level. There's something that stirs inside your personality when you watch films like that . . . maybe I'm too fucking stupid, but I cannot explain what it is but that something is what we try and translate into bits of our lyrics.

You don't see an awkward match between the basic rock energy and the crazed pseudo-gothic melodrama that's lumped on top?

B: No, no, no, melodrama, fantasy and energy . . . I mean, what more do you want? They go together, like, great!

OFFSTAGE you're very polite and easy-going, yet onstage there's this corny aggression – for me another part of the deceit or manic-compensation of heavy metal.

S: It's not corny, it's just natural, it's just what seems to be entirely right.

B: It's like you're building yourself up all day and then just letting it all go during that two hours. You have to visualise what's happening . . . I shut my eyes and think of the people in the audience and it's like a huge sea and the waves come rolling over you and you're part of it, and it's like you're part of this huge great thing . . . you can call me an old fucking hippy, I don't care. The whole thing is just absolutely great. I suppose it's like a meditation and it's like when I'm singing and there are no distractions, there's a little voice that you become aware of that's singing along with you and you're aware of the crowd. . . .

Shit, I'm making it sound fucking religious, like it's a way through to God.

Or are you saying "Heavy Metal is important", despite me claiming it's severely diminished?

S: It's not going to change the world. But I fink it's important for anyone to fink at some point in their lives, fuck it, I'm going to have a good time, whether it's going out and getting drunk or playing football or seeing a band or screwing a bird . . . letting the barriers down . . . and kids can come to a heavy metal concert and have a good time without worrying who's looking at them or laughing at them. They can just do what they feel like doing at that time.

B: All this is getting a bit serious and theoretical . . . basically you get on that stage and you have a steaming great time and you come off and you think . . . what!!!! That was fucking great!

Is there room in a heavy metal band for, say, a gay guitarist?

S & B: Gay!!!!!

B: If, say, some geezer turned up . . . put it this way if he could play fucking amazing guitar then he'd be in. . . .

S: . . . As long as he doesn't interfere wiv me, I don't give a fuck!

B: Excuse me, but a lot of people buy Judas Priest records . . . you know what I mean . . . I don't want to spell it out, y'know . . . I mean everyone knows, but no one fucking cares. . . .

S: . . . We're not talking about all Judas

intimidated by them. I feel they're adults."

American youths seem to be adult at 15 these days.

"It'll pass. It's just a phase. The next group of people will dislike that so intensely and so thoroughly that they'll fight through."

So if you're not an adult, then what are you?

"I would say that I was part of a prolonged adolescence."

Moving towards what?

"Middling adolescence!" He laughs. I switch the tape recorder off. "Yeah, that's far enough."

A clump of dust falls from his hair.

Haskins: "Was the review artificial?"

The day's labourer: No. It was based on fact.

Jay: "Were you there?"

The day's labourer: Yes, in the fourth row. I set about taking each element of my opinion of Bauhaus and blowing it out of all (so-called sensible) proportions, which in a way is what you do, the exaggerations. I tried to structure the review in a way that parallelled the way you maybe work.

Jay: "I don't think we're quite as abusive or hysterical as that review."

The day's labourer: That's exactly what I took you as being . . . I object to the waste of words pouring from the pop papers saying nothing at all. I think it's stupid that pop journalists can impose their own banal world view on to the most exciting things, forcing in a banality where no such thing exists. I hate the fact that pop journalists refuse to question the limits of their routine or deal with the indulgences. It's just a churning on for no good reason. It's a moronic padding, building up bashing boredom when the whole point is to oppose such a

Priest by the way. . . .

It's not the fact that people have their good time with heavy rock that causes the antipathy, but that there seems to be a very muddled, messy worldview, and quite often an active prejudice against gays or blacks or women or. . . .

B: There's no prejudice against blacks. You don't see a lot of them at our gigs but it's like they have their own culture, their own community. I suppose it's a bit intimidating when you see a whole load of white guys all in denim, in the same way that a white guy will be intimidated walking into some heavy rasta joint . . . plenty of ganja and guys thinking they look 'eavy in their bobble hats. . . .

Have either of you any racist tendencies?

S: Well, put it this way, I don't know where you're from, but I mean in the East End it's, like, there is a lot of darkies because it is a working class area I s'pose, but, er, I mean I've been to school wiv some of 'em and some are great, some of them aren't. There's good and bad in everybody. I dunno, there's been a lot of problems round the area and I fink being honest about it . . . I dunno . . . there's not many of 'em I get on wiv to be honest wiv you. Some of the ones I do get on wiv are fucking great.

Would you say that you're a racist?

S: . . . Erm . . . well, like it depends . . . erm . . . maybe . . . I don't mean a racist in the sense of a right . . . put it this way, it's not a colour thing. Believe it or not, it's not . . . Y'know, it's said that the Australians hate the English, you know what I mean? And that's not a colour thing 'cos they're white, right?

Right.

S: It's just a racial thing where some cultures cannot seem to get on wiv others, and the fing I feel is that when people go to live in another country they should, er, y'know, when in Rome do as the Romans do as such. Try and integrate into that fing and live in a certain way. I admit you've got to keep a certain amount of your own culture.

Do you not have a respect for other cultures?

S: Yeah, I do . . . but the fing is if I went to Australia and they hated me just because I was English and not because of what I was like as a person, I wouldn't like it. But then again it's nuffink to do wiv colour 'cos I'm the same colour as them. . . . If they don't like me it's because of the way I am, so fair enuff.

With the black and white thing it's not a question of colour, it's a question of you not getting on wiv someone who's a different race or whatever. All round the world there are wars because certain races just cannot get on wiv others, they just cannot live togevver . . . I fink that it's pie in the sky to say that racial integration can happen. It's been proved time and time again that it can't.

A GOOD LIFE has landed at your feet, but do you still get frustrated and disappointed with certain events or happenings or situations?

B: Well, yeah, like the racial thing is a bit of a serious grief because fuck knows what anyone's going to do about it. There's loads of bad news about. . . We were over in America when the riots happened and I can understand that kind of thing because I can understand being concerned. I can understand feeling that there's nowhere, nothing, nobody to care . . . that you might as well be fucking dead. There comes this point where you think you might as well be dead, you'd be better off, so bollocks to everything, let's just fucking go for it.

Ultimately, though, I've got a fundamentally optimistic feeling about most human beings. I really feel that most people, apart from politicians, are quite nice people. I think all politicians are wankers and that most people just want to get on with what they do and they want to be happy and be friendly. . . .

What about heavy metal's apparent attitude towards women – is it a "sexist" attitude?

B: Not really. . . .

S: There are only two songs that we've written about women as such and both are really, really tongue-in-cheek . . . fantasy fings about going wiv a prostitute which not everyone can say they've done. I'm not saying we have, well, I haven't. . . .

B: Don't say nothing about Hamburg!

S: But it's like a fantasy fing and it really is tongue-in-cheek.

Does heavy metal omit girls because of its rituals and its undertakings?

S: What I really don't understand is why there aren't more women that come to our gigs – not just our gigs, but heavy metal gigs in general. Guys go to heavy gigs cos they like shaking their heads and the aggression fing. I feel it's a shame that there aren't more women, do you know what I mean?

B: I think that heavy metal is a male orientated music, but I wouldn't say that it's sexist.

S: It's, like, disco music is female orientated 'cos birds love to dance. Let's face it, the majority of geezers who go to discos they might think the music's all right, and they might even buy a couple of disco records, but the majority of them go to pull birds. The birds dance, the geezers have a beer and pull.

B: I didn't go to heavy metal gigs to pull a bird. I went to see a band. . . .

Why don't girls go?

B: 'Cos they can't get pulled! I dunno. . . .

Don't you feel that girls will look at Iron Maiden onstage and that it's something they can't possibly take seriously: this grotesque parody of sexuality.

B: Well, I just fink it's unfair that girls don't fancy us more. Perhaps we're all fucking ugly. . . .

B: I wouldn't say that . . . I *can't* see how it's grotesque. . . .

But wouldn't a girl look at you and laugh at the straining, whereas a boy-virgin will look at you and identify with it because he thinks that this is what appeals to women, poor sod?

B: I've no idea. When I'm onstage I don't even think of appealing to women. It doesn't enter into my thoughts in the slightest bit. I'm there to project the music that's being played.

Are you trying so terribly hard to be a man?

B: Not really. God made me one of those, or my mum and dad. . . .

To be a "man's man".

B: I don't feel the need to have to go around proving that I'm more macho than the next . . . nerk. I really don't feel the need to be a great macho beefcake.

That's exactly what it looks like you're trying to prove.

B: I'm not! Ha ha ha ha ha. There's not a lot I can say about it.

What are you trying to do?

B: Expend a lot of energy so that I have a good time and enjoy myself and let myself go and as far as possible accentuate the music and what's going on in the music. I want people to have lots of enjoyment through what we do and I don't see why it has to be analysed.

YOU FINISH this world tour in November – what's beyond that, and do you take each month as it comes?

S: You can't really say what's going to happen. I take each month or whatever as it comes. Y'know I just want to play for as long as possible ontstage. I want to go to different countries and play to different audiences. So basically I'm having a good time at the moment and I want to have a good time for as long as possible, and I don't want to fink about somefing else.

It is similar to a football fing. You know that at 32 you're going to have to give it up . . . Y'know, I don't really regret that I didn't make it as a footballer. I couldn't really be dedicated to it. Cos, like, when I went round to West Ham, like, it's my favourite team, it's all I ever wanted to play for, and when I got down there I found that it wasn't really what I thought it was. You know what I mean? I didn't want to go to bed at ten o'clock in the evening. I was at that age when I wanted to go out and have a few beers and meet a few women and that. . . .

Which is what you've been doing ever since.

S: Well, yes and no . . . .

thing.

The Bauhaus review was me splashing around in the stale mess of all this pop writing and at the same time attempting to establish a new reason for doing such a review. What originality can there possibly be in a criticism of a pop show? I tried to charge something up. Part of it was as a preparation for meeting you. Why not? Maybe we can talk now. Be annoyed. It's better than sleeping. Be pissed off. It's better than plugging your new records.

Haskins: "So that review was just an exercise. . . ."

Jay: "In provocation. . . ."

Murphy: "But people read that. . . ."

The day's labourer: Of course! Hopefully it will make more sense and do more good than the bland words that just dissolve into nowhere. Words can't be wasted all the time. Some words, even in the pop papers, have to stick around. Or stick in someone's throat.

Jay: "When this interview comes to light are you going to indicate that the review was merely a piece of provocation?"

The day's labourer: Obviously . . . The intention here is to open up a clearer picture of Bauhaus. Surely you would prefer a complexity in any approach to you to fan-nish simplicity. Some people feel that the case for Bauhaus could be wrapped up inside two sentences. I'm here to take it much further than that. Impressed?

Ash: "It's impossible to tell anything about us that's proper inside half an hour."

Obviously not. But can Bauhaus claim to have any distinctive value?

Ash: "A distinctive value only to a certain amount of people. We personally can't do anything about that, because people are only going to draw off something they want, what they accept,

WHAM!
October 25, 1983
The limits
of explanation.

1

a. "It's selfish. Totally selfish. We may not be mindless but we're totally selfish."

b. *The true being of a man is his* deed: *for in it individuality is* real.

c. "I've wanted to do this since I was 7 years old. I didn't suddenly think, oh, I've got a great talent."

d. *You can measure the reality of an act, a man, an institution, custom, work of art, song, in many ways: by the constancy and quality of its effects, the depth of the response which it demands, the kinds and range of the values it possesses, the actuality of its presence in space and time, the multiplicity and reliability of the sensations it provides, its particularity and uniqueness on one hand, its abstract generality on the other – I have no desire to legislate concerning these conditions, insist on them all.*

e. "We're not different. Our situation is different."

And pretty banal.

"I think most people's lives are pretty banal. There's nothing exciting about the fact that people have our pictures on their walls. That kind of thing's been going on for years . . . so, well, I think glamour is pretty banal, but it can still be enjoyable . . ."

You're banal, George.

"Yeah, I'm banal, as far as what goes on the record . . . but I enjoy the music and a lot of other people enjoy the music, so I don't care."

What do you care about?

"I care about me, I care about my family. I care about making sure that I'm still here in five or ten years' time. Y'see, I'm about as human as most people are. I don't think you have a grasp of how human most people are. I don't think that you have a grasp of basic human requirements. You seem to use the word "banal" as derogatory. But life is banal . . . if you understand, you know that it is banal and that there's nothing wrong with that. . . . It's just life. It's just the way people are, people are banal, their lives are boring, and they just try to get through life as enjoyably and as *simply as possible*. . . ."

f. *. . . the content of an aimless consciousness is weak and colourless . . . the work is futile, the thought is shallow, the joys ephemeral, the howls helpless and the agony incompetent, the hopes are purchased, the voice prerecorded, the play is mechanical, the rules typed, their lines trite, all strengths are sapped, exertion anyhow is useless, to vote or not is futile, futile . . . it is the principal function of popular culture – though hardly its avowed purpose – to keep people from understanding what is happening to them . . . in every way they are separated from the centres of power and feeling. . . .*

g. "I do enjoy this kind of conversation . . . I like coming up against questions like these. But I don't think it means anything to people. No one wants to know about the things you're going on about. Enjoyment is what matters."

But doesn't such single-minded attention on the juices of enjoyment become repetitive and desperate? Doesn't such small determination to enjoy, enjoy, enjoy actually nullify the possibilities of pleasure? Don't curiosity, complication, adventure play their parts. . . .

"Yeah, those things, but why should we be the ones to put it about? Why should we? I want us to be happy."

h. *Knowing. For most people it is precisely this that is painful. They do not wish to know their own nothingness – or their own potentialities either, and the pleasures of popular culture are like the pleasures of disease, work, poverty and religion: they give us something to do, something to suffer, an excuse for failure, and a justification for everything.*

i. "What I think we're celebrating is simply what certain years of our lives meant to us and what they mean to most people. Valid things . . . energy and optimism, y'know. . . ."

what they relate to. Obviously we don't think we're just another band lost amongst thousands." The despair had grown.

I ask Chrissie Hynde if she's thrilled to be number one. "Personally, not so much, I'm glad everyone worked hard to promote the single, and that obviously someone out there likes it, y'know, but right now I'm thinking about the song we were working on last night, you know . . . all I know is that I've got to do 'Top Of The Pops' today, mime the damn thing again, and it's a song we've done for a year. I mean, can you imagine standing there miming to your own song, not even performing it. . . . It's no ego boost. It's just part of the job. Last night my flat mates were raving on about how we've been thrown out of our flat, we've got nowhere to go, and I'm saying YOU'VE GOT NOTHING TO DO, YOU'VE GOT NOWHERE TO GO, YOUR LIFE'S A SHAMBLES – BUT WHAT AM I GOING TO WEAR ON 'TOP OF THE POPS' TOMORROW! But then I feel guilty, like I shouldn't say no I don't care that it's number one. It's very rare that I get any satisfaction out of anything that I've done . . . oh, y'know, I'll never seem very positive, there will always be things that I cannot like about me. Like if I hear my record in a public place I just want to go and hide . . . I feel like I'm on display . . . you know, then I remember when I was a hobo and I could do what I wanted when I wanted to and no one would bother me . . . the days when I really found happiness in my life. People always ask are you delighted with your new success, and all the trappings of success that outside people are attracted to are exactly the trappings that make me feel nervous, you know. . . ." I know.

Leading towards what?
"Getting older."
The end.

2

HERE comes trouble. W. Ham United stroll into the photographic studio ready for action, the type of action they can really wrap their teasing eyelashes around: make-up. George and Andrew, a couple of stubborn-looking vikings, although I'm told that they're "pop's terrible twins", carry their dressing-up bags with the kind of nonchalance that only a second division member of The Style Council Europe-Tourist Brigade could believe was spontaneous. Their rehearsed nonchalance is calculated along safenik paper-deep 1983 pop lines – an old-fashioned mixture of shyness and arrogance and ignorance and screwy neo-adolescent suspicion transformed, due to a few radio plays, into a dull-eyed assurance.

W. Ham United: princes of the superlush era, two under-sophisticated con-men out on one of this century's most eccentric capers, used to being flattered, used to humble attendants, spoilt like a threatened species, a metaphor of modern limitation, kids kidding around and taken seriously by people who should know better. I wonder if I can bring them to tears? Certainly won't ask them what songs they'll be singing on their tour.

Let's talk about humility: no trouble at all.

3

HOW can you feel in any way satisfied or inspired being a prime part of the current charty gay abandon, all this flimsy jingly sing-along?

George/Andrew (in touching harmony): **That's what pop music is all about!**

What, a sing-song?

A: **That's what makes pop songs popular,** because everyone can sing along with them. There's nothing wrong with that.

G: **What fucking right have you got to say that we should sing something that is socially important?**

I haven't said that, don't insult me!

G: **What are you saying then?**

I'm just wondering about the extent of your ambition. You must at times get pissed off with music that is popular, not just indifferent, because everyone can sing along with it. You have to draw the line somewhere – do you have standards?

G: **What are you talking about . . . your standards are what you enjoy.**

Tell me something about your standards.

A: **If you like it, it's all right. What you enjoy, it's all right.**

Comprehensive stuff. No second thoughts, no doubts, no feelings of restlessness.

G: **What are you talking about? There's obviously a great difference between the way *you* look at music and the way *we* look at music. We look at music as something to enjoy, not as what the pop song means or what it represents, or whether it's better than pop music made five years ago. All that's not for us.**

I'm just an argumentative bitch, I just have this feeling that it's positive for energy to be used in a different way than how it has been in the past; I like movement rather than self-satisfaction.

G: **Look . . . we like pop music . . . we make pop music . . . why do you expect something from us other than pop music?**

I don't expect anything else, certainly not moral action – I sometimes think – this is all – that within the pop song context you might want to appear a little less common. . . .

A: **But we're not writing songs for you or for anyone else for that matter, so we don't give a toss what you say because we like what we do. . . .**

G: **What the hell are you going on about?**

I'm finding it hard to be polite. Instead of just having people sing along with your songs, and blink in the glare of your teeth, wouldn't it please you to think that maybe you'd intrigued, provoked and enlivened your audience?

A: **Why do we have to intrigue, provoke and . . . whatever else it is you're going on about. . . .**

So what do you want to do then? Sorry I'm so curious.

G. **Why the fuck should we have to do anything?**

A: **Fucking hell, we play music for ourselves.**

G: **We enjoy it, our audience enjoys it, why the fuck should we provoke them? What the fuck's that about? Ego, that's what this is about. For Christ's sake, most people have an ego, most people who are in pop music are there because they have an ego . . . the whole business is built on ego, vanity, self-satisfaction and it's total crap to pretend that it's not.**

The "ego" you're talking about seems pretty threadbare to me – it's hardly as though you have the nerve to pretend you're God, just the courage to revel in your own small-minded big-headedness – and if there's ego, self-satisfaction and vanity, why not initiative, inspiration and irritation as well? Wouldn't it be more fulfilling to your ego if you were bolder, bitter, better – you talk of ego but you just mean self-congratulation; you don't want your ego fuelled because of any candour and brilliance.

G: **What the hell are you talking about? Why do you have such resentment of big pop success?**

I don't. But why should "fame" always be vacant, a crude unimaginative outlet for self-advancement?

G: **To be a huge success means that you cannot intrigue, provoke and all those things you go on about. Because the public don't want it. You just can't get past a certain number of people by being provocative because the vast majority of people just aren't interested in that.**

Does that piss you off?

G: **Why should it piss me off?**

I'm thinking of depersonalisation, deflation, moral coma, that people just want to shrink into themselves. . . .

G: **It's human nature. . . .**

A: **Look, why should it piss us off if we're happy. . . . We're OK. It might piss *you* off. It doesn't piss us off.**

G: **What are people supposed to do with their lives apart from enjoy them? I prefer to forget those people who want something interesting and just play for those who want to enjoy themselves. I don't want people to say that our music is incredibly innovative or new, I just want them to enjoy it. . . .**

You don't want people to be stunned by the remarkable effort you put into your music, exhilirated by your spectacular stamina. . . .

G: **What the hell are you talking about?**

4

ANDREW laughs at me. Wham! chuckled – scoffed, even! – at me quite a lot during my gracefully uneven abuse of the docile, shameless efficiency that is their entertainment. I, in return, blushed – I'm not beyond blushing, it's one of my greatest weapons. They practise a loveless overinsulated cynicism towards those of us who enjoy a state of permanent dissatisfaction. I suppose it was inevitable we wouldn't get on, me enjoying lively minds, and Wham! enjoying . . . enjoyment.

Through their sour passion for enjoyment and their rejection of irony and curiosity they do not demonstrate strength but simply obstinacy. (Andrew laughs at me.) Just because the feeble ego-blast of their music is enjoyed by thousands doesn't mean that the thinking ones amongst us shouldn't mock its lack of excitement and invention; nor do we ignore the fact that their complacency towards any purpose or resourcefulness in life means their music will never include

What gave you the conviction to start making records?

"It wasn't rebellion. I only got into what appeared to be rebellion because I wasn't able to do what I wanted. I just wanted to play. I couldn't play here and I couldn't play there and I couldn't do this and I couldn't do that, and that's why I became, like, annoyed at it. But before that I was just idealistic as far as you want to know. And we started the Stones to play THE BLOOOOOOSE . . . which is a pretty weird thing to remember. But that's why we started. And also in those days we were pretty naive about the press. They sort of pushed us into an awful lot of things that we didn't want to do. When you look at those old press cuttings it's pretty amazing what they got you at. You were put up as being such and such a thing, and of course you began to play the roles, unbeknownst to you. Seduced by the likes of the *Daily Mirror*. It becomes that you play the roles that are forced upon you. Being dirty and all that crap. It seems so long ago and it is."

Once you'd got through all that you must have come to some decision about what you were?

"Well, then you don't know where you are! Then you think, fuck it, I'm fed up with being pushed around, now I'm going to try something different. But by the time you reach that point you are an incredibly rich man, or you appear to be so. I wasn't actually. Unfortunately. I didn't get any money until . . . I mean, I spent a lot of money, but so did everyone else; it's all relative. We didn't have any money in the bank until 1972. I'd spent it all and owed it all in taxes. Although it would appear that I was very rich, in actuality I wasn't. Most people in entertainment are not as rich as people would love to imagine that they are. That's just a fantasy."

the forces that could lift it beyond being small if cheerful. (Andrews scoffs at me.)

Wham!, defensively, thought that I was demanding that they explore insights into themselves or the society that impinges upon them: no, hardly. I just thought that it might be a delight or something if they really truly exhibited themselves as very hip/beat, very imaginative, very candid, and performed directly from the guts and the nerve ends instead of playing at all that. If they have to be around, there's no reason why they have to be so lifeless.

"You wouldn't say these kinds of things to Modern Romance," *protested George. What the hell was he going on about?*

I can hear Andrew laughing at me, shaking his head, the terse smile, such a grim snob. . . . The dumb defiant laugh becomes the symbol of 1983 pop's timidity, its retreat: Andrew laughs at the thought that the way he works might be careless, an avoidance; is unimpressed by the suggestion that a true depiction of the dislocated age we inhabit could intensify his music; is tickled by the idea that there can be an elastic and surreal response to cruelty and ugliness, instead of a desperate and unreal attempt to duck its existence; is annoyed when you wonder whether "entertainment" could benefit from an invasion of crazy tensions. . . . No, Wham! are just out to earn more and more eager congratulators.

Wham! are just a little too belligerent in wanting you to believe that they haven't a care in the world nor a thought for it. They might yet realise how thick they are. Isn't that so, Andrew? Spiteful indignant laughter snorts down his nose. And then all of a sudden you feel embarrassed for the boy because he is such a fool and is so proud of it.

Andrew laughs at me.

5

YOU TEND to laugh a lot at the things I say, Andrew. Is that because you're a condescending little slob?

A: **Yeah. . . .**

G: **You don't think you're condescending!**

A: **Your whole attitude towards us is condescending. You don't understand, you don't make any effort to understand.**

You think my mind's made up?

G: **Yeah. . . .**

I never knew that I was capable of making it up.

G: **Everything you do in this life is for yourself as far as I'm concerned. The way that you should go about it is so that you don't harm anyone else. That's my view, right. Your view seems to be that you want to make other people's lives more interesting and worthwhile and that just doesn't make any sense to me. I'm being totally selfish, but I never detract from other people's lives.**

By being truly totally selfish and obsessive then, a by-product of your work will be that it is of intense interest to other people. . . .

G. **Are you mad? Look, I don't hurt anyone to satisfy myself and so that's all right.**

So Wham! is more pleasure than pain and you don't hurt anyone else?

G: **So Wham! should be pain.**

I didn't say that.

A: **What the hell** *are* **you saying? What's all this pain?**

Well, is it an input into Wham!? If there is no acknowledgment of pain there can be no understanding of pleasure . . . just one of those tensions . . . I mean, there's no obligation here, boys. I was just trying to arrive at a snappy little definition of Wham!

G: **Well, most people don't want to know about pain. . . .**

A: **Chuckle, chuckle, chuckle. . . .**

You chuckled again – you're making no effort to understand me!

A: **Well, what you're saying is funny.**

G: **I don't think it's funny. I just don't see why escaping. . . .**

I certainly never said that escapism is a

disgrace. . . .

G: **We've both got personal lives, right, and there's plenty wrong with my life. I make up for my problems and all that on stage, on record.**

How?

G: **I'm not going to tell you how!**

Why not?

G: **. . . Because I haven't thought about how.**

Maybe I'm being hard on you, here. Maybe you're not used to it.

G. **No, I'm** *not* **used to it. Look, I'm perfectly willing to accept, right, that all I'm doing when I get on the stage is enjoying my own music and satisfying my own ego, but don't presume that because we've got success everything is rosy and it's all great and that we're forgetting that there is a lot of pain in life . . . I know that there's pain in everyone's life and the way I get away from it is up there on the stage. There's nothing wrong with that.**

Another snappy little definition of Wham! – two plastic male models with odd things attached?

G: **Well, I mean I wouldn't mind . . . If I thought I could be a male model and enjoy it, then I'd be a male model. It wouldn't bother me as long as I was enjoying it.**

It would get you through life?

G: **That's right. As long as I enjoyed it, it would be all right.**

6

WHAM! stroll into the photographic studio. . . . You can tell by their faces that their minds are made up: life is for simplifying, down to the last losing trickle of vanity and vacancy. I'm going to interview them after they've been photographed. Their faces are made up: up to the last wipe of prettiness. Some preliminary photos are taken, but they say the light's not right. So the talking begins and – guess what! We fight. All right?

7

George: **What the hell was he going on about, Andrew?**

Andrew: **Fuck knows, George. Let's get these photos over with. Look as though you're enjoying yourself.**

So, in 1972, why continue? Any illusions must have been shattered?

"No, they weren't shattered enough that you didn't want to try and continue to build on something."

On what?

"A very shaky foundation! You've already set yourself on a very dodgy course which has zig-zagged in and out, you've had a lot of trouble, so you want to try and keep yourself level-headed a bit after you've had this experience."

Then you weren't particularly fighting for or against anything?

"No . . . I don't think that's necessarily what musicians do. They just have a good time. You're placing too much emphasis on an imaginary cultural side that only really exists for writers who need something interesting to write about. Some people want to make music, some people want to listen. That's about it really . . . it can be made out to be complicated, but really it just isn't at all."

Can it change people's lives? (Strummer) "Well, whenever one of those yank journalists asks me if I think rock and roll can change anything I always say no, no, no, not at all . . . but really we all know that The Song is the be all and the end all of everything. It is in my life any-way. If I write a song, even when I'm walking down the road, well, it is like that song, no one can take a song away from you, even when you're sitting in a Kentish Town prison cell. At least you've got a song, right, and that can seem to be the most powerful thing ever. I think it has got the power to change . . . I mean people go to clubs and they hear songs and that's where the information can come through to them. . . . It's got to be the only thing. It's about sharing human experience, and having new

DURAN DURAN
July 25, 1982
''The Golden Age Of
Rock AND Roll'':
a salmon screams.

SO I'M surrounded by the five fluffy Duran boys, blinded by their bounce, dazzled by their cheek (bones), and I do what any responsible star-writer would do. I ask to look at their socks. Simon, Andy, Nick, John and Roger lift up their trousers: Simon the singer's are the worst – woolly!! – Nick the synther's are the best – sheer! "*Music Life* from Japan asked us what our favourite cars were, and what kinds of girls we liked."

This is the sort of challenging poser these light-weight poseurs love. So I ask them what are their favourite ice lollies.

"Strawberry mousse . . . Cornetto . . . 99s with flakes . . . Funny Faces . . ." emerge out of a bubble of Brum and Geordie accents.

Do they eat cornflakes after sex?

"I eat Thornton's Continental chocolates after sex," says Simon, or was it Nick.

"I always have a cigarette after," admits Andy, to jeers of "cliché!" from his Duran-maties.

Now the Duran Airy are poppy stars, is their love life better?

"Do you mean do we get more shags? Of course."

Dear, dear, dear. Does it vary throughout the country?

"No . . . the girls all look exactly the same and they wear the same clothes . . . we've had quite a few Lady Di futurists. I'm into Lady Di futurists," said Nick, or was it Simon. "When are the *NME* going to put Lady Di on the cover?"

How long do Duran Trifle want all this pop starlight to last – a quick thing over in a year, ravishing and wonderful?

"We want it to last and last!"

Because you're greedy?

"No, because we enjoy it," says Roger, or was it John.

"I don't want to be a has-been by the time I'm 21," says Nick, definitely. "That's two years away . . . I'm dreading being 20. . ."

I think I want to be cynical to Duran Frill's faces.

"No, it's all right, you don't have to bother. . ."

You're surrogate Moody Blues.

"Cliché! That scores five out of ten."

Are you surprised with what you get away with?

"I choose to ignore that remark," says Nick, earnestly.

Is it difficult being five boys so close to each other?

"If you mean are we up each other's bums – no we're not!"

How are you going to avoid becoming fat and rich overnight?

"We're going to be rich and when we're rich we'll buy a gymnasium and that'll keep us fit. Also when you're rich you can eat really nice foods like smoked salmon 24 hours a day. That won't make you fat. One of the perks of this job is getting rich!"

A quarter of a mile away from where we're sat, there's a riot going on.

SIGNING AUTOGRAPHS in HMV record stores is a thing that has to be done, it seems. It's expected. It's now part of the day when you tour.

At 3 o'clock on a Saturday afternoon at the Birmingham HMV in New Street, Duran Smile are squeezed behind some tables faced by scores of young girls and a handful of young boys holding out armfuls of record sleeves, posters, articles, tickets. . . . Girls with blood-red lipstick, white faces, frizzed black hair, drowned dreamy eyes, wearing waves of black, take snaps with cheap cameras. Duran's handlers have trouble keeping the crowd orderly; Duran Teeth soak up the pleasure-pressure with warm pride, adoring to be adored.

Duran Scream embody the new age of teenybop. They say that the demands and desires of the consuming teenager have not altered over the last ten years; punk, if anything, aggravated the lust for the made-up pop star, the wanting to look up and beyond, perchance to dream.

"It's coming back to what it was like before punk. . . . During punk and just after there were no bands like us or Adam playing Odeons that any age could go and see. . . ."

knowledge and insights into it, and the more people know about things, the more we're moving on towards equality and that . . . the more we can protest. Songs can lead to progress, so they've got to be important."

"We've seen some of your stuff," continues Jaz, "your praising of Sting's fucking transcendental fucking experiences in India, right. We've seen quite a few of your fucking articles and personally I don't think you've got any right to write like that. How can you write like that about us? What do you actually know? What I can see of your taste by the way that you write, you haven't got a fucking clue, have you? You don't know what you're fucking on about."

My brain seizes up. What do you mean?

"Well, you're into pop, aren't you, the traditional form of a band. That's the way I see it by the way you write, like you're into the traditional fucking form of a rock band."

I stare at him passively. Youth will tell me later that Killing Joke are so anti-tradition and so far outside the business it's a major achievement. I think "tradition" in the way we use the word as an insult is foul as well, but this doesn't mean you have to end up as stodgy and as unglamorous as Killing Joke.

Meanwhile, Jaz has a Sting on his shoulder. "I can see by the way you praise Sting, and all that sugar shit, it's nothing to do with our way of life. We live here, we play the music we want to play, right. . . . And a couple of journalists have decided to really put the boot in, because they don't like us personally. I don't know why it is, but it's fucking not on."

I wipe the sugar shit from my eyes.

Tell me about The Jam's Eton

"I've got two sisters", says Andy, who's interested in guitars, "aged 13 and 15, and they're just the same about pop music as I was at that age. Posters on the wall, off to see Adam; their appreciation of pop is exactly the same as mine used to be. It would be a big loss for kids if they couldn't go to Odeons to see groups.

"In the record shop signing away, it's ridiculous the way we were all horrible and sweating by the end and getting crushed and everything, but it's worth doing because all the kids obviously got something out of it. If they didn't want to they wouldn't be there yelling and shouting, and it's great because it makes them happy. They'd enjoy it all, and they will be at the show tonight."

Duran Suave are committed to dragging glamour and fun and games into pop music: simplistically and selfishly, not so much Ze as Bay City Rollers.

"The whole idea of show business has been torn to shreds by punk, but at the end of the day what I always remember was I wanted to go out and be entertained from the second I walked in the hall. I wanted a big show. Things got out of hand when you had to spend £7.50 to see Pink Floyd and plastic pigs in a big barn. That's crazy, but there is an intermediacy between scruffy clubs and arenas."

Where will Duran Bigwig draw the line?

'Well, for this tour our tickets didn't cost more than £3. We're losing out but I don't think we warrant charging more than that. Last night in Oxford the whole bloody theatre was dancing, and it was a seated hall. Every night on the tour people in the balcony have been standing up, and I've never seen that at gigs. Especially Hammersmith. . . ."

Duran Ditto love playing live; the new nightclub latitude is just a part of their act.

"The groups we tend to get bundled with might not like playing live, but we really enjoy it. We're a concert band. When Chic came over to play here they don't do Top Ranks, they play Odeons. You can dance to our records every night of the week in clubs, but come and see us and it's something different. You pay a little more money than you would down the Locarno so we try and put on A Show."

Are Duran Distant aloof?

"You can be close to your audience and personal with them which is what we do on stage, we talk to them, we're there in the same building as them, but they haven't got great big spotlights over them. One of the main reasons Gary Numan took off was that he was the first guy to come along who actually placed himself under the spotlight as pop star.

"This appeals to us . . . the Hollywood untouchable thing. I think kids like that too. There are plenty of bands catering for people who want to hear about how bad life is. We're not interested in that. The entertainment is escapism really."

AS THE Duran fans peter out and the five fop-tops prepare to sign off, someone mentions, as casually as if it was raining, that it's rioting.

Outside in New Street packs of Rastas and bald boys are marauding. The small batch of fans left in the shop are hurried out and Duran Shocked slip quickly into the Odeon a hundred yards away. Gangs of youths line the pavements around the theatre, the shopping centre becomes a no-go area protected by railings and police, straggling shoppers walk down New Street a little uncertainly. Saturday afternoon's sport is over within a couple of hours, leaving faint traces of tension. On the 5.30 Radio One news bulletin it's announced that 400 youths have stormed New Street. It was more of a jog than a storm. Duran's manager despairs: "No one is going to turn up tonight now."

Because it's their home town show, Duran Spoilt are brutally disappointed. A life's ambition is being disrupted by what they term "irresponsibility".

"I've always wanted to play the Birmingham Odeon," John tells me. "I saw all my first gigs here – Roxy, Ronson – and now this."

Do Duran Butt think about things other than lolly pops, girls and money?

"I hate people slagging us off for us saying that it's only entertainment. They think we're naïve and so we mustn't consider things outside. We do think about important things but to ourselves. We all have our political views but they haven't got anything to do with what we're doing now. If we were working in banks, it really wouldn't have anything to do with that job. You'd get the sack if you started giving people the heavy vibe.

"I think it's bad to preach to kids because we've got a really young audience, they're at a highly impressionable age, and it would be tough on them if we started lecturing. We have a responsibility *not* to tell them things. The main responsibility we have is to give people a good time, to give them what they pay for."

Do they find the rioting exhilarating?

"It really annoys us that it's our home town and we've got a gig tonight . . . you come down home after a really hard tour and then this happens. . . . It's so irresponsible . . . it reminds me of Baader Meinhof, they don't even know what they're doing.

"Hey, let's stop this. It's getting political . . . we avoid political interviews, they're so boring. This is getting smutty. Let's talk about bottoms."

INSIDE THE Odeon just before Duran Daft's sound-check I walk with John to the front of the theatre to see how the riot's getting on. The two girls, maybe sheltering from the storm, are in the foyer and run delightedly towards the bright bass boy. Little squeals, sparkling eyes. . . .

''Have you got anything for us?'' they ask.

"You can have him," says John pointing at me. The girls are totally unimpressed and prefer a twopenny piece out of John's pocket (imagine) to me. What do they want that for, I wonder?

''Because it's his!'' they exclaim abruptly.

What's so special about him? A gasp or two is supposed to explain it for me. John walks back inside the hall, leaving the two girls' lives in the balance.

I tell him Duran Dandy's appearance on the *Whistle Test* was appalling, that it confirmed all our best fears that Duran Pomp-It-Up-Like-Suckers-In-The-Night are gummed-up glammed-over techno-rock twits.

"It's difficult to come out good on that programme. And every time we're on the BBC they use dry ice – they seem to think we're the perfect group to use dry ice on."

It's not often the BBC are right.

Later Simon tells me that one of the best things about being in Duran Vain is the dry ice between the legs. **"But what's the point in turning the offer down?"**

Duran Unsated are open to all offers. They have little objection to anything so long as it gets them out to more people.

"We want more and more people to know about us . . . we've done *Cheggers Plays Pop*, the *Whistle Test, Top of the Pops*, we're doing the new Peter Powell thing . . . and I've always wanted to do the *Test*. It was nice to give the badge you get to me mum."

For a lot of these new teen tarts the game is enthusiastically copying out all the antics of previous generations because it was what they dreamed of at the time. Like playing the Birmingham Odeon for Duran Dream: it's an inexorable process. It's inevitable.

I get John on my own on a back row in the stalls and!!!! ask him if the group, officially a year old on July 16th, anticipated the recent shifts away from rock, grey independence, submission, austerity towards pop, disco, colour, lights, action.

"We must have done, but not consciously. We were just never really into that grey, small-time independent thing. Our heart was in the

Rifles.

(Weller) ''It's a piss-take on class . . . it's an imaginary setting and that, the two classes clash, like the trendy sort of revolutionary saying in the pub, come on sup up and collect your fags because there's a row going on down the street, and it's like the revolution will always start after I've finished my pint. That's how a lot of people feel. That's how I feel. It's always round the corner. It's a lazy attitude but in another sense it's a realistic attitude . . . there's all this going on in the world and that, nuclear threat and that, internal fights with my missus and that, but as long as I've got enough for a pint I can tolerate that. I don't think there's too many people who feel differently to that.''

Does thinking about the wider issues scare you?

''Sometimes, but I also think what the fuck can I do about it. The sheer fact I put protest on to plastic isn't going to change anything. I could put protest on to plastic and send it off to all the leaders in the world, but they're not going to hear it and even if they did they wouldn't do anything about it. They'd take no notice. So all you can really do is operate within your own limits, for your own people.''

Leading to what?

''A bit of solidarity I suppose.''

A direction?

''I don't know about any direction. That can sound pompous, saying I lead the way, as the generation's spokesman. I never try and tell anyone how to do anything. There are feelings behind my songs obviously, but I wouldn't say any of them are blatantly opinionated. But you have to be careful in my position not to take it too far. I don't think many of us have ever got much chance of breaking out from being owned. There's not much you can do about it, unless

early '70s. Quality, big studios, sophisticated production, all of this has become important and that's great. For us the whole thing is a total concept, it's not just making crappily produced singles ... the image, the recording, the presentation, the clothes, the whole lot is very important. Some bands just want to be single groups or album groups or live groups – we want to be everything."

It's easy to talk about it, and easy to imitate it – this grand dream of quality. It's harder to achieve, or enhance. But there's been no failures, no black spots, to suggest to Duran Ownway that their definition of show business, their entertainment aesthetic, is in any way flawed. There has been nothing to tell them that their judgement is distorted, their music and presentation obvious or lightweight. Just a rash of reviews from *clever* rock writers whose value is rapidly diminishing – Duran Precious are heroes of the movement away from reading the self-important words to looking at the pictures.

As far as Duran Jelly are concerned, and it's not far, pieces in the rock papers can be packed with sharp cynicism: as long as they're accompanied by clear photographs, preferably in colour, then that's their equivalent of a good review. Photographs can turn people on, words just get in the way. Words are an ordeal, photographs possibly a temptation.

"We can't stand negative journalism."

Have they ever received what they think is constructive criticism?

"Not in the press. I mean at first we get this image in the press of being created by EMI to battle Spandau ... they'd picked out the five prettiest polaroids sent into their office."

I thought this was true!

"Shit no. But there are too many people who do think this. You didn't really think that did you?"

No, I was fiddling about. Would have been lovely, though.

"You little liar! We have to prove something on that score because there are those who still say that we were to Spandau what The Clash were to the Pistols. We hate that ... then again The Clash are still around."

———————————————

AFTER I'VE been talking to John for a few minutes the rest of the group gather around: they can't bear to be apart, or can't stand the thought of not featuring in the interview. Five smooth faces, five lush hairdos, ten lively eyes ... the Duran Hearts laugh and play, the Duran Pussycats jest and pester. They've never had it so good. They confidently think their audience has never had it so good. . . .

So how frivolous is all this?

"It's all of our lives, it's all we've ever wanted to do. We enjoy what we're doing obviously and it's all that we've got. So it can't be frivolous. It's very important to us. Obviously there are frivolous things, we can be frivolous. Like putting Dairy Box on our contract rider, and prawns."

Three Duran Lads totter off to see how the riot's doing: two stay put, putting it all out of mind. It's all a lot of play, though. Is Duran Love a lucky escape? The three strays return to tackle this problem.

"I feel incredibly lucky that I've got this job to do," Simon says.

Andy gets touchy. **"If people think we're lucky, we're not really, because we're doing a job in a sense that we have to work."**

Simon continues: **"I feel incredibly lucky ... thankful ... I dunno, that I'm doing this and not putting dustbins on dustcarts."**

Do Duran Diane place much emphasis on clothes?

"This is another thing. . . ." Nick the pussycat snarls. Slightly. **"What I've got on now is what I wear when I wake up in the morning. I don't think anyone in the band overly dresses. We're all very much ourselves."**

You're taken to be clothes-pop.

"I don't mind people thinking we dress up. You can't object to people putting labels on you because they're going to whatever."

Has being associated with cults with names helped Duran Right-time-right-place?

"To a certain extent, especially in the early days. We were surprised to be tagged new romantic or futurist because we're not like that at all . . . it's pop, and more Blondie than Led Zeppelin. . . . Give us that hour on stage; we can convince people that we don't need to be labelled to help us. I think honesty wins through in the end. I think honest is something we'll always be."

How can people appreciate this "honesty" – how does it manifest itself?

"People think we can't be honest because we've had success so quickly . . . how can we have integrity if we're so successful? I think that is just sour grapes. Perhaps we were lucky that we came along when all the record companies were looking to jump on the futurist bandwagon and we'd been put in that niche, so from that respect the look helped us. But the honesty is there, and it manifests itself as people going home after they have seen us having really enjoyed it, or listening to our records and loving them."

"That's all people ask of a group, to get enjoyment out of it. And we believe that the product is really good. On this tour the audience has been incredibly young, they're all really enjoying themselves, and as long as we can play to people enjoying themselves and if we're enjoying ourselves, I don't see any harm in what we do. Because it is honest. You'll see later."

HOURS LATER Duran Din dish out what is paid for. Despite the day's troubles the Odeon is almost full: hundreds of Duran-kids kept off the street. Modern Duran are an '80s Osmond family: wholesome and kind of holy, but it really depends on how you define "honest". Hard working? Duran Damp are not timid or lazy.

If you've never heard Magazine, Simple Minds, Japan . . . then Duran Fun Fun must be mighty and magnificent; Duran Flash In The Pan as a first love must be brilliant. I'm twice as old as most of the audience, months away from the pension, very possibly the wrong sex, and too familiar with the grand Magazine things . . . I even know about the very beginnings of Roxy Music.

It is simple to criticise the Duran energetic attraction, to moan about the implications and complications of Dilute To Taste, but no words can cripple its force, its promise, its prettiness. Only The Time of The Revolution can halt Duran's darned drive. Duran Efficacious are a symbol of the futility of attempting to control or organise the Pop Mass. It seeps everywhere. It saturates reason.

The teen stars of today are smart: they've a lot to go on. Duran Fluke are classic effective innocents. They succeed where their elders and betters Simple Minds fail; they're pretty and they're not yet confused; they've reduced it all to entertainment instead of deciding or pretending that there are more "important" things. They may celebrate superficiality; they may be the kind of encouragement they think *their* pop can be. It's all so easy for them. How can anyone tell them it's not? They won't shorten anyone's life. In the face of darkness they glow and grin with a happiness lighting up the lives of the little girls. As the fighting gets closer their resolve to escape gets firmer.

"I want to thank you all for turning up," singer Simon says from the stage after a few songs. "We know it must have been difficult for you."

The crowd crushed up to the front having one of the first times of their lives scream as if for murder. Here we go. . . .

"I want you to remember what's happening out there has nothing to do with what's happening in here."

He could as easily have said, let them eat smoked salmon.

you are talking about revolution. All you can do is remind people of what goes on . . . and just not accept any of it. . . ."

The writer puts his tape recorder away. The musician eases himself out of his chair. The photographer gets his equipment ready. The musician shakes his head as he recalls bits of the interview. "Fifteen-minute sets," he marvels. "If I had to pay £8 for a fifteen-minute set I'd trip out. The economics of it – I would feel so guilty. Even if I did a 45-minute show so packed with emotion and intensity and everything it needed to have, it still wouldn't seem right. People have to work hard to get their little money. The best experience I've had as an audience member is when I've seen a musician get excited and inspired and go over time. Forget about time . . . forget about time and then you can think HEY! and an hour and a half has gone by and it seemed just like ten minutes. That's the stuff!"

The photographer scans the room looking for likely places that the musician can pose. The musician stands looking a little lost near a window. The writer tells him that 45 minutes of his music seems to go on for two hours.

'Well, have a nice rest!''

The musician and the writer laugh, loudly. They'll never see each other again.

What happens if you're just a flavour of the year and you lose your people?

"I don't think you have to lose them at all. You can do what Sinatra did. I think you can do what Bowie did. I think if you're good enough, if you show that you're willing to make more effort than anyone else around. I'm not going to stand still. It's always useful, and in a way comforting, to look at what has

PHIL COLLINS
December 18, 1982
"Anyone would think
I had made
some extraordinary
suggestion."

THE SOFT and bitter Phil Collins has a punishing hangover.

He was up until six in the morning drinking and watching exclusive videos, celebrating with friends his successful solo performances at London's Hammersmith Odeon.

Ten hours later, a dark anxious afternoon, he's blending rough and smooth into the warm roomy furniture of his extremely comfortable hideaway house – a Sony Trinitron in the lounge, and one in the kitchen, perhaps just because Cleese acts for Sony.

Collins is edgy and over-cautious. At first every question I ask – favourite soap, preferred skin – provokes a response centring on the fantastic aspect of Genesis' secret trendiness.

There is, he needlessly gloats – though I suppose some people are impressed – a surprising number of unexpected musicians who have approached him, made sure no one was looking, then confessed to being a fan. People like Topper Headon, The Dead Kennedys. . . .

There is, he says, a powerful club of what he calls closet Genesis fans.

Not even the fast realities of world-wide success and a beautiful house in Guildford can stop the hard hurt of his group Genesis being considered by many as the crushing bores of our time. Perhaps Collins would rather be super-trendy than hopelessly popular; somewhere stirs faint understanding that pop is a matter of factless unpredictability.

The dull daft hysterical ravings of critics and writers as they crudely distinguish between "brave new things" and "cowardly old things" reaches even the still, safe place where Collins reclines.

Soon, it's not as though I begin to believe in him, just that I feel strangely sad for him. Is he on the edge of being found out? Quite rich, nearly lost, wanting to laugh with him not at him, half heartedly expecting considerable generosity.

I lean forward in my chair; he's laid back. It would suit him to be sucking on an antique pipe with a shining golden labrador curled up at his feet, as sleepy and dutiful as his fans. There would need to be a coal fire about to burn out.

"FROM JOHN Martyn to Frieda . . . Via Mike Oldfield, via Robert Plant, with Eno and Gary Brooker thrown in . . . if I was to talk about all the LPs I've played on, producing John Martyn and Frieda . . . well, it isn't that far apart. . . ."

JUST WHO the hell do you think you are?
"Well . . . I've had this running battle in *Melody Maker* **with the letters. . . . It's actually come as quite a shock to learn just how many people don't like me.**

"We did this gig in Philadelphia with Elvis Costello, Flock Of Seagulls and Blondie; it was a carefully planned bill, everybody wanted to play with each other. But in the press it was just Elvis having a complete breakdown of taste by wanting to support Genesis. It wasn't even support; it was just a bill and we happened to be last.

"And then there was this letter in *Melody Maker* **saying how great Elvis's music was, and this reply by Adam Sweeting was something about how more people should think that way and then Elvis wouldn't have to debase himself by playing with Genesis.**

"This came in the same week as Julie Burchill calling me the ugliest man since George Orwell, which I took notice of. It all came in this week when I thought, fuck, is this abuse for no reason? It was all totally out of order, I thought.

"And then Gabriel gave an interview to Richard Cook, and Cook said it was a magnificent gesture for Genesis to play Milton Keynes, but he was sure that we looked at our wallets first. Which I thought was a really stupid thing to say. We did it so the fucking bands could be paid.

"Anyway, I wrote this letter to *Melody Maker* **saying: Please, I know Elvis, I know his drummer, we had a great time after the**

happened in the past. There is always an initial boom, an explosion, and then it's just a matter of whether they bottle out. . . . You know, between me and you, Marco and I haven't even scraped the top of the barrel yet. There is a lot more going on inside us that hasn't come through yet and will not come through for a while. People don't use the term Ant–Marco. I hope that in ten years' time they'll be using it in the same way they use Lennon–McCartney. They don't at the moment and it can be very disheartening. Y'know, I have turned down film offers that most people would have given their left legs to do because there is a standard that I want to maintain. I want to do a film, but I'll do a film remembering those people I admire – De Niro, Brando. . . ."

What scares you about what you are now?

"I don't think there's anything particularly scary. It's just that when you're at the top there's not many ways that you can go. You will either stay there or you will go down. And I don't want to end up like Mohammed Ali, y'know, that's scary. You can see someone disappear. I don't want to be somebody who cuts his mind off from the fact that there's always that pitfall and there's always a very easy way down every time."

Are you scared of losing your looks?

"I think you're scared of actually wrecking your body. I get scared of the fact that over the course of touring America, Japan, Australia, Europe, you can actually feel inside that you're five years older. You know that your skin is as white as a sheet. You know that you have really punished your body, abused it. I take as much pride in my body as I have to, to get up in front of people and perform. It's a case of stamina; it's a case of keeping on your

gig, no one felt it was debasing – so fuck off! Get off our backs! Right? For Christ's sake.

"The next week there was a flock of letters saying how dare Phil Collins, the egotistical megastar. . . . It was very anti and I was amazed that there was that much venom from people. And I read that letter about me being an egotistical megastar while I was on a tube . . . nine o'clock in the morning, on the tube, not being driven about in a chauffeured Rolls Royce. . . ."

I'm surprised you pay much attention to the careless drifts of today's pop writers, let alone know the names of even the minor ones.

"Well, I do. Someone said, does criticism bother you? Well, of course, everyone likes to be loved. You wouldn't like it if you went out of the door and I said to my lady what a wanker . . . you wouldn't like that, would you? So for something to be printed, and for it to be a stupid misrepresentation, is very frustrating and upsetting.

"I mean, Julie Burchill, I don't know why she wrote that, it was an extraordinary thing to write . . . and knowing where I come from, knowing where my heart is, to have Cook saying they must have checked their wallets first. . . ."

The Burchill comment I can sympathise with if you'll pardon the expression . . . the thing that Phil Collins becomes, or anyone in your position becomes, is a symbol of banal security. I don't want to be too straightforward about this, but he is no longer a human being, he is a target, a representation of something somebody might not believe in. . . .

"Sure . . . but doesn't . . . well, in this case she obviously doesn't believe I'm going to read it. . . ."

Exactly – you're a target, you're not real. . . .

"Right . . . but when you read something that hundreds of thousands of people are going to read – and now the boring single from the ugliest man since George Orwell – you just think . . . why?"

You're not "allowed" to feel that way.

"Well, it's extraordinary . . . and of course

I read the fucking papers.

"I rang up Richard Cook after this thing with Peter Gabriel and I asked to speak to him and he wasn't there and I spoke to Danny Baker and he said, what? Phil Collins the drummer, on the phone now? And I said, yes, can I speak to the editor, and Baker was shocked that I'd rung. Anyway, I spoke to Phil McNeill, is it? And he was going, well, this is all very unlikely, and I said well, if you think this is unlikely, I'll ring up every time I get pissed off. . . ."

Do people forget that you're real, a soft fleshy human being with ups and downs and ins and outs, not a hardboard target?

"Possibly . . . but what really annoys me is that people assume that I'm something I'm not. I'm not what people think. Definitely not."

But it's one of your functions to let other people take it out on you.

"Yeah . . . huh . . . but I'm not that unfeeling. People who know me know that."

Maybe reducing everything to mean-spirited gossip puts people like you in your place. Or again maybe the trivial, thoughtless attacks get in the way of the serious criticisms and considerations of what it is you do. . . . I would want my displeasure with your operation to be taken as something a little more serious than just another undramatic spiteful jibe, for it to be clear that I'm more concerned with the neutrality of what you do rather than your baldness.

"Sure . . . I said to Virgin that I wasn't over-keen on opening myself up to someone who appeared to be overfriendly, but who then butchered me afterwards. . . ."

One of the silly sly tricks of the profession, I'm afraid.

"It's happened lots of times . . . I said what I would like to do was find someone who wasn't particularly a fan and to actually. . . . I wanted to give it one more chance otherwise I wouldn't bother doing these sorts of things anymore. What's the point?"

– –

"I THINK my music is different from a lot of people's music, purely because I'm taking black and white and making it something different . . . maybe I'm kidding myself . . . I don't think I am. Hopefully it's something that's worthwhile. I believe that it is."

When you use a word like "worthwhile", what do you mean? It's one of those words that in a rock context or conversation has no meaning whatsoever, it's just a dribble. It's a nothing work, like "commitment" or "honesty" or "original".

"Well . . . of some use to somebody is what I mean. . . ."

So you do want to be of some use to people?

"Well . . . I've never really thought that I wasn't, I suppose. The couple, for instance, who are sitting in the audience. When I'm singing "If Leaving Me Is Easy", it's a curious thing, but I know the guy has got his arm around her and he's almost saying to her let's not have this happen to us . . . it's a corny thing, and again I wonder, should I be embarrassed by it?

"It's not a public service I'm doing, but presumably you can be of use to people . . . but 'worthwhile' was just a word I slipped in because it's a word that I usually use and, yes, you're right it's just one of those words."

"MY AUDIENCE last night was made up of, like, 18-year-olds in Motorhead T-shirts and 35-year-old couples . . . so, I mean, I've no idea of the type of audience I appeal to . . . really . . . I don't even really think about it . . . one writes one's music for oneself . . . it's a natural thing, it's there. But that sounds a very negative thing, that's not what I mean. . . .

"There's two sides to it – well, there's more than two sides to it: there's the Genesis side, which I'm not really interested in talking about because I feel it's just . . . something we do for pleasure . . . Oh . . . I'm not making sense. To be honest, I don't think too much about what people are listening to my music for."

Do you do it, this, whatever it may end up to be, for it's own sake?

"Yeah . . . I suppose so . . . I don't know anything else. I play music for its own sake, that's why I don't strive to get away from it . . . I don't ever try to get away from it. If I'm not doing something by myself or with the band, then I'm invariably doing something with somebody else. . . .

"So it's not like music is what I do when I have to do it; it's what I do all the time. So when somebody says to me what do I do apart from play an instrument? Or, what do I do apart from music? I don't do anything. Which can be described as boring, but at the same time . . . inside that there's a lot of different things that I find don't make it boring. . . ."

If what you do apart from music is very little then what kind of experience, attitude, perspective, thought enters into the music to give it any unusual appeal or interesting energy?

"Well . . . I wish I'd been more together for this . . . I dunno . . . I don't know what I think, this is awkward. . . .

"My music is written as a result of the things that have happened to me. There's two ways of looking at music; well, there's a lot of ways, but lyrically, for instance, there's the music that takes you away from what's going on . . . and with the band I think we have got ourselves a tag of being a band that takes you away from what's going on.

"So The Clash remind you of what's going on . . . and with us it's good old entertainment. You come to see us to forget what's going on; it's an escape. . . ."

Those two sides, legends in their way, for me Genesis do neither – they don't take you away in the way that ruptures reality or enriches experience, and they don't point their fingers . . . it just hovers.

"What we're doing is just for us . . . We write our music not to help anyone, not to encourage anybody to do anything, we just get together and we write music. We do it for us, so I don't feel any responsibility to help

toes all the time. When I stop wanting to get out of bed, I'll let you know."

Is success important for Peter Gabriel?

"Oh, I think . . . erm, yes. But it's changed shape. When I started off with Genesis, and this seems to be so for a lot of musicians, success had more to do with it than anything else. There was a lot of ego tied up in it. I wanted to sort of scream at the world and yeah, there was definitely a lot of ego momentum there. When I left Genesis I think the whole slant of it changed quite a lot and now I have different criteria."

Gabriel mentions screaming at the world. Although he seems to me not so much to do that as indignantly berate it and prance through its horror with mild outrage; using the word "scream" suggests that Gabriel feels a very deep need for expression.

"I felt I could repress the middle class English person with soul music . . . I wanted to sit at the piano for hours and hours and scream or whatever it was. Just release emotions. This was one of the main attractions of rock music for me; perhaps another just being the raw excitement of it."

Would you consider yourself to be more sensitive than most?

"Erm" There is an incredibly long pause. "Initially I was going to say yes. But over the years I've thought more and more that beneath the façade, people are very much the same. We're all frightened of certain things. There is no real us and them. When people strip themselves psychologically you see the same basic lumps of humanity."

He stops himself. He looks puzzled. "That's not very well expressed. Everyone has their problems, their fuck-ups . . . some people can see them better

kids get out of their situation or whatever. People happen to like our music, and that's a happy coincidence . . . it means . . . that people enjoy us!"

Why?

"Well, you should have a dozen fans in here and ask them, I suppose."

Don't Genesis just add to the dead weight of it all, and contribute mightily to that deadening - taking music and its implications for granted?

"Well . . . mm . . . the thing's . . . I dunno . . . There are certain elements of Genesis that I don't like. There's bits that each of us don't like. There's one thing I would like to stress and that's. . . .

"Well, there's 75 per cent of me that believes passionately in what Genesis do, and I care totally about what I do personally. I just sit down and analyse it too much. It's too much of a natural thing for me to go in and write with these guys . . . ugh. . . ."

So what don't you like about Genesis?

"Well . . . the sort of . . . grandiose stuff . . . A lot of Genesis fans like that area of our music. . . . Really it's just entertainment, that old word, I don't see why everything has to be used to move forward. . . . I mean, I am getting better at what I do, so I'm moving forward in my eyes . . . maybe I'm not capable of doing much else . . . it's quite possible I'm not. I obviously don't think about it."

— —

"IT'S LIKE at some of the big gigs you can feel that you're insignificant. . . .

"I went to see Bad Company in Dallas and I was surprised how many people were throwing up. There were 15,000 people: 5,000 of them were throwing up; 5,000 of them were there to score dope, and the other 5,000 were there for the music. That was a rock show as such. We attract people who like the band a lot, so they come and listen to the music. . . ."

— —

"WE USED to be a band to take notes to, and a lot of people still think of it as being like

that. . . . We used to hate playing universities because you felt like you were being marked for each song, eight out of ten for this, nine out of ten for that. There are many people who eventually get to see the band who come away saying it's a lot less pompous than they thought. I do feel with the Genesis fans that there's something of a reverence. . . ."

Do you find that reverence disappointing?

"In some respects it's great that it is here and there, but at the same time it gets depressing when you think well, are they really listening?

"There's a certain type of fan, in the old days it used to be the trench coat and the fishing hat with the albums under their arms . . . but they're the guys, even though they're caricatures of themselves, that did help us carry on doing what we wanted to do. So we feel very grateful to our fans. Let's face it, if the band doesn't sell records, if no one comes to see the band, then you can't carry on. They helped us carry on, so we do the best we can for us and for them as well, I suppose . . . but . . . erm . . . sometimes it gets annoying. . . ."

— —

WHAT IS the value of entertainment?

"Well, I don't know. What I find curious. . . . For instance, on my records I have pictures of my kids, and that to some people is very soppy; it's embarrassingly trite. But I don't see why one has to be embarrassed by that sort of thing. I'm not, and it's, like, not . . . it's not a hip thing to do I suppose. . . ."

Would it be more embarrassing to you if you felt your music could be explained away as extraordinarily non-extreme – the embarrassment comes in that your music is trite and cosy.

"I suppose some of my music is cosy."

And that doesn't embarrass you?

"No . . . I'm not embarrassed . . . A song like 'Why Can't It Wait Until Tomorrow' is a pretty cosy song, but it's got a nice feeling to it, and I get the required reaction from people. So somewhere along the line I'm hitting a nerve. Obviously there are some people around not moved by that, yourself being one of them. But . . . I don't consider it safe . . . not myself. I'm just trying to do the best I can."

So in the context you're in, you take risks?

"I don't think about it in terms of taking risks. To be honest, something like 'In The Air' – it's as simple as hitting a chord and thinking, well, what sounds good coming after that? That'll sound nice coming next. . . . So, it's just interesting for me to do it. I don't think of it as being . . . I don't take gambles or anything. I just follow my nose a bit."

Don't you feel because there's so much competent, adequate music about – I'm using those words as prime insults – that it's important for you as a skilled musician with interesting contacts and a massive audience to possess a greater urgency in what you do?

"Well, I'm not complacent about what I do at all. . . . I mean, I live and breathe the thing, I do love what I do. . . .

"I'm aware that by inviting a writer like yourself into my home I'm laying myself open to you going out and looking at my Mercedes, looking at the decoration of the house, and seeing it all as being a kind of, I'm all right Jack, and saying that the complacency which might appear in the house is reflected in my music.

"Look! I've never done anything else except be a kid actor for a while, y'know? *I'm a very simple kind of person*. . . . I've got a son and a daughter, and my son hasn't got a father any more, 'cos I'm not his dad any more and therefore I get very upset, and I'm a romantic person, and I am a sentimentalist in a way, so therefore I like to give a little bit and reflect that in my music there is something that is . . . that is *me*. . . .

"And so my albums come out in that shape and *it might seem cosy, it might seem trite, but that's me*, and if people don't like it, they don't have to listen to it. I make records for me primarily, y'know? And after 12 years of being with the band – and it seems like a

sentence, but it isn't, y'know – I've got a few things together. . . . This house wasn't expensive when I bought it, and it's only my girlfriend who's got it to look like a house, because she's a lady y'know, and she makes it a house. But it's not like . . . *the complacency that appears in this house is not in my music."*

– –

HOW SERIOUSLY do you take yourself?

"I think I take myself very seriously. I'm cynical, but maybe that's good. . . . I'm not as good one-to-one as I am in front of 20,000 people – there's a certain kind of, y'know, if you put on a funny hat and coat, then the person will become different. . . . And I like to go through that; it's why I wear braces on stage. It's, like, it makes me feel I'm a bit. . . .

"Well, they do say comedians are the most miserable people in the world. . . . I'm not sure if I take myself seriously or not. . . . I should know."

Do you take yourself seriously in as much as you take seriously the public image?

"Oh no. In reply to that, I don't take myself seriously at all."

What do you care about?

. . . I'm still saving up for a rainy day.

"That doesn't quite answer your question . . . I'm convinced that what's happened to me won't last . . . so there's no way I'm going to sit back and relax. Maybe I should enjoy life more . . . I don't buy much. Most of the things you see here I've had for years.

"I took very seriously my marriage breaking up; I took very seriously what was happening then . . . I used to go upstairs and cry my eyes out over my son, because I was thinking that he would no longer have a father and *everyone wants to love their dad*. It's the normal way of growing up, you have a mum and you have a dad . . . and suddenly I was thinking: Christ, this is my heir and he ain't going to have me. Like I take that seriously . . . *life just goes on."*

You're not a great theorist.

"I'm a man of principles, I think . . . I'm not

than others . . . I'm not very happy with my string of thought."

What are your fans wanting from Marillion? From this rock??

"To quote the last lines from 'Fugazi' itself . . . 'Where are the prophets, where are the visionaries, where are the poets, to breach the dull and sentimental mercenary?' People need the visionaries. . . ."

Who do you consider to be visionaries?

"Joni is. Jim Kerr is. Bono is. Kate Bush could be. Annie Lennox definitely is. These people are giving us depth, something important. . . . I mean, you look at the history of the musician, and the lyricist. I mean, they came from when people couldn't read, when the only way to send history through generations was through song and words . . . the only way to encapsulate wedding, death, battle was through song. . . ."

So you see Marillion as a sort of folk music?

"Yeah, that's probably a very very valid statement. Folk music. I'll go for that."

Is The Big Fish a manifestation of your personal refusal to live out a routine existence?

"Yeah . . . aah . . . at least at the moment I have the ability to shout . . . or to whisper. . . . To be in a situation where I couldn't even whisper, it wouldn't be so much boring as totally frustrating."

You like people to know that you're about?

"Oh, I'm about all right. And that's your problem."

Very clever.

So what are you saying – give up, or don't get so worked up about rock and roll?

"Neither really. Whatever it is you do, if you want to keep one step ahead of the pack or whatever, you keep moving.

a very cosmic person. *I'm not a great thinker or intellectual* . . . I'm a believer that if you treat someone with a bit of respect, then they will give you respect back . . . I'm constantly amazed that people kick me in the teeth 'cos I don't think I deserve it. *I believe in fair play."*

You're a very decent man.

"I'm a boringly normal guy . . . I don't listen to records much. I've just got a music centre, not an expensive system, and it took me ages to get round to buying a fan heater. . . .

"I like to go down to the pub for a couple of pints of Guinness with my mates, who are mostly older than me . . . and I like the fact that I can get on with guys down the pub who are 65 and not talk about music. . . . It's a great leveller my pub actually; I'm going to buy a pub for the landlord, 'cos he's such a great bloke. It's like a living room . . . you go in there and you talk to people at face value and you either get on with them or you don't. And if ever someone comes in and says, oh, Phil can you sign this! I clam up . . . it embarrasses me. . . ."

Pushing further out that idea of you as unashamed entertainer, can we begin to explore the possibilities of a new kind of middle of the road that you represent?

"Well . . . should I be embarrassed that couples come to my gigs? That this guy has his arm around his girlfriend . . . I don't think I should be. . . . But what I do has a harder edge than Barry Manilow. . . ."

How does this harder edge manifest itself?

"The harder edge is in the music."

A quality or complexity?

"Well, there is a depth to the thing . . . I've written some nice love songs though, ballads – the word ballad again conjures up Barry Manilow or Jack Jones."

What would be embarrassing to you about being compared to Jack Jones?

"Well, there's the schmaltz side of it which I cringe at . . . which is why I like Steve Martin, the way he deals with that. I mean, I've never seen the Barry Manilow show, but my rigger's just come off a tour with him, and he said you don't have to like it, but it is a very professional thing . . . it does what it's supposed to. . . .

"I call that middle of the road, but then middle of the road has got a bad image like entertainment. Middle of the road. Well, *my music is not extreme. . . ."*

In the days of A Certain Ratio, Southern Death Cult and the Banshees, then you are decidedly middle of the road.

"Mmmm . . . but that's also because people assume that if you're 31 and play in a group like Genesis then that's what you are. . . . that's what you become. I think that's very unfair. I don't think that 31 is old.

"I've got my slippers on – right? – but . . . I mean, shit, I started off doing coke. *I go out and do things other people of 20 do* . . . it's not as if I'm suddenly a different person. . . ."

You don't seem to have much of a rigour, a disgust about mediocrity.

"I hate mediocrity as much as anyone else."

Take away the safety barriers and perhaps you are mediocre.

"Well, sure . . . but if you talk to musicians I'll think you'll find 99 per cent of them say that we've done . . . something. Mediocrity and sitting on the fence is something I have a great aversion to.

"But I've got no real reason to spite Barry Manilow. I don't listen to his records. I would probably feel pretty spiteful if somebody locked me in a room and made me listen to all his albums, then I'd probably think, bastard, what's he doing this for? There's enough room for everything. *Everything serves its purpose."*

– –

DO YOU CRY EASILY?

"Yes. Oh yes. . . . That's an interesting remark. . . . It's curious, part of human nature, that if somebody is depressed they do not put on a happy record, they put on an even more miserable record to make them even more depressed. . . .

"And although I went through a lot of pain – I don't mean Lennon pain, but I did go through an awful lot of bad times when my marriage broke up . . . 'cos I went to school with my wife, and I went out with her on and off since I was 13 . . . and every man wants an heir and I had a fantastic son, and I have a daughter as well, and I couldn't believe it . . . I spent hours and hours on the phone when she left here. . . .

"Oh, I cry at the end of *Romeo and Juliet*. It is easy for me to do that. I don't know why, 'cos it's not as though I had an unhappy childhood or anything like that. I am a romantic person, which is why a lot of my songs are cosy, as you say. . . ."

From a man who cries so much can we expect anything more?

"Aah . . . I don't know about that, it just happens that crying is something I'm very capable of doing."

————————————————

"I AM constantly reminded by things . . . what a lucky boy I am to be in this position."

————————————————

WHAT NOW would be the adventure?

"Well . . . I mean, my, it sounds funny to think of adventure and then bring it down to *the morose level of records* . . . I would dearly love my next record to be radically different, but then you would probably not agree that it was radical . . . A lot of people have asked me to produce them. . . . The Nolans, Manhattan Transfer, Air Supply . . . loads of them. . . ."

You are seen as the new expert at MOR production, turning shit into chocolate.

"Oh, I hope that's not why they're asking me. But maybe you're right. It would be interesting for me, a further development in my capabilities as a record producer . . . to go into the studio with someone like The Nolans, or whoever, and try and make something *worthwhile . . . oh, there's that word again. . . .*

"God! I don't think I'm middle of the road. I mean, I've got a normal shirt on, a normal pair of trousers, maybe it's just that I'm so

normal. Maybe I am middle of the road . . . oh, but I don't think I'm that middle of the road."

Maybe not.

"Maybe not. . . ."

Do you think you're funny?

"I like Hancock, Steve Martin, Cleese . . . humour as opposed to jokes. I've introduced comedy into my show. If Steve Martin ever pops over here, I'll have to re-think what I do. . . .

"Erm, yes, I think I'm funny. But if I was reading that in print, Phil Collins thinks he's funny, that would embarrass me . . . because there's plenty of people *who don't think I'm funny at all*. It's something I enjoy, that side of the set every night."

I would say, Phil, that you're funny in a middle of the road sort of way.

"Thanks. . . ."

————————————————

PHIL COLLINS has been asked to produce Victoria Wood's LP. Amongst the many photographs of entertainers decorating the walls of his house there are signed photographs of Norman Collier and Steve Martin. As I say goodbye to Phil Collins I keep a straight face and refrain from crying by imagining Bernard Manning producing his next LP.

Never settle. There's a temptation to settle. Ignore it. People will always say to you, 'What are you still working for?' "

Exactly!

"Well, fuck you. Let me just do what I want to do. Don't tell me where to stop. I'll know when I feel like it."

Does it really irritate you when people ask you why are you still hanging about?

"Well, not as much as if they say why did you do it in the first place. There's no real difference in the way I feel between then and now. It's a load of old bollocks to accuse me of being complacent. Because I'm still in there. I may not be in there as much as I was when I was 21, but I'm there. See, people imagine and fantasise that you've got all this money and birds and swimming pools – and they imagine that once you've got all that you should stop. It doesn't work out like that."

Just who the hell do you think you are, Mr Fry?

"I'm somebody who gets more death threats than love letters. . . . I go to the local burger shop and the girl in there gives me a free hamburger. She just says 'oh, we want you to have it.' And that touches me. That may sound foolish. . . . In fact, it was in a sandwich shop where I'd done a fair amount of shoplifting in my poverty-stricken periods. People want to give you things, and they want to cuddle you . . . and they want to take your arm off. They either want to plant a kiss on your cheek, or a fist."

Is it just part of all the oddness?

"Yeah, I sometimes do think it's very odd. I've always felt things are odd. I've always felt quite conspicuous. I've always felt at odds with this odd world. It's odd that my hair, lips and skin should excite. It's odd that four undernourished dudes can

JIM KERR
October 3, 1981
Growing pains and
the heart's desire.

HERE WE GO AGAIN. . . .

Daylight. What day is it? Should I get up? Is there anything to do? What am I going to do? Where am I today? Liverpool. . . .

It was the Royal Court last night. Not much of a response, why bother with an encore? Why does everyone look so bored until it looks like we're not coming back on to the stage? What's it like outside? Do I need to shave? Rotten colour scheme in this room . . . boring hotel. Maybe I should go back to sleep. Fine dreams. A day off today. Some photos to do. Still, the first week of something that's going on for three months. I can't even think what's happening tomorrow.

What is?

What town?

Have I got any clean clothes left?

It's not that late really. . . . Really, all this is getting more and more like a respectable job, the petty worries and all that. All the things I wanted to get rid of . . . I can't face going out and playing much more, especially in this country. It's getting so oppressive and divisive. I hate . . . I dunno . . . I just feel there's some kind of betrayal.

This whole procedure, roadies, trucks, big halls, hotels, buses, I can't go through with it much more. But then it's so hard to find the alternative. Yeah, I mean what is the alternative?

This whole tour date planning for months ahead, it's like Dr Feelgood or the fucking Rush. So then why do I do it? We just use the channels that are already provided yet try and do something new and more emotional. . . .

I dunno. It's like those two passions, there's that spirit we get playing that we just don't get recording. Last year was so terrible we just didn't want to play Britain again. Yeah . . . I think if I was going for the big alternative I wouldn't sign to a record company, I'd get

sponsored by a magazine or a vodka company. I think some sort of radical change is needed. I suppose we're not doing much about that side of it, but who is. . . .

I never honestly thought we'd end up this far in, so tangled up. You're in Glasgow and you hear the first two Roxy LPs and then you hear "Real Life" and you think, Fuck working. You see a couple of great films, read those kind of books, and more and more you get the feeling that you just have to do it for yourself, find out for yourself, and in a way you're play acting. But you get the chance and you go for it.

Early on you think, what the fuck ever gave me the backbone, the absolute cheek, to think that I could ever do anything? That horror I have . . . I dunno . . . I do think that people are getting more anxious these days to be adult earlier . . . that word youth is dodgy, this supposed voice of youth that sounded out for two decades . . . what has the voice of youth got to say for itself? What has the point of that voice been? Where is the value in what I'm involved in? . . . Has it been one word, a sentence, an act of violence? What is supposed to be going on? What are we reaching for?

▬▬▬▬▬▬▬▬▬▬▬▬▬▬▬▬

MAYBE IT'S just one moment that can carry you through, that you hold within yourself for the rest of your life. Maybe pop music is like a drug, maybe it does you bad. Drug . . . that's a complimentary word for it. It's more a tranquilliser for a lot of people, an anaesthetic. I don't know. . . . Too many words, too much analysis . . . that's why I loved what

count for something in a glamorous way. At the same time it's just false modesty to just say, oh, gee, thanks. You can't excite people for an hour and a half in a show and then just shrug it off. You can't just innocently ask, oh why are people mobbing the coach? Why do they stand for hours in the rain waiting for a signature? Why are they very affectionate or very aggressive? I can see why people show us respect or disrespect; I can see why people want to stitch us up in the music papers; and I can see why our records climb the charts in the USA . . . but it doesn't make it any less odd. It doesn't make it comprehensible. I'm glad things are still odd."

What do the teenies see in you?

"A shoulder to cry on . . . a father figure . . . ha! . . . first sex . . . um . . . a hero . . . I don't know, all of those things mixed up I should think."

Is that odd for you?

"As I live and breathe it is, yeah . . . But. . . ."

But?

"Just but. . . ."

Ash: "Bauhaus won't last forever . . . it might not exist next week. It might exist for another five years. You can't say. But we're not totally obsessed with it anyway. Individually we have other interests. But we seem to be climbing the ladder slowly, so we continue. . . ."

Perhaps Bauhaus are healthy. Maybe they have no wish to move the question of "creativity" out of the shadows; they genuinely don't want to make heavy weather out of something that should be left to find its own rhythm. Perhaps they are healing people. I wouldn't like to say. I am only the day's labourer. As such you keep your mouth shut. And quickly forget a group lost among many: all committed and idealistic and small . . . Ash: "You know what? It all boils

Morley wrote about Peter Hammill. As fashionable as fuck. All that straightforward way of approaching things and passing on information that just clogs everything up and we've come to accept all this banality, banal music and banal ways of discussing it, and that phrase just brought it right down to what it is.

When I went on Radio One a few days after I read that, on *Rock On*, just the name gives you some idea of what's going down, it was probably Ted Nugent the week before . . . and the guy asked me the usual questions about how most bands who've been around as long as us would've quit without the conventional success and usually I'd have given the polite rap but I just goes, Well other bands make crap LPs.

I liked that. I'm fed up with patronising myself. This has to be stressed . . . if anyone is going to make music it may as well be Simple Minds. Who else are we going to look up to in this day? That's a better way to feel.

What did Morley say? The difference between sincerity and authenticity . . . some groups are content with being sincere, we have to be authentic. The punk thing seems long ago. I've learnt that there's much more than what was suggested back then. You have to go for it. For what? Does it shine? Is it a glory? Aye . . . it's a glory.

People who are truly in love with the world are as cynical as fuck, they don't accept anything straight . . . because they care. I care. I just want to . . . that line in "Love Song": "*America is my boyfriend*", it's so throwaway, it means nothing and it means everything, it's just great. It stands for the whole fucking glory. I hate people who ignore ambition and possibility. I just love . . . celebration.

Today I'd like to have lots of money . . . just today. There are all those people who've helped us and who I owe things to. Not possessions, but I just feel today that I'd like to buy people loads of things . . . I don't have to, they don't expect it, but I'd love to . . . I want a lot of money today. I'd have had that thought a year ago and been ashamed. Today I just feel uplifted. I don't feel guilty. A few years ago it would have been philistine if you didn't have the ultimate conventional social conscience, but now you're allowed, in some ways, room to come in at problems in different ways.

I can sum up all that rock guilt in one line and I can go deeper than just a moan. I accept it both – pleasure and protest, the beauty in fear. Celebrate, that's what it is, there's so much to go on. You have to take things head on. Think of the amount of people I've met who I wouldn't have if I'd listened to those people who said I was being stupid and pretentious. I've never really been stopped from doing anything I wanted to, there's nothing that's been out of bounds in terms of . . . well, there has really. . . . Greatness. . . .

LIKE PAUL SAID, that "Empires and Dance" was a genuine high and with the new LP we haven't moved on much, just consolidated that whole.

Yeah . . . I think this has been the end of some kind of phase for us. There were those big leaps between the first and second and the second and third and with the fourth it wasn't nearly as big a move. We've reached the end of something. . . . I don't know what the next starting point will be . . . that Greatness – I think we've got that at our fingertips. . . .

Last year there was hardly anything up there with "Empires and Dance" . . . in time it'll be looked upon up there with the big ones. It just shines so bright, lines, sounds and feelings that come through . . . at the end of last year we'd just come so far from being termed the wet and wimpy mascara boys and we were being given some true respect. Then it changes and people expect so much from us.

I don't think our songs go on too long, people are missing the point and associating us with totally the wrong images. Our songs deal with trance and gathering forces and motions, and that's just developed maybe to its limits . . . but think about the repetition in my life . . . think about the shape and agility in the songs that is being overlooked.

These people talk about the abstraction in my lyrics . . . just what is abstraction? It's as elusive as the word pretension; using that word to soak up everything I do, it's just a lazy response. Still . . . reviews used to matter, now you can just throw them away . . . the standard is appalling. . . .

Morley said he'd read a review of our Manchester show that made him ashamed to write for the same paper . . . just so condescending and simplistic. . . .

There is like . . . well . . . Chris Bohn gave me one of the biggest kicks in my life in terms of that go for it when he came to us all cynical and then went away saying the lyrics to "Empires And Dance" could have been words to "Lodger" if Bowie had been younger. That just like elevated me.

Then a year later . . . don't one year give us this king thing and the next year say we're wasted. Don't call us top of the class in one year and then dunces the next. The gap hasn't been as big, but we've not crumbled, we've not lost our way. Just what are the expectations, what do people expect from popular music? Chris Bohn, what is your expectation of Simple Minds . . . what should I be writing about, Chris, that has value and vibrancy and where would the difference be to what I'm writing now?

Don't give us the crown and then snatch it away. We deserve better. Do that to the fools.

We know our position. We're not bullshitting anyone and there's no way we're fat and lazy.

▬▬▬▬▬▬▬▬▬▬▬▬▬▬▬▬

WE'VE ONLY been together three, four years and this is the first time we've slowed down after tremendous acceleration . . . like the two LP idea was our own because we had to get all our ideas out of the system ready for the next stage. What the fuck does hype matter? In this bloody world faced with all the crap and superficiality, does it matter if Virgin or the *NME* hype something that has some soul and depth?

The thought of doing a double LP, you just get visions of Masters of Rock and The Clash, but how could we get all those songs out? Of course we know that two LPs at that price is going to get us in the charts. I'm not denying that, and I'm not ashamed of that — there are three or four songs on "Sons And Fascination" that are as good as anything put out this year. Am I ashamed of that? No fucking way.

What's it matter who's hyping you? We control the lust in the music. Everyone's hyped by some force, myth or matter. I could say that the second record is a gift to the people, a gift to our fans. But am I going to

down to getting that shiver down the spine. When you get that shiver, you're getting somewhere."

I ask Peter if he feels that it is important for him to continue. We had been talking about the frightened, restricted rock industry, and people like Peter's position within it. "I have no crusading feeling . . . I don't feel I belong to a privileged group of conscience-prickers. I think . . . integrity is important. . . . For instance . . . the Crystal Gayle television programme the other night had as a guest B. B. King . . . the whole show I think was sickening . . . it smacked of insincerity. But as soon as B. B. King came on there was a tremendous dignity and integrity. With those two things the box was transformed. I think it's very important for people like that . . . in this business that's how they should function and be able to function . . . how people should function in the charts and the record business. With dignity . . . and I don't always think I'm that clean and honest, but I like to think I'm trying."

How does artificial intoxication enter into all this?
"(Sylvian) Not very much that is artificial. The only thing I do is coke. But I only use it because it appears to speed up the mind when I'm in such a low state that I feel I need to use it, when I feel trapped and my mind's too slow or lazy to work. I sometimes turn to that, but it doesn't really help. What helps more, to a certain extent, is recovering a contentment of being, even on a superficial level . . . a contentment that relates more to an excitement than people would think, thinking of the word 'contentment'. Not necessarily thinking that deeply about what's happening around and inside, but continually

say that? Fuck no. It's just a collection of songs that's over two records. There it is. We'll be lucky to break even . . . a Top 20 LP for a few weeks doesn't matter much. I'm not ignorant. It represents an end of something for the Minds.

What happens next? We travel a few thousand miles and we'll end up with something different. We always respond to change, we get impatient. We've done four LPs . . . it's weird, probably pathetic. No one could have expected that. . . . Paul says we've been fucked up because we've toured so much and produced such strong music and we're broke, but it's that something that has come to exist within the Simple Minds that is important. No one gets inside us.

Right now I'm broke, but that's just a hangover from past bungling . . . we're doing all right in Britain, we're doing all right in Europe, we're taking off in American discos, we're going to Australia . . . we're going to make lots of money and as it is we're having a great time and there will always be excitement and possibility . . . we have made something special for ourselves. . .

I'M THE FRONT person in the group and I get all the attention . . . Paul just interviewed me yesterday . . . but Charlie and Mick and Derek, it seems not enough to be just musicians or technicians these days, but for me to have the courage and drive to get on a stage and perform I have to have total trust in the people beside me . . . and they're good. They're no way just a backing group. I'm getting to be just like the pulse behind what they do . . . in interviews I always go on about musical heroes, but right now Burchill and McNeill and Forbes are my heroes. . . . The next stage will emerge out of the great strength we've established amongst ourselves and we're going for an energy that's twelve times greater than what we originally envisaged.

We're not scared to take on any task and what we've achieved in the past has given us the confidence to just go for the next giant jump into some area that might once have appeared hopelessly out of reach. Simple Minds has meant confidence, yeah, and we will take on absolutely anything. For the heck of it. It's a word I wouldn't have thought of using for a few years – but for the sheer *anarchy* of it. For the fun of it. For the necessity. For the vitality.

Any shame I've had about feeling this way about what I'm doing has turned into celebration. Any nervousness I feel about performing or walking down the street relates to the confidence by keeping the edge, keeping us looking. Bands do make crap records. We don't. There's not many bands who've progressed like us. Because we're fucking good. We've got vision, courage, tons of it. . . .

I look at the things that are so floppy and milky and I see that we're part of something crappy and unlovable and we just want so much to be better than all that. We want to make something that people can touch, that isn't manufactured. We want to exploit the industry ten times more than it can exploit us. If the *NME* says to us you can't go on the cover because you've missed the boat we can just tell them to stuff it up their arse . . . none of that matters any more.

We have a spirit now and nothing can break it. We have this spirit and it's helped us break away from all the silliness and faddiness and it's not spirit for the sake of it and it's giving us more and more confidence.

The past two years have elevated me so much. I don't apologise now. I'm more dynamic. I couldn't speak to a person before unless they asked me something. Now I bawl and scream like a madman and I will not feel contrived or embarrassed or any shame. We've got something iron solid, whilst other groups are relying on flukes and bits in time. . . .

I've found something that I have to do, a way of growing up, owning up, and I'm going for something. I don't stop for no one. We have taken a long road compared to some groups, but we've got this energy that just exists and it's strong and we can see it. We're so fucking good and we're getting better all the time.

Yes, I am going to get up. What shall I wear? What can I find out about this world, anyway?

conscious somewhere of those depths. You can find that by living in an absent state for a while that at the end of it you can see yourself more clearly. This is what's happening at the moment . . . I'm living in the absent state, aware of my situation, content up to a point to be meandering, ready to take up the next stage. It's this absence which allows the human spirit its vital space, which enables the mind to construe essence beyond the narrow and shut horizons of our material condition. And I step forward. . . ."
Dust to dust.

Pop journalists are cowards. It's easy to wield the nasty pen in sweet isolation, to exploit the inevitable bias, to always but always have the last word, to evade the inherent hypocrisy of rock criticism. The group that has been torn apart rarely has a chance to answer back without their words being tampered with. Perhaps it is this awareness of a cowardice that is the something that prompted me into a dense den with Killing Joke. Their side of the story must be heard to even things up. It's odd how worked up we can all get. "I think we deserve a bit of your time to establish the facts. Killing Joke is an attitude. Nothing more. Our music gives you a tension. I don't know if we get it on record, but live we capture that tension that everyone feels at the moment. If you're living in London, that's the way it is. We're tension music . . . that's all it is. We use the music as a method to balance ourselves, as well as playing music that we like to play. The feeling of a guy in the First World War who's just about to run out of the trenches, right, and he knows his life is going to be gone in ten minutes and he thinks of the fucker back in Westminster who put him in

STING

April 12, 1980

Is there anybody there?

GETTING OUT of Bombay was one of the hardest things I've ever done. I'm certain that everyone is staring at me; that they're all whispering and watching behind my back; that they're all waiting for me to fall – or at least to trip.

I was escaping India, the dreamworld or the real world, and I knew that I was running away and so I was panicking. There was a threat. I could come to no decision. I felt impotent and pathetic. Fraudulent. If only I could see further than others.

India is a place full of ghosts. The air is thick with madness and lethargy.

I had been in Bombay only three days. Most of that I had spent tripping wide-eyed and unconsciously through the unkempt streets, markets, bazaars, parks and alleyways of the laughing misery class.

I had sensed the estranged hierarchical attitude of the stoic upper class, but had always been with a party – other people with whom to laugh and share . . . an absurd circus of rock stars, film makers, TV people, journalists: enough people to camouflage the confusion; to maintain cheery comforting banter; that kept the Indian impatience, its monstrosity, a distant, bearable dream.

For three days I was on the press trip to end all press trips.

It was part of the exotic section of The Police's triumphant world tour. I was promoting The Police. Summarising this or that.

The experience! I tried to discard the feelings of frustration and submission, the vague feelings of sell-out (and mostly managed it). This was a sign that I was beyond hope. I lost all sense of reason. But for three days I was with my people and I got on with my job: interviewing, reporting, looking, listening. I had a great time.

But then these rock stars and film-makers – this troupe forcing history into the books and on to the screen – jetted off to Cairo, Egypt, setting up more history and having more fun.

I had to get out of Bombay on my own. And I couldn't shut my eyes all the time.

But I didn't want to. I wanted to stare and rationalise – or at least believe I was rationalising. But stuck in a sticky taxi-capsule lurching maniacally towards Bombay's ramshackle airport, I was paralysed, embarrassed and, ultimately, humiliated. Everybody must've been looking. You know how alarmed I felt. I was sweating more than is natural.

What the hell was going on?

I LEFT the hotel seven hours early to make sure of my flight, as I had been warned about overbooking. I took no chances. I panic easily. I suffocate slowly.

The Taj Mahal Intercontinental is a soothing westernised haven. It is set deep inside, but far away from, the constant Indian pressure and commotion of natives looking to sell wares, drugs, girls. Indians just looking crowd around the perimeter of the magnificent hotel grounds, but they're kept at bay as if by an invisible barrier (but actually by six discreet Indian policemen).

I walk through the lobby past relaxing tourists and emerge into the outside glare and wet heat. Yellow and black taxis are lined up. One is ordered for me. It pulls up. I clamber in. It curves away. Scatters some Indians *Screech*! Honks horn. Scythes through crazy traffic.

At least the taxi is some protection from the weirdness outside.

Bombay life has no order. It is so disordered it is magnificently disciplined. The city is an out of focus confusion of an antique present, a precious past and a disjointed future. It's a city that never stops. I could grow to love it. All the beauty and all the ugliness the world could ever muster has collapsed into an agonising and challenging heap called Bombay.

In vivid afternoon daylight, looking with a panicky glance through a taxi window, Bombay is like any major city, except it's been left to rot and crumble. When it falls down no one will rebuild it.

Roadside hoardings advertising fluoride toothpaste, the best brand of cigars, mentholyptus sweets and Cadbury's chocolate, mock the charismatic crisis of Bombay with explicit cruelty.

The taxi takes such a ridiculous route to the airport that I begin to think it doesn't exist. I sit in the middle of the small taxi's back seat, lean towards the shoulder of the driver in a futile attempt to disperse the irrational panic in my stomach, and try to look straight ahead. I hold my breath. Sweat. No one likes me.

Every time the taxi stops at traffic lights, at junctions – and that's every three minutes – the beggars descend and collect around the taxi.

that position. That's the feeling we're trying to project. The Killing Joke. . . . What we write is what we see. We are fucking grossly misinterpreted!"

What did I do wrong?

Two hours' fishing is enough. It's like, a couple of hours with Cope, Geldof, Bono, is fine but you wouldn't want to spend a holiday with one of them. It's not so much that Fish preached, just that he reached into areas of fretting simplification and coarse idealism that you only get away with in the new rock. After my research and a two-hour conversation I now know more about Fish than you, although I'm not sure that I want to. I know that he's half-crazed, and that might be a good thing. I know that he's pretty clever, and only occasionally could that be a problem. And I know that he's just another in a long line of reasonable passionately non-reticent rock eccentrics. Just what we need. Oh, and there's no stopping him . . . talking.

"I could bitch like fuck about, say, Boy George, but I still appreciate what he does. It's like I don't like Max Bygraves, Des O'Connor, but as professionals they're fucking incredible. But how many people are actually aware of what Marillion do? That's all I want. Bitch like fuck about me but at least listen."

That could be an impossible dream.

"It looks like being."

And that's your problem.

"Very clever."

Did I say something wrong?

Has Mick Jagger got security for life?

"No one has security for life. Security doesn't lie in money. It lies in a lot of other things. Money doesn't hurt, but sometimes it can be a terrible burden to some people. It ain't to me. A lot of people that I know

They've spotted me. It's not pretty.

It's not easy to slot into any perspective that I know. It's no use writhing in pity. Who can handle the confusion? Where to direct the hate? Is there any use in getting worked up?

Some of the beggars are limbless, a few tragicomically contorted. There are those who drag bony children; others carry cute babies close to their bodies, half hidden inside their robes. They are not stigmatised. They present themselves naturally.

Sitting in this taxi, willing myself on the plane or in London, because all of a sudden the alienating closeness, the brilliant and nebulous difference of the place, was affecting me. I had nothing I knew to cling on to. The beggars floated towards me, weaving in and out of other cars, and performed their trade. I was lost.

The people of India are victims. Do we remember as a matter of courtesy? How do we deal with it? How do we act? Western guilt and ignorance mixes with Indian principles with degenerate illogic. Begging is an Indian tradition; truly a trade.

These thoughts do not ease the emotional uncertainty of the visitor, the tourist. Those Indians who are comfortably off, and those who are richer and snugger than you or me, are enthusiastically quick to dismiss the innumerable beggars that cling to likely targets. They make a racket clicking their tongues. "But these people earn more money than the poor fellows working in the factories," a well-off Indian would explain.

Some of the beggars are melodramatic and too well-rehearsed in their manner. A lot of them use exactly the same gestures and timing, as if they've been taught in the same drama school. If you presented these with a full set of clothes, they would be back the next day in their same carefully torn rags, I am told.

Those Indians who have a good home to live in and more than enough to eat, are quick to point out that the hundreds and thousands of natives who sleep in inches of brown dust on the city's pavements do so out of choice. It is another half truth. Given the *choice* of horribly crowded and unsafe tenement buildings or a pavement where you can stretch and pretend you have privacy, most choose the pavement. It's not the sweetest of choices.

THE TAXI pulls me through the outer limits of the city: a warped parody of Moss Side. What is worse? The makeshift shacks leaning against each other for support, or the isolated tenements that look like a Hulme housing estate turned inside out — walls bleeding, crumbling, black? It's here in the ruinous outer limits that the beggars come in droves. Trapped in a turmoil whether I was giving chocolate to the starving but unable to reach hundreds of millions, wondering whether I was supplying a comparatively rich racket or what, I end up with my fingernails clenching in my palms giving nothing. Now I feel bad about it, except the whole scene flickers out of sight, desperately out of mind.

I stared straight ahead, leaning over the driver's shoulder, but he was no help. He looked menacing. He had a leathery, gnarled face, a droopy moustache, green teeth, eyelids that could crush an arm.

A beggar paws my expensive suede jacket. I stare straight ahead and he curses me. Apparently my head will fall off tomorrow.

The driver murmurs to every beggar that signals, weeps, chuckles and sighs. Is he pointing out my callousness? Telling them to go away? Sharing a giggle. Can he understand my confusion? Like a dog sensing fear, he undoubtedly senses my pathetic silliness.

A little child is pushed through the back of the taxi. She whimpers. I clutch some rupees in my pocket. But the taxi quickly pulls away. I rub a thumb over my forehead . . . and collect a strip of grime and perspiration.

We reach the airport that's set in the midst of this desperate wasteland. From the outside it looks like a row of garages. I'm visibly shaking for reasons I only half know. The taxi meter registers 16 rupees. The bandit driver snarls 60. Outside a horde of eager porters surround the taxi ready for my bags. I point to the meter, having been warned that I will be conned. But it's stupid arguing hysterically over 60 rupees (just over £3) for a journey that would cost three times that in London.

I throw the money into his lap. Drag my bags out of the car. Almost fall over. Stumble into the departure lounge. Into what I wildly presume will be a bland, anonymous airport land, somewhere clean and comfortable. But the chaos I trip into is no comfort. Where do I go? What do I do? No helpful signs. No obvious people to ask. I spend the next five hours in a state of high panic and paranoia – pacing around, gibbering. . . .

Five and a half hours after reaching the airport I get to my plane seat. Smiling Japan Airlines. Escape. I sit back and shut my eyes.

Pop music. The Police. India. Taxi drive. Beggars.

What the hell was *that* all about?

THE FIRST time ever I met the Sting. . . .

Was at The Who gig at Wembley Stadium and it was also around the time of *Quadrophenia* and Sting had a seat in the royal box. I was at the bar, absentmindedly sucking some white wine, when I half-recognised an agreeable looking guy who was standing next to me. But he was carrying a small, three-year-old boy and that threw me off. Then he said something to me. He recognised me. Now I'm not going to pretend that this never happens and when it does that it doesn't cheer me up. I'm not going to pretend that I'm not corrupted.

So this guy with the boy recognised me and introduced himself as Sting. Oh, I thought, unimpressed.

He mumbled something about the Ted Nugent article I had written. I'd argued with Nugent about "Roxanne" – I'd called it, bitterly, polite, and I'd never thought of The Police as being anything other than polite and certainly nothing to do with me. The Sting softly told me that he'd stuck the pertinent part of the piece into his scrapbook.

It appealed to my London-bred conceit. I can be a bit of a show off. Sting and the kid departed in a searing wave of cool. I gulped down the rest of my white wine.

It was the first time ever I'd seen his face . . . really. I began to think about Sting. Within two months it was as if I'd never loved a pop star as much as I loved Sting.

Stars are as much a part of rock 'n' roll as the progression and the sex and the poetry and the

introversion and the communication; and rock 'n' roll would be grimy without them.

I'm where I am because of Marc Bolan, so I could never lose the part of my heart that flutters for stars. But the stars have got to be right. I am also where I am because of punk, so I know how destructive stars can be. The power they have can go either way.

The real stars look larger than life and see the world through a personal magnifying glass: with a lot of spite, sadness, drama, defiance. They're not meant to be just pretty pictures. It would be patronising and vulgar to say that there should be no such things as stars.

In the latter part of the '70s there had been no new star who had the sublime glamour, spring, looks, mystery, sensitivity and relevance of The Ideal Star *and* who also had punk enforced principles. Johnny Lydon isn't a poet and poster star; there are too many shadows.

I tried to make a few of my own: Pete Shelley, Howard Devoto (the closest . . . so close). Then it began to get desperate: Gary Numan! I soon lost interest. I began to moan about the true new pop – beat, heart, melody, love and yearning, chilling life modes, dress, style, charm – it was not where it belonged, in the charts, on our walls.

Bob Geldof is not a real post-punk star. Siouxsie comes closest. Most of the new pop stars who would be are being shoved into the underground. The Industry is still in control. People older than me still run the media.

I was thinking about Sting. And then – "Message In A Bottle" made my nose bleed, helped shape a new vision – I realised that everything I wanted was already there. The cool. The mask. The soul. The beauty. The music. Those words. The voice. *The Star.*

Sting! More so than The Police. Sting had beaten everyone.

The Police. I hadn't liked the name, the image, their record label, their ages, the smoothness of their music. I hadn't liked their summer success. I was lazy. I didn't look through the gloss. I didn't like Andy Summers, this has-been; and I didn't like the brash and ludicrous Stewart Copeland.

But Sting introducing himself, not one bit bothered by all the nasty things I'd written about the group, had swollen my head and made me think.

"Message In A Bottle" was released with its crystal clear communication and startling struc-

have terrible trouble because they have a lot of money. They don't know what to do with it. They go overboard. They spend it all and then they're worried. It's fucking hard if you don't have any!''

What does money give you?

''Freedom to move around is the most important thing. I don't have to worry where the next meal comes from. But of course I feel more security than someone who is out of work.''

Do you feel totally safe?

''No, not at all.''

Scared?

''A little bit. By politics and their effects. You feel rather helpless. Of course. I don't feel there's an awful lot that you can do for the economic and other problems of a society. There's a little bit you can do. Not an awful lot. I think to think so would be inflating your own position.''

You don't like to do that, do you?

''Naah. I used to think I could do an awful lot. That's probably when I was taking too much acid.''

Why did you first take acid, Fish?

''Experience . . . it was February 1981. I wasn't scared. I did it on my tod. I went through an acid peak in 1981. It got absolutely ridiculous . . . I was doing four or five acid tab trips and started to realise that I was just burning. I just stopped it. It influenced me. It made me a lot more aware. I had the bad trips . . . the whole crucifix bit and all that shit . . . and that scared me completely. It took me a long time to do it again after that. Perhaps this is the wrong sort of thing to say in an interview . . . we're talking to people who are impressionable. . . . It's too dodgy to talk about. There are too many people doing the Jim Morrison thing. Too many people thinking that it's cool, and it's just not fucking very clever.''

ture. It clicked. The Police (Sting) were only right as a supergroup. Were the only right supergroup: the tension, aggression, vulnerability, superiority. When they were obscure and struggling, supporting Chelsea, rushing off to America, The Police smacked of insincerity and conspiracy. But The Police as supergroup . . . were important and, if we only looked, refreshing!

Sting transcended the whole blue and frothy Police myth. He beat back the notion of star as something stupid, to be reviled. He was part of the rock 'n' roll tradition, yet the looks, the voice, the intimacy, the intelligence and developing perception contradicted it all. Sting with The Police as star in the charts and on our walls *was* the fantasy and *mocked* the fantasy.

Sting didn't hide the fact that he was smart.

THE SECOND time ever I met the Sting. . . .

Was at ten o'clock in the morning in India. I was jauntily walking through the large lobby of Bombay's Intercontinental hotel, foolishly kidding myself that I'd got used to this decaying and fantastic country. Walking towards me was the Sting. I paused. I tried to pretend I hadn't seen him. It didn't work.

Since the last time I'd met Sting I'd elevated him into something special and here I was fooled by the personality that I'd made Sting into. He said hello. Stewart Copeland was with him. He said Hi. I stuttered. They went off for breakfast. After recovering I went in and joined him.

Just as I expected, Stewart Copeland ranted and raved about the charts. Sting sighed, tried to read, stayed mostly silent and restless.

Later on, during one of two conversations I was to have with Sting where I was beginning to look at him as if into a mirror (his will strangely imposes itself, yet is quite selfless) we were talking about art and innocence. I ask him about the immense cool of Sting. It cannot be ignored or played down. It is not intimidating, it is merely . . . spectacular.

He shrugs. The cool makes The Star. His voice is soft and accentless; husky from recent throat trouble.

"I don't feel like a star, myself. I just feel like I always did."

But you do build up this coolness, I push.

"I know what the effect is and I know why I choose to do certain things," he muses. "Just cool! I just think about how I look. I care about how I look, and I care about how I present myself. Like this morning when we met, I cared very much about what you thought of me at breakfast.

"Maybe it's vanity. I feel that I'm being watched and I enjoy it, therefore I have a task to do it at all times. I mean, it's no great burden on me. If anything I find that it's a pastime, just to maintain that kind of cool. . . ."

I let him know that the second time we met I was nervous.

"I know! You moved away! You thought you'd pretend you hadn't seen me!"

The first time we met I was very cynical towards The Police so it was a different thing. The Sting lets some more of his secrets slip.

"I went up to you at Wembley with the sole purpose of introducing Sting because I didn't think that Paul Morley had ever thought about Sting and it was a good opportunity to get you to. The excuse was the article about Ted Nugent. . . ."

Bastard! It did have a profound effect on me.

"I know! I know! I thought it's put the cat among the pigeons."

It worked. What a sucker!

"I know it worked. I tell you how I know it worked because not long after the photographer Pennie Smith came along and said Paul Morley sends his regards, and I thought, 'It's worked. I've got him.'

"It's interesting how personal meetings can affect things. Like I met Elvis Costello once. I was walking down Kensington High Street and this guy leapt out of a car to buy a newspaper. He was in front of me and he's small and he was trying to pass me and he looked up and saw that it was Sting and he was trying to scowl at me and I just shrugged. And he fucking went off and I thought, 'Well, that's the first meeting, wait till the second one!'

"And there's this thing building up about his hating The Police and I'm just dying for

the next meeting, because I'm going to get him. Metaphorically. There is no way I'm going to be drawn into a slagging match. The next meeting I'll get him to love me."

Sting chuckles, presumably plotting again.

"And that's the ultimate cruelty."

IN THE lobby of the hotel The Police troupe is slowly gathering. It is the 26th of March, my twenty-third birthday. The day The Police play a special concert in Bombay, the first rock concert in the city since Hawkwind played ten years ago. It's a cultural occasion; a significant event.

Because The Police in Bombay is being covered by a posse of film, TV and journalist people, there is always a wait for everyone to assemble before the pack takes off. "Who's not here?" shouts The Police manager Miles Copeland, intensely fluttering as usual. Those that aren't don't answer. Those that are sit on a long seat facing the hotel reception. Elongated drummer Stewart Copeland sits at the end. His brother Miles resigns himself: those that are coming will come when they come.

He sits next to his brother. In many ways Miles is the fourth member of the group. "With the belief they have, I think Stewart and Sting and Andy would have made it in the end, but probably not as big. Me, personally, I'd like to think that part of the success of The Police is up to me!"

His brother Stewart has his say. His American accent is slower. "If you like the music, then we get credit for that; but if you respect our success, then Miles gets a lot of credit for that."

Miles takes off. "The Police is the ultimate dream for everyone, y'know. It happened without hype: the kids discovered the record in America, the record company followed afterwards, but it was the import that was taking off in the charts not the record. . . .

"It is a group that did not get into debt when it started happening, so the first royalties actually went into their pockets. Erm, for me as a manager, they look good, they're cooperative. If you say, 'Hey guys, we need a photograph,' they're all there. They're ideal. Obviously, I'm speaking comparatively. . . ."

"The things that make us co-operative," butts in Stewart, "the things that Miles says are good about us, that we're good boys, are just little things that you've got to do, extra parts of the job. And we definitely get paid for it, to shake another hand. It's not such a hassle."

There's a three-way pull inside The Police. A flamboyant blend of steadiness, tradition, ambition, rivalry, calculation, dedication. Out on the left is the champion Sting. Out on the right are the breathless Copeland brothers. Andy seen-it-all Summers is a placid, but influential, buffer for this rivalry.

The personality and cool of Sting dominates the group, is the *phenomenon*. But it is the workings of the Copeland brothers – third brother Ian runs an agency in America which gave them their early dates there – that has pushed The Police into their sturdy, unprecedented position. In many ways it has also given Sting his stardom. But whereas Sting will talk about breaking down barriers, looking to challenge stereotypes, the Copelands talk incessantly about facts and figures and markets and success in the abstract.

A lot of things that are bad about The Police are rooted in the Copelands' activity. Sting suggests this rivalry is stimulating. I ask Stewart about it.

"We've got different things that drive us, that keep us pushing. His is a kind of sense of rivalry and mine is something different. There are different things that I want out of life. I have a different plan for getting them. And I have different kinds of talents for getting them, different things to put into the ball game to make it happen for both of us.

"During the three years that we've been working together, Sting and I have evolved a way of working with each other that brings the best out of each other, and it's mostly just out of making it hot for each other."

What has success and The Police given to the drummer?

"The fact that I get to do anything that I want to and if I want to do it really seriously I can shun other responsibilities and get really involved in it.

"Ordinarily that would not be possible because I would have to earn a daily crust. Things like making movies; such as going to Bombay; such

What is your value of yourself?

"I value myself lightly."

Never take notice of what people tell you?

"Now and then. That's when you learn to be more modest about yourself. What the media says about you, and going on the road, they can make you feel very immodest. You start getting all this attention, and that's when I start going round the bend. I don't like it. It all seems to affect me, because my personality changes, warps."

You become horrible?

"Yeah . . . I become horrible on the road. . . . I become rude, vulgar, loud-mouthed, immodest, self-centred. . . ."

The Mick Jagger we all know and . . .

"Well, it's a load of old bollocks."

I don't know what came over me.

It could have been pity. It could have been strength. Perhaps it was just downright idealism. Did I know better than them all? Was I examining others in order to examine myself? Using their achievements and attitudes to work out for myself what might be going on . . . I could have been just creeping around a little. Or did I just want somebody, anybody, to confirm the validity of the system? Any *system*. I must have felt I was practising a realistic dissidence, this being the trademark of anyone who has a new idea in business. *Any* business. Should I have signed every piece I wrote with the words "your humble and obedient servant"? Steve Harley didn't think so. Simply, I was up to no good. That's what he said.

I asked him if he deserved stardom. Now, when you ask a question that the interviewee feels is a gross blunder it's not as if what he is demanding is a truly dislocating determined

as, well, making records, which is what I'm best at. I mean you can have a pretty good old time and it's been like this for the last year."

Does his immense popularity crush his impetus in any way?

"Oh, no, because it's really only different in degree from what I've always known. The feelings I have about my current popularity are pretty much the same as when I first headlined at the Marquee with my own group . . . and you swagger into the club and everyone knows who you are. And it's exactly the same now but to a different degree."

Does he think about responsibilities?

"Sort of. Every now and again. When I'm in a pious mood I do feel that I have to kind of remind myself. I have to kick myself every now and again. I've been doing that regularly up to now and I don't know what good it's done. We're doing this gig in Bombay for charity and so that all seems OK, and I can relax, my karma's all right.

"I suppose I'm guilty of a certain amount of vanity . . . shit! . . . y'know . . . you really got to struggle to get where you wanna get and when you get to the top you're bound to want to thumb your nose up at people!"

WHILE WE'RE sitting in the hotel lobby waiting for everyone to gather for the gig at the Rang Bhavan in the very centre of Bombay, I'm wondering – why India?

Sting said it was about challenge, adventure, initiative. Then he'd talked about Miles Copeland and his "vision", a long term project to introduce rock 'n' roll into countries such as India with a view to "westernising" such places. Is he serious? Sting had said Miles had "a sort of right wing drive".

But when I asked Sting how he related to his manager's apparently half-political ambition, he was cautious.

"I'm into his energy. I'm enjoying the adventure and Miles isn't in charge by any means. We will argue about things . . . Miles' energy and Miles' ideas, whatever the end is, are useable. There is no Police spokesman.

I speak for myself and him for himself. I think he's probably one of the most dynamic managers in rock and roll, he really digs it, he thinks of great things to do. . . .

"But he does have this idea about Russia. All Americans are frightened of Russia, and I'm sure it's the other way round.

"Miles' idea is that the world is in two camps and that there is a political solution to the world. I don't believe that. I play along with it . . . I think the solution needs to be more spiritual. . . ."

Later I tell Miles what Sting has said. I ask him about introducing western and capitalist values into the eastern world. His deceptive face breaks into a stiff smile and he answers as if addressing some distant persons, half preaching, almost reciting, drawling like a wet Jimmy Carter.

"I believe in the word capitalism in a different way to maybe how some English people would use the term. In England the word means oppression and everything like that. To me it means freedom of the individual, and to me the great thing about England and America and our western way of society is that the individual can pretty well make up his own mind, at least compared to other countries – i.e. Russia.

"I find socialism oppressive because I don't believe The People when they start talking about The People; they really mean a few people dominating everybody else in the name of 'The People'.

"Erm, I grew up in the political life. My father (a top man in the CIA) was involved in various aspects of politics and the way governments run and all that, so I obviously have an interest in it. I grew up in a lot of exotic places and as a young kid I met Nasser and I hob-nobbed with rulers of various countries.

"But I'm not trying to inject politics into what I'm doing in music. But the fact is if western music gets played in Russia and gets played in India and gets played in China it tends to liberate all those individuals to a degree that it's revolutionary music. It's kids standing up for themselves.

"Look at England. Music is used as a form for changing society; it's a revolutionary force and our society has the freedom to do that and it can influence events. In the '70s a lot of pop stars altered the course of America in the war with Vietnam.

"But if all the Russians and all the Chinese and all the Indians get into western music, it means really that they get into western culture, which means they become oriented towards the west as opposed to the east.

"But I did not get into this business to do that. I'm not playing India because I want to change India. I'm just saying maybe that's a side-effect that in the end is a good thing.

"I happen to believe in the values of our western society as opposed to anything else that is being offered. I don't pretend we're perfect, but we certainly are better. Somebody like me is free to do what I want to do in England. But I wouldn't be able to operate like this if I was in Russia. So I have to believe in the values of our society.

"But The Police are not in India for any ulterior motive on my part. We're here to have a good time! It's fun! It's a new culture! It's exciting. It keeps the band fresh. They're playing places nobody else has. We're doing something nobody else has. We're doing something good, I think. All the Indians are real excited that at last all these rock groups they hear about are gonna come over and they're gonna get a chance to see what it's about."

▬▬▬▬▬▬▬▬▬▬▬▬▬▬▬▬▬▬

"LET'S GO!" Miles Copeland commands loudly and the huge white limousine which is totally incongruous amongst all the tiny vehicles in India, eases away from the hotel and heads for the open air theatre where the gig is to be. I'm in the back of the car with the two Copelands. Andy Summers is in the front. Sting is lost.

The two Copelands are chattering on about the endless tapes of conversations and idle chit-chat that Miles is building up from the whole tour. "I'm catching all those little moments so that in ten years from now when they do The Police story, syndicated all over the world, I'll have all these little bits."

Miles grins like a little boy. Stewart begins "We're laying the foundation . . ." and Miles completes, " . . . for The Police tapes!"

But the atmosphere of happy tourists cruising along Bombay's evening streets soon comes to a horrific end.

"Oh my God," groans Miles loudly.

The car has pulled up at some traffic lights. An armless girl beggar has presented herself at the car window.

"Shit!" spits Stewart. "Can you imagine showing your deformities to everyone?"

We all try to stare away. No one knows what to say. "Oh God," Miles repeats. The car moves off. "But if you give them money you're actually encouraging it, and I think it's not to be encouraged. . . ."

"Where do you draw the line?" wonders a shaken Andy Summers. "Where do you stop. You can't give it to one and then leave seven million out. . . ."

The incident is soon forgotten. Deep down everyone needs consoling. The car pulls up outside the neat open-air theatre and Miles is back to his good self.

Two hours before the concert and there are already queues for the sell-out concert. Three and a half thousand tickets have been sold.

He looks gratefully at the queue which is breaking up and beginning to surround the car. "I see that there are a few foreigners here come to check the stars."

▬▬▬▬▬▬▬▬▬▬▬▬▬▬▬▬▬▬

THE THIRD time ever I met the Sting. . . .

Was on a high balcony of the Taj Mahal Intercontinental Hotel, and by now we must know that Sting knows what he's doing. But how. Overlooking the Arabian Sea and the majestic Gateway to India, Sting and I talk about Joy Division. Sting may like the group – "The LP blew me away" – but he also knows full well that they're my favourite group. It's a calculated move for us to talk about them immediately, yet still honest. It's part of that Cool.

In the lobby prior to The Police pack going off on some outing into the Bombay maze, we arrange when we'll do the interview, when we'll talk about Sting and Pop, and I say that I feel slightly silly discussing the pop phenomenon in Bombay.

question. Interviewees don't want to delve into the cheats and promises of the entertainment lark. Really, they just want to be allowed to amuse themselves and, they think, others. Harley screeched at the simplicity of the question, but the truly mischievous would have crushed him. "Don't ask such stupid questions." I obeyed, but didn't bother asking him about the influence entertainers have over their consumers. Harley helped me see the lightness. The chatter of pop is one hell of a sales talk. I just had to ask: Was there any more to it? Was that wrong of me?

Don't you want to talk about the new LP, Mick, "Emotional Rescue"?
"Just put that it's out, in big letters, at the top of the piece."

"I do think," says Gabriel, "that there will be a tendency again, that musicians will use music as a tool for learning about themselves. . . ."

I left Harley where he was, and he stayed there for ever. Out of a fumbled thirty-minute conversation, which I began with a curtsy and ended with a nagging, I decided that I knew all about him and his ways. That's what happens when you ask questions and then later on compile the asks and the answers into the final say. There's an unclear power, a world to rule, and the interviewer has to appear very healthy in spite of everything. The interviewer must know it all, in the most tactful manner. They have a lot to take care of, if they mean it. They must never lag behind in life. They must make their own contribution, and never trust the facts of the matter. Even as they ask the questions they must see through it all, and see it through to the little end.

"Oh no," Sting shakes his head.
"Pop is important."

HAVE YOU always loved pop?

"I always hated rock in my teens. From about 15 to 25 I stopped listening to it. But I loved the '60s thing and the whole heavy punk thing."

It is the idea of The Star that interests you in the Ray Davies, John Lennon tradition and not the Plant, Gillan sort of macho thing, and you want to find new ways of adding to that tradition because of what it's given you?

"Yeah. I think we add . . . I think the whole school of pop and rock groups take their inspiration from the generation before the last one. We hate the groups from the last generation and so we take our inspiration from somewhere else, and carry on from those people.

"Or maybe we're just trying to get as far as they did. The Beatles are definitely the blueprint for almost any group."

Is that an old-fashioned thing to say?

"It's true, whether it's old-fashioned or not, because they did it. They did everything. They did it long before we did. The whole perpetuation of the myth and the idol and the star thing, they had it. . . ."

And tried to do something strongly within that. . . .

"Yeah, I think the Beatles changed the shape of history."

So Pop is important!

"Oh, it's vitally important.

"I mean, being English from the age of five onwards I've been as interested in who's at the top of the charts as I have been in which Prime Minister or government has been running my life. I think England is probably the only country in the world where it's that important. I don't think America cares that much about it.

"England as a community is very very pop orientated. I think it's the folk music, the folk culture of our time. People just take it seriously."

I can come close to blows over it. I can giggle at its silliness. And here I am in the middle of Bombay trying to discover whether one of the biggest pop stars in the world is "serious" or not.

"Well, you can look at it objectively and say, 'God, this is a load of crap. This is a load of noises on a piece of plastic.' But there's something about the music that is indefinable, a magic to it that you can't laugh at."

BUT NOW you are what you are it's important that you resist becoming aloof.

"Well, we've got a good start. A lot of groups have an image that is very hard to adhere to, like the stony-faced idol who can never be approached. I think Gary Numan has this, and it looks great at times, but how long can you keep it up? It's not long before people are sick of it.

"We get up on stage and we laugh a lot and we tell jokes and we banter with the audience, and I feel very natural. I feel very ordinary, in fact. I think that will stay longer than the cold unapproachable icon. That's attractive for a short time – unless it changes all the time, like with Bowie, which is fascinating, it's a work of art. But there's a lot of pressure on him. He can do it because he's a very clever man. We don't have that problem. We're just ourselves."

How does your work in films move into this Sting as Star angle?

"I try and keep it very separate now. I've been offered lots of movies lately where the two worlds merge. I was offered a film by Francis Ford Coppola to play the singer in the film, the lead, and it was very attractive. The pedigree of the film was impeccable, but reading the script it was like the stereotype rock star with stereotype rock star problems, which has nothing to do with me. I find that too dangerous an area to work in. Too much a risk. . . . The goal at the end of the movie was not worth the risk. What I would get out of working in that movie wouldn't be worth the price of failing in it."

What inputs went into the *Quadrophenia* mod?

The character was very enigmatic; lots of secrets in there.

"That performance was ... me, actually. Definitely part of me and very easy to do.

"I'm not an 'actor'; looking good on screen is just a matter of intelligence. I was lucky in that film because I was in it just long enough to create a big impression and not long enough to blow it. It was perfect.

"The Police did a lot for that movie actually. The week it came out in England we were number one. I know for a fact they waited until The Police had toured Australia before they released it there."

How do you relate The Police Sting and the film Sting? Do you feel there's a common goal?

"Yeah, I suppose so. I think Sting is separate from The Police."

That separation has been a seductive development.

"Yeah ... I've developed ... I think the other two are developing their own personas. I'm standing back a lot now and letting the other two take the limelight, because there was a sort of imbalance – and I don't apologise for that. I was the singer. But I'd like my career to be a long one and I don't really want to stay just a rock 'n' roll singer. I think there are more graceful ways of growing old. And acting is one that appeals to me. I don't think I would go back to teaching."

You taught for two years. Was that a good apprenticeship for what you're doing now?

"Yeah, learning to stand up in front of people and not being an arsehole, although I might seem to be one. Self-confidence in front of people. Entertaining, I suppose.

"I think the phenomenon in the classroom isn't teaching, it's learning. I think what you have to do is create an atmosphere where people can feel happy and want to learn things, and I think the rock 'n' roll thing is similar. You create an atmosphere where people can let themselves go, get worked up if you like. It's a sort of ritualised release. We get back to the placebo thing: wouldn't they be better off on the streets, bringing down the government, killing off old ladies? I don't know. Music made me give up teaching.

DO YOU enjoy being involved in other people's lives?

"I feel a lot of responsibility, actually, I don't know how much I'm in their lives. I feel a responsibility and that's a reason that I want to avoid the stereotype. I feel that responsibility very strongly, because I think rock stars let people down in many ways. It's not that they're not intelligent, it's just that they stop thinking and that is disgraceful. That's an insult to people who follow them, to the people who buy their records.

"The average Police fan is spending money on me, he believes in me, and he expects something from me, and I feel a responsibility to that kid. I don't want to serve him up the same old shit.

"First of all I want to please myself, and it would please me more to think that I'm giving more satisfaction than cynically saying 'Oh, any old shit will do!' But that's such a danger and it happens so often.

"It happened to pop in the '70s. It wasn't the artists themselves who were being cynical, it was the industry who created Mud, Sweet, Alvin Stardust, The Bay City Rollers – absolute puppets. They had no intelligence whatsoever, in the real sense. The puppet-master was just breaking them in. And on the other hand, on the serious side, you had Led Zeppelin doing the same thing, but pretending they weren't.

"So that's why The Sex Pistols happened. And that is why The Sex Pistols are probably the greatest group since ... *The Beatles*! They were! They were totally relevant, totally right. . . .

"I personally owe a lot to The Sex Pistols. I wouldn't be here if it wasn't for Johnny Rotten. I don't suppose he gives a fuck whether I've said that or not, but I do actually feel that without any of that initial push there would be none of this and we'd still have Gary Glitter."

What about The Police's appalling record because whenever a wreck of rock is asked what new wave group they like, they always say The Police. Cozy Powell did last week.

"Cozy Powell, Paul McCartney, Ted Nugent, Keith Richards . . . just another area of society where The Police has infiltrated!

Did Steve Harley teach me all this inside thirty minutes? No. But when I asked him "What do people want?" he had this to say: "Me."
See?

Are you telling the truth during this interview?
"That's for you to find out."

Silence. Gabriel looks hurt. His stare returns to the mark on the wall. I crack my knuckles. Slowly, Peter's breathing grows steadily louder and slower. Is it hard work for him to expose himself? The question seems too bare. I think Peter has given up. Nothing more to say. Wait. A flicker. He's dragging through tattered memories. . . . shaking away the dust. One long deep breath. Talk. "Yeah, especially I think on a social level, with friends. I mean in a sense music has always been there as a vehicle, erm, almost a therapeutic vehicle."
To purge yourself?
"Yeah." He giggles to himself. What's up? I ask a little over-pleasantly. He grins broadly, showing ugly yellow teeth. "There was one occasion after I'd moved to London. I disappeared to the gents and I'd just been in conversation about repression and so on . . . it was just beginning to bug me, and I just left all my clothes in the gents and walked back through the room with nothing on and . . . er . . . was ridiculed for quite a while afterwards. . . ." His voice trails away.
Does he find life complicated?
"Er, no, not especially. I think it's a struggle."
Peter looks puzzled. So does he hide behind his music?
"I don't feel that I'm still . . . well, maybe . . . I was going to say that I don't think I act anymore, but perhaps I do when I sing in the first person about situations which obviously aren't

From 8-year-old girls to 30-year-old rock afficionados."

Why do you think these wrecks who perpetuate the stereotypes flipped for The Police, despite you being opposed to those stereotypes?

"They weren't the only people to like The Police, Paul."

But those who were moving to break down these stereotypes are hostile towards The Police and those who relied on them for their continuing audience were in favour.

"Yeah (sigh). . . ."

This has never helped your reputation. Did these rock elders merely identify with the craftsmanship of the records?

"Yeah, I think so. I think they identified with the polish of the records. The way we put them together.

"You're right. In many ways that's another albatross around our necks. Fucking hell! Keith Richards likes us! Oh shit! But Frank Zappa likes us . . . there's light and shade in the whole thing. I think it's nice that Paul McCartney likes us! I'm greatly honoured! It's just another degree of hipness depending where you're standing.

"But I'm most interested in new groups and what they think of us . . . like Gang of Four . . . like, well I know that Joe Strummer doesn't like us."

What's needed to be done is separate the too-good-to-be-true public image from the actual — what Sting is from what he seems to be. Few bother to penetrate the nasty Police myth. It's the same laziness they accuse others of having.

"I think it's a slow process. The initiative is with us to convince these people. I'd like to convince the *cognoscenti* that we're worthwhile listening to even though we're a pop group. Because I feel that we're in a position where we can make what was once crass worthwhile, and I think they can do the same thing.

"Why not sell great music to masses of people? Why not? I think it's a great objective to have. The easiest thing in the world is to appeal to a minority. It's much harder to actually appeal to a lot of people without compromise, without going for the lowest common denominator, but going to a reason- able level of art. I think that's what bands should be aiming for."

How do The Police oppose stereotypes?

"In the way we live."

How about performance and presentation?

"There's still a lot of tradition in The Police; we're still on the boards and we go through a lot of showbizzy things. I like to get the audience singing. It appeals to the nightclub entertainer in me; it's definitely part of me.

"It's not a rock star stereotype. I feel that the old god who stood there and went through his act totally aloof to whether the audience was there or not is something that I'm against. I am a musical entertainer. I don't demean people. I don't demean myself.

"Like, we played at Leeds and you could hear the audience singing the songs louder than the group, and we play fucking loud. That got the old ticker going. I just enjoy it. I don't think there's anything wrong with that.

"If that's a stereotype, it's a good one. I want to get rid of negative stereotypes. The ones that almost destroyed rock music."

SO WHAT is integrity? Do we knock The Police for visiting India, does such an exercise put them out of reach, or do we admire their curiosity? Their determination? Their innocence? Is it just part of the game? How frivolously or how sternly do we look upon their visit?

I was never happy with the idea of interviewing Sting in India. There is abuse everywhere, the poverty and ruin of India savagely warps the straightforward interview. I just wanted to talk to Sting about pop and pleasure and protest because in our world these things are important and are becoming more important. An interview with the Sting that uncovers the extent of his strategy and his cool sensible head is important . . . as far as it goes. Forming the interview in Bombay — which in many ways left me so impoverished it was hell — was indulgent.

The Police's two-day trip to Bombay — the things they did, the sights they saw, the people they met, the autographs they signed, the beautiful meals they ate in upper-class houses, the constant filming and interviewing and photographing – was almost like the farcical fantasy of a lunatic. Nonsense.

The concert itself was performed for local charities and promoted by a dozen delicate ladies called Time And Talent who usually present sedate classical music concerts. They were highly delighted with what was happening, and happily posed for pictures with the tolerant group.

The machinery and patience necessary to set up the concert was enormous. The Police spent their two days in Bombay wandering through receptions, eating meals, visiting record stores, buying musical instruments, shaking hands and signing autographs. They performed their task without scorn or visible condescension. So polite. It's their job.

I did the interview with Sting in two parts, and during these conversations we entirely forgot about the circumstances and the commotion, the sweet ladies, the despair all round us and the nonsense.

I still wish we'd done the interview in a cold white-washed room in London.

▆▆▆▆▆▆▆▆▆▆▆▆▆▆▆▆▆▆▆▆▆▆▆▆▆▆

"THIS IS the sort of life that we're leading now. We've been doing Japan, Bangkok, Hong Kong, and I think this is an ongoing sort of thing. The band has always had a sort of pioneering spirit about it, just to do things for the sake of it. The reason we went to America was not because we thought we could be big in America but because it was something to do. We were languishing in London when we did it, and it was the same kind of thing that drove us to do it as this has been. This thing isn't about making money or anything. It's just an exciting thing to do."

You impose structures immediately around yourself and then work towards them – like being photographed, for instance, which is happening all the time and yet you always make sure that you look good, you always pose carefully.

"I think there's a stereotype that a lot of bands fall into, a lot of individuals in rock fall into, that of being bored, aloof, indifferent to anything else but being on stage. That's a mistake. You end up being manipulated: the Keith Richards syndrome I call it. You end up being a vegetable.

"I want to be seen to be in control of my own life. I do not want to be thought of as this rock stereotype, which I really abhor and don't want to copy. I want to appear very positive about what happens to me. Because I am. I am very concerned. There are too many pressures and you can see them all the time. The pitfalls in this business are so obvious if you just look."

What kind of opportunities do you now have in this position?

"The constant challenge is *what* next? In the space of two albums we've sold more records than people do in ten. In England our album is quadruple platinum or something.

"The constant challenge is to forget that, because it is a distraction, it really is. You've got to try and come up with music that is valid and relevant, not just feeding the industrial machinery that all of a sudden is all around us. The cogs are so well-oiled that as soon as anyone's a success the world immediately becomes what you want it to be, and you sort of have to get outside of that. I don't want to make music where my heart's not in it.

"A band like Joy Division are on the periphery of the whole thing, they don't have the whole industry behind them, they've got to fight it. For what they want to do, they're lucky to be in that position. It's a very creative position to be in.

"Whereas our position is entrapment. You have a vast army of people dependent on you for a living. The record company expects you to produce so many singles a year, so many albums, so many units, and they're depending on you. And the radio stations want it, and the fans want it, and what you really want to do is make music that you like, music that reflects you, *not* the industry. It's a problem.

"See, in many ways this is a dream. It's escapism, and I'm not saying that's a bad thing. . . . The Police are an anachronism in many ways. We've achieved overnight inter-

my own . . . In real life . . . I'm losing my thread again . . . re-direct me. . . ."

What's up?

"I think uh mentally I'm still there . . . on . . . The operating table."

In control?

"I'm the body, not the doctor."

What's up?

"I think fantasy and reality are always very confused and I think the confusion between fantasy and reality is one of the things that interests me most. I mean it's like going east and west with fantasy and reality, to either pole, and if you go far enough in one direction you come to the other. If you go far enough into reality you go into pure fantasy, and vice versa."

When I imagined talking to David Bowie, I would wonder to myself – what is it that you're showing people?

"One thing at a time. That's for sure. I suppose overall I want to show what I'm worth. Life's like that!"

Do you want your audience to trust you?

"*Never*. In a way what I wanted was for them to think they were cleverer than me. It's like . . . he who stands aloof runs the risk of believing himself better than others and misusing his critique of society as an ideology for his private interest! One must never forget one's own fragility, nor how little *the image* is a substitute for real life."

You're joking!

"It's a living. That might be going too far. . . . The deserter seeks refuge."

Tell me about your "talent"?

"Well, it's a reaction against one's training. Have you noticed? From the very beginning they want you to go this way, and so you never do. You go back and then you find the point from which you can go forward again . . . *talent* . . . a bad word national riches and fame and success and that is a kind of Elvis Presley dream. It shouldn't happen in this day and age. We shouldn't be able to make this amount of money and be loved by this many people.

"I feel very strongly that this is an anachronism. A time warp if you like. It's like the '60s."

Superstars are coming back — it's sticking at Rats, Blondie, Police, and that's no good.

"It does seem to be happening. It's closing up."

So what do you feel about that?

"I think the lifeblood of the whole business is new groups, and that's why the early '70s was so frustrating to someone like me. . . . Led Zeppelin . . . Deep Purple . . . and you couldn't get a record deal unless you'd been in one of those groups. So the only people who were getting record deals were about 20. I couldn't bear that! And then there was the revival of interesting new groups that we sidled in on, and now it's beginning to close up. It's getting harder and harder."

So have you reached this point by being honest — you mention the words "valid" and "relevant".

"I don't feel compromised. The music that we make we enjoy making, and although there is a certain amount of craft in it. . . . We just happen to be making music that is successful, and I don't think we've really compromised. I enjoy making records that I think are going to get into the charts. That now has become inseparable."

What about the distance between what you're trying to achieve and the way that it's finally received?

"It's a challenge. In many ways it's a challenge. Without challenge there's no gig in Bombay. The challenge is in the hurdles you have to go over to change. And the challenge at the moment is to forget the distractions and the distractions are the charts."

Do you break down this mass into individual listeners? The energy and intelligence you put in the music might be being wasted.

"Well, it's one of the things that upsets me. That I know if we recorded three minutes of the band farting it would probably be in the charts immediately, and that kills the will if

you like.

"So what I'd like to do is place demands on that mass of people. I would like our next record to be slightly a bit . . . off. I have plans in that direction."

ACKNOWLEDGING that there is little you can constructively do about the new superstars, part of your responsibility has to be to constantly move into unexpected areas, introduce the innovations being made elsewhere in rock into the chart consciousness. "Message" and "Moon" stand up next to what, say, Gang of Four are doing in terms of inverting rock tradition.

"Gang of Four, yeah . . . well, you see, I am into that school of bands. That's the sort of knife edge if you like where pop and rock is going. It's not yet a commercial end, but I feel that you have to be aware of it. In our position I know realistically where we stand, we're with the Rats or the Blondies, but I'm very aware of where the actual musical barriers are being broken. I'm not saying we rip people off, I'm just interested in what other musicians are doing."

How do you feel that The Police introduced reggae moves into a white consciousness? A lot of people consider you diluted the music.

"Maybe we did. I'm not apologising for that. We're white Anglo-Saxons. But I've always loved black music. I feel we add something to it."

Anything you can put your finger on?

"Whiteness, I think. It's, like, the Stones in the '60s were just as valid as John Lee Hooker. I mean, there is a sense of guilt, all white musicians feel that sense of guilt, that sense of duty to the black man, and whenever we meet black musicians, y'know, we're interested in what they think of us."

But haven't you taken the reggae thing as far as it can go?

"Yeah. People call us a white reggae group, which is a bit of an albatross around our necks. I think it will always be there intrinsically in the music because I think we're good at it, but not as overt as it has been."

Do you place qualitative or quantitative demands on what you do? You say that getting into the charts and writing songs is inseparable; you also say that the charts are a distraction.

"The music we make we do the best we can. It's not a sort of cynical, 'Oh, that'll do', or 'Let's go for the lowest common denominator and sound like Slade and it'll sell millions anyway.'

"We don't do that. This music is the best we can do. We try as hard as we can, and it just happens that it's commercial as well. Six months from now it might not be and six months before this happened it wasn't and that's just an accident of fashion or fad.

"I also think it has a lot to do with our image. I think that's inseparable from the music now. The *Gestalt* of the music is very simple. Three blond hairs, the macho name, albums that have a very camp title . . . it's very cleverly put together. I'm quite proud of it. The videos are good; it's product. As that, I think it's impeccable.

"Yeah, we do have quality control."

But is this package empty, or are you offering challenge: are you being subversive?

"We're interested in making people think. If you want to get into our lyrics, they have been slammed sometimes, but I think the lyrics to 'Message In A Bottle' are subtle enough and well-crafted enough to hit people on a different level from just something you just sing along with. I think it's a quite cleverly put together metaphor, it develops and it has an artistic shape to it. I'm very proud of that song. I've never thought of it being subversive. . . ."

You're talking in terms of making the next single "a bit off". You imply that you want to unsettle the chart norm. Why's that?

"Because I think we have to place demands on our audience. There are so many pressures. One is the artistic pressure inside: I want to make something that's good and I want to make something that pleases me first of all. That's the whole thing. It has to please me. Second, there is the thing of wanting to sell records – you can't get away from that.

"There are so many influences on us, there's the press, and we're very aware of

everybody who listens to our records – everybody will listen to the next Police LP very closely either to pull it down or to say that it's the greatest work of art since the ceiling of the Vatican or whatever.

"You're asking: what drives us artistically? I suppose it's ego. I have to say it. But it's, like, we don't have any choice. In this position as successful songwriter in a successful group you start losing alternatives, and you constantly have to look for new ones. That's why I say that the next single has to be an alternative, a direction that we really shouldn't take, that the forces around us say we shouldn't take."

Can those forces halt your natural drive?

"They couldn't. We're in such a position now, financially, managerially, logistically we're in command. There's no way people can stop us doing anything. The only thing that stops us is the responsibility to the whole thing. At the same time we still want to take chances."

These claims can be easily made. Do you really see these chances being taken?

"I'm on this tightrope. I feel it would be so easy just to say, the next album all we have to do is get ten songs, all the usual clichés, and it will sell millions. That's dead easy. But I want more than that. I'm already comfortable. I want something that I can't actually put my finger on."

███████████████████████████

THE BAND walk about Bombay. They push their way along crowded, crushing streets, constantly surrounded by beggars and the curious. They're also constantly being filmed, as the Old Grey Whistle Test is assembling a documentary on the group.

Strolling nonchalantly through the teeming rowdy streets could look really bad on film, especially if it's edited against the group.

"It's our film," Sting claims, **"and we have control over what the *Old Grey Whistle Test* does.**

"But when you're out there in the streets, what can you do? What's the alternative? I

. . . it's all very boring to go on like this. . . . I know all the answers by heart. Six stories in all the world, and even less questions. What would happen if your tape recorder wasn't working?"

I would make it all up.

"Of course. Then perhaps I would say things that would surprise, things I'd never dream I would say. But I'm still here!"

We hope.

"Oh sure. It's all that counts."

Tell me about your last twenty years.

"I've seen pretty people disappear like smoke. I had the satisfaction of speaking for the many that I am. A few uncommitted crimes, babbling self-advertisement, drawing power, a heart of gold . . . definite potentials. I'm very good at concentrating."

Is that all there is?

"What strange places one wakes up in! You see, what I usually say at this point is that I am far from being a genius and must rely on hard and faithful work. . . ."

Of course.

"For me to say that . . . it's almost a surprise. Huh. That last huh wasn't a joke."

Tell me about your future.

"I don't think that I am over-anxious about the future, though I do quail a bit sometimes before the probability that I will be lonely . . . getting older, lonelier, crankier. Oh, good, the tape has stopped turning round. Just in time. Does this give you a license to lie? What needs to be said . . . such a man has no social role only a positive commitment to being alive . . . it was an adventure or a crack-up of the spirit."

What are you defining?

"I'm celebrating myself!"

Should we rejoice!

"It's better than sitting still."

We hope.

"No man is an island, etc. etc."

find it very hard to take an attitude out there apart from stunned amazement. **Either you break down and cry, or you ignore it. It's just what they say in the books, it's the old mystery of India.**

"But walking around Bombay, I just felt odd. Strange. I keep thinking of The Clash and the pictures they had taken in Belfast, standing next to the soldiers. Copping this attitude. It looks good . . . but what does it mean? What do you do? Not come to India? Ignore it all?

"But I enjoy being photographed wherever. I was also aware that there was a kind of madness about it, all these people living with their nerve endings hanging out."

What about being in a place like Bombay and not being able to walk an inch without it being filmed or snapped or spotted by a journalist? Publicising this thing, don't you feel it trivialises it too?

"I don't think you trivialise it. I think it would be a waste if it wasn't being photographed. We do what we do and we're seen to be doing it, because we are doing it.

"As for this concert in India, one way out of it is that we are doing it for a charity, however vague, and we are actually promoting a few rupees for the people. We can sort of salve our consciences with that.

"I wrote a song called 'Driven To Tears' – what are you left with when you're faced with atrocities? You see it all the time in the papers, but what do you do? Basically . . . all you can do . . . is cry . . . really. Then again that's a bit of a futile, useless gesture anyway."

████████████████████

WHAT ABOUT the money, Sting? The hundred billion dollars.

"I haven't really got it. It's on paper. We've sold five, six million albums and I got 20 pence each. It's a lot of money, but I haven't got it yet. I still live in a two-room flat in Bayswater. I don't have expensive tastes. Next year I'll be rich and that's when the rot could set in. Very easily. I'm very aware that money corrupts."

So why don't you ease back, forget The Police, try something else, if the money could possibly distort the songwriting you say you care so much about?

"I enjoy making money as well. It's a complex thing. It is inseparable, which is why it's so difficult. I enjoy making money; I enjoy playing the game that is the charts; I enjoy the success; and I also enjoy the abstraction that is music; and it's a constant battle. But I also enjoy that challenge. I also enjoy that."

So you enjoy being comfortable and enjoy being uncomfortable at the same time?

"Yeah, I'm a workaholic. I could never stop working. When I stop this tour it's great to be back with the wife and kid, but pretty soon I want to be back on the road again.

"It's the old musician's thing. See, my life's comfortable but difficult. I can't go shopping anymore. I can't scratch my arse in the street because people are watching. . . ."

Do you "enjoy" being a celebrity?

"I enjoy being the centre of attention. But this is something I enjoyed before I was famous. I enjoyed being a bus-conductor for six months after I left school."

I suppose you were always joking with the old ladies.

"Oh, well, it's a situation where people are looking at you and you have the ability to entertain them because you're standing up and they're sitting down. So you have a sort of captive audience for a while and you can ponce around or you can tell jokes.

"Again, it's creating an atmosphere, and I could do that and that's why I think I was a good teacher.

"Where I did really badly – and I've had lots of jobs – was where I didn't have that facility. Like, I worked for the Inland Revenue for a while, in an office, from where I almost got the sack. It's almost impossible to get the sack from the Inland Revenue but Sting almost fucking did – just because it's so isolated from that function for which I feel I've got a talent. I'm not particularly good at one to one for some reason. It's a weird thing, but give me more than 20 people and I'm fucking magic."

Do you need that attention.

"I must do. Yeah. And I need it more and more everyday. I also need success. It's like a drug. When I first started in the business two lines in *Melody Maker* was incredible, but now I have to have the front page, otherwise it doesn't mean anything. Then it has to be the front page of *all* the papers. Then it just escalates."

So within your life now it's reasonable to expect front pages all the time?

"Yeah, you expect more and more.

"It's a situation I never actually aspired to really. When I left teaching I wanted to be a serious musician. I was a muso basically – beard, into Charlie Mingus – and I wanted to be respected in the jazz world. I really did. But the horizons just kept receding. Your objectives go further and further away.

"Like the first objective was to get a single out, just to make a single; the next was to get on the Radio One playlist, and it took us ages to get that; and then it was for just one person in *NME* to like us.

"And then it just happened: breaking in to America, a complete dream, before England; and then to come back to England and the accolade. You find yourself a celebrity overnight.

"I fit into it comfortably because I enjoyed it at every stage and I enjoy the stage that I'm at now. I'll enjoy the next stage whatever it is."

You think that it's largely money that damages rock stars?

"Yeah, I think so, and that hunger . . . that need. It's, like, animals that kill for a living are cunning and intelligent, but an animal that just eats scraps has no challenge, has no goals. They just become stupid.

"I am intelligent. I want to maintain my intelligence. So because you have to stay hungry at the same time that you've earned a massive vast fortune is why the band are doing things that are strange – like playing to 50 people in Hong Kong."

Going out of your way to pick fights?

"I think so. Also within the group there's a healthy antagonism because we're all very strong egotists. I don't stand there and say, 'Right, we'll do this and that' and it's done.

There's always a struggle. It's not easy being in this group for any of us. We keep it hot for each other.

"Stewart and I have an intense rivalry which is at times destructive, but is often creative. We like each other; it's not as if we hate each other. We have lived in each other's pockets for three years. For our first American tour there was the three of us in one double bed."

What about the Sting going over the top as glamour boy?

"Oh! that's another danger. It is for sale. The whole thing is for sale. We appeal to the anorexic 14-year-olds. In many ways that is what puts the Gang of Four out of influence, because we have this kind of overt pop image.

"It's inseparable, it really is. It's helped us get to the position that we're in, but I just want to make music. We'll lost the glamour image very quickly. I'm 28, for fuck's sake."

▬▬▬▬▬▬▬▬▬▬▬▬▬▬

THE CONCERT itself is close to miraculous, vaguely reminiscent of an open-air gig in Regents Park. Sting had worried that the audience was just going to sit still, confused, shocked. In the end it was almost too easy a triumph.

It was good to share, but there was no sense of conquering India.

The event could have crumbled into something ugly. It was a sell-out, and excited people without tickets clamoured to get in. There was only one small entrance and so huge uncontrollable queues built up, ticketless and ticketed. The mass outside the gates thought the tapes that were played before the group came on were the actual performance and they panicked.

Miles Copeland calmed things down. They all got in: from the craziest hippy to the Chief of Police.

The gig was exciting! They danced! They sang along! They cheered! They didn't spit! They screamed for more! What a lovely sight.

Afterwards backstage it's like any gig. Young Indians crowd around the group, asking for auto-

"Look, I could have a traumatic life if I wanted to . . . easy . . . I could make life very difficult for myself . . . but I don't think it's going to do me any good . . . I'm not opting for the easy life, but I'm certainly not opting for one that is more difficult than it should be."

The Rolling Stones perpetuate the idea that it's plain and easy to escape, plain and painless.

"That's what entertainers are for! Entertaining people so that they feel really better . . . what else can it all be about? You seem to want it to be more . . . complicated somehow . . . I don't see it. . . . What you do is work out your frustrations to show that things can always be better. . . . This doesn't mean that life is a bed of roses, just because you're a rock and roll star . . . it can always be *better*. That's what the entertainer is going for . . . the *better*. Why should it all be so difficult?"

I have to know it all.

I wrote about Steve Harley as if I knew it all. I did, of course. I was dead alert. I made him look a fool, kept my distance. What a way to start! By making up the inadequacies and sadness of Harley I was somehow calculating the thrilling guiding truths of pop music; to be so annoyed about someone or something means that you feel there's some transcendent opposite, where there are no bothers and no uncertainties. To be so damning means that you are right fussy and expecting untold revelation. To be critical means that you have a perfection in mind. Revelation? Perfection? From pop music? Apparently. Everything is possible.

At the end of the Steve Harley piece, which so impressed the *NME* editors with its comfortable arrogance and certainty, I used a Henry Miller quote. It was a quote I would have liked to have

graphs, offering sincere congratulations. An Indian journalist wanders around until he hits the right person. "How did you get your name?" When he gets to Andy Summers he asks: "What is your favourite beat group?"

Andy Summers passes me by as I chat to an Indian about The Boomtown Rats and *Melody Maker.* "So that was India," Summers shrugs dismissively.

Later still at the hotel Miles is telling us about how the people who'd paid for the front row, 100 rupee seats were confused when all the people moved in front of them and started dancing.

"They were complaining they'd paid their money and now they couldn't see, and why didn't all these people sit down? I said, 'It's rock 'n' roll, you just got to let it happen.' They understood."

"Oh that's cool", says Sting. **"They'll know next time."**

Next time?!

"Oh yeah. There'll be a next time."

OK? SO WHAT ABOUT FUN?

"That is the main thing. I think, you've got to keep having fun, finding fun. It's like every-time I pick up the bass I have fun with it. I find something to play.

"You've got to keep having that experience. As soon as you stop having fun, music dies. There's no point to it. Just nothing. Then it becomes a chore.

"It really is fun for us. Sometimes it's exhausting, it's really hard work, but it's never a chore. I think I'll always have that. I hope so.

"We were talking before about why do people get corrupt? Why do they fall down? Why do they lose touch? I think they've lost the sense of fun, the joy of playing. I think drugs have a lot to do with it."

You don't take drugs?

"I'm not puritanical about drugs; I think drugs should be used. I've used cocaine to get me on stage when nothing else would do it. When I've been travelling 17 hours on a plane and done two shows the night before and nothing else would get me on the stage, I had a snort of cocaine and I think that is a justifiable use of a chemical. I'm aware of the implication.

"As far as sitting around with a lot of pals listening to Grateful Dead albums and sticking it up your nose, y'know, *forget it*! I don't want to know.

"I've never smoked tobacco, so I don't have any inclination to smoke dope. The only time I've ever taken hash is when I've eaten it, and then it's given me nightmares! I'm interested in hallucinogenic drugs as things to be used. I'd never be so stupid as to take drug after drug after drug.

"For people who write songs, part of their task is to experience things. I get a lot of inspiration from low-life. You get a lot of low-life being on the road: prostitution, gang-sters, dodgy parts of cities. That's a good input to get: to go and experience it."

There have to be people like you who do?

"Yeah, I mean, the other night I went out in Sydney. There's a great part of Sydney called King's Cross which is a real zoo, and one of the streets there is a total gay street. I'm not gay, but I'm fascinated by that and I walked down the street and it was fucking heavy just to see those people looking for love and affection in a way that I find alien. Just to go down that street; I needed to.

"Maybe it's just curiosity, but there's also a part of me that says, I can use this. I can use this as an input later on. Like today, seeing those kids begging. It's very preda-tory in a way, but any situation, whether it's positive or negative, you can use."

You're not singing songs of extreme experience?

"No. They're metaphors about loneliness. Everybody feels lonely. Who do they think I am? Maybe they've been fooled by The Cool. I suppose that's it. I've succeeded in fooling them. Jesus Christ!"

You can feel lonely doing something as manic as this world tour?

"I feel lonely making love to my wife. It's like we're all here, but we're totally isolated; no matter how close you are to one person or a hundred you're always totally isolated. And I find that compelling as an image."

The melancholy tone of the lyrics is an unsettling contrast to the exuberance projected in the music and the visuals.

"Mmmmm. We don't just project one image. We are exuberant; we are friendly; we are open; and at the same time we are, everybody is, isolated. We're isolated all the time. I do get lonely, I'm not that social.

"I think it's a reaction against being on stage . . . being what is really everybody's friend. When you're on stage it's like being everybody's brother."

How much longer can you go on singing songs about loneliness and playing the white reggae?

"Yea, it's . . . change, we'll have to. . . ."

Presumably all you're experiencing in the rock star fish bowl is more loneliness?

"I suppose we have to get more and more subtle in the way we treat the subject. I am obsessed by it. I don't think I'll ever lose that. I just think we'll get better at disguising it. That's one objective I have as a songwriter, is to kind of vanish behind the handiwork so that the song exists on its own; forget who wrote it.

"I think 'Walking On The Moon' is a good metaphor. Nobody thinks it's good because nobody really thinks about it . . . to them it's just another set of lyrics . . . but it's a really good metaphor for feeling good. And I'm not sure what the song's about."

How does Sting as Star intrude into your personal life? You were married and had your son Joe before you were a household name.

" '76 was a crucial year. I decided to have this kid, live with this girl, quit my job, move to London. It was all a big trauma. And then I saw The Sex Pistols, had my hair cut, dyed it; it was like an acid trip without the acid. It completely turned me around. . . .

"The constitution we set our marriage on was very flexible. I said, 'Right, we'll have this kid, but I don't ever want to say to him that I gave up the best years of my life for him', because it was said to me. I wanted to carry on living my life to my standards; and both of us were like this.

"We're rich enough to have a nanny, so we've been very lucky, and our relationship is strong because of these separations. It keeps it fresh.

"I've been married four years and I'm still in love."

FOUR HOURS after tidying up the last bit of business in Bombay all The Police except Stewart Copeland (who joins them hours later) flew to Cairo, Egypt. To do it all again.

I came away from India as pale as ever. As nervous as ever. Nothing has changed, everything is changing. The Police did something, achieved something that may have a profound effect. It may mean nothing.

There is still India. There is still greed. There is still hell.

There is still Sting, and somehow that seems to be important. To me.

For no logical reason – except maybe the Sting interview – I came away from India not thinking that pop was sillier than I imagined, but that it was far more valuable.

At the end of it all I don't know whether I'd been tricked by Sting . . . he'd used me! To add yet another new dimension to Sting. Sometimes looking at Sting was not so much like looking in a mirror, but like seeing right through and seeing something that was simultaneously compelling and repelling.

However, I spent the first three hours of my twenty-third birthday discussing POP with Sting, and for a while it didn't seem like I was getting old. Present from heaven! And there I was, piling all sorts of pressures and contradictions and compromises on to him, saying that whichever way he turned he faced problems, that no one was paying serious attention to him, that he was losing himself in the industry, that he was fighting a losing battle, that he was living . . . hell.

"No. It's not hell," Sting smiled.

I don't suppose it is. Hell is what you make it.

put at the end of every interview I wrote – especially when I got worked up. Whether I liked the act in question, and it's acting up, or not. Because the point is NOT BEING BORED. The search is for the jolt, the *moment*, that comes and goes and must come again. If this entertainer can't make the moment for you, some other must. The beauty in that moment is the most important thing, and what it slips to you. When everything matters because nothing matters. That moment being the opposite to the sales talk. What those who talk in clichés call "the shiver down the spine."

When I smashed into someone because I thought they let us down I would have used the quote – with cynical regret, or a note of triumph – you can't fool me! And when I charged on and on feeling I could almost define, even design myself, the *power* in the moment. I would also use the quote then – to prove my gallant objectivity, to prove my head was level: I'm no fool, it's only a pop song, after all. . . .

"What if at the last moment, when the banquet table is set and the cymbals clash, there should appear suddenly and wholly without warning a silver platter on which even the blind could see that there was nothing more and nothing less than two enormous lumps of shit?"

Somewhere, the right answers must already be recorded.

IN

Addition (AL) One

Notes

1. Here, then, is what I think of thought: and we shall thereby approach the very heart of the matter.
2. We need to interpret interpretations more than we need to interpret things. (Montaigne)
3. What is the spirit of the age which an ideal journal can articulate while mere newspapers remain on the surface?
4. The pop (i)deal – wanting to make *all* things new.
5. The pop (i)deal – enthusiastic misunderstandings.
6. To flaunt one's superiority is, at the same time, to feel in on the job.
7. The critic's arrogance derives from the fact that, in the forms of competitive society in which all being is merely there *for* something else, the critic himself is also measured only in terms of his marketable success – that is, in terms of his *being for* something else. (Adorno)
8. In the end I fall into a kind of trap.
9. A kind of trance.
10. The pop (i)deal – whatever next?
11. All arguments stem from confusion, and all arguments are a waste of time unless your purpose is to cause confusion and waste time. (Burroughs)
12. I suppose so; there are certain things that you just cannot find uninteresting.
13. . . . a certain ignorance, a certain naivety, a boldness that springs from this naivety, but a naivety that is not simplicity of mind, and an ignorance that does not rule out knowledge, but assimilates and rejuvenates it.
14. But rather than a sermon, this is a warning, a friendly appeal for vigilance, and I admit it can be turned against me.
15. The pop (i)deal – confidences and confessions.
16. The whackings and teasings are a mild form of shock therapy to jolt the listeners, the "enjoyers", out of their mental habits and to hammer it into their heads that they must act spontaneously, without thinking, without self-consciousness and hesitation.
17. I suppose so; I don't do it deliberately.
18. This is very difficult to describe, but I would say, in a general way, the main answer is to be *interested*. Unfortunately, we use this word so often that it has lost a great deal of its meaning, the meaning being how its root is defined in Latin; *inter-esse*, "to be in".
19. *Ecstatikos* is a Greek adjective meaning 'inclined to depart from'.
20. The pop (i)deal – "the penny has dropped".
21. Buzzcock's "Spiral Scratch" EP exposed the horror of boredom, intensified, compressed, pinpointed and exploded it; Robert Wyatt's "Rock Bottom" made us laugh at things that should make us cry; Tim Buckley and Nick Drake sang to us from inside the dark labyrinth of the world; Iggy Pop engaged himself in bad tempered black magic; Brian Eno sparkled with mischief; Marc Bolan was *out* of this world; Peter Hamill tore me to pieces; John Cale was relaxed, harsh, almost childish; Josef K. could go on for ever, with their pained surprise and the vague conviction that life could not be wrong; The Smiths' "This Charming Man" eased us into the solitude of timelessness; New Order were supreme *remote* control. Perhaps the answer is that such things as these account for the fanaticism. There's more. . . . Beefheart's breathing. The lies of Devo. The sore Siouxsie. More!
22. The pop (i)deal – it's a secret.

To be continued ....

Addition (AL) Two

Killing Joke ....November 15 1980

Jerry Garcia...March 28 1981

The editor of *New Musical Express* at the time, Neil Spencer, estimated that this article caused 30,000 people to stop reading the paper. There were no thoughts as to where they had gone, but if it was true it is in one sense, along with such happenings as Queen's "Fat Bottomed Girls" and John Blake's arrival at the *Daily Mirror*, the day the music died.

Marillion ....April 28 1984

Soon after the publication of the piece, Fish rang the commissioning editor to thank him for editing out the numerous references to his coke taking during the interview. I had included his drug use feeling that it was an important part of any true portrayal of *this* character.

Gary Numan ....March 20 1980

Martin Fry ....December 25 1982

Midge Ure ....September 13 1980

Bauhaus..March 20 1982

The group taped the interview themselves and later used a tiny fragment of the recording on one of their 12″ records – a part where I mentioned the stupidity of the interview process (I was in a tight spot at the time). It was a deliciously obvious and inconsequential thing to do.

Adam Ant.. January 16 1982

David Sylvian ....November 20 1982

Paul Weller ....November 3 1979

Mick Jagger...June 28 1980

The Clash .... October 20 1979

Fire Engines .... January 7 1982

Depeche Mode ....February 25 1982

Chrissie Hynde .... January 26 1980

Peter Gabriel ....July 5 1980

The Gabriel piece, which pushed out the idea of Gabriel as madman and me as his sickly keeper, caused Gabriel to refuse to speak to the paper for five years. It was apparently too much a crack on the head of the "interview" as advertisement.

After the 1980 interview with Duran Duran, they also refused to talk to a *NME* writer for five years – agreeing to an interview with Chris Bohn only after they had long mastered how to act aloof and artful when their mouths dropped open. By then they had also perfected the up-to-date knack of surrounding their light-weight musical sensations with the works and images of shrewd-ish graphic designers and terribly sophisticated video makers. A kind of protection racket; modern teenybop acts learning from punk, and after, little but the values of good *design*, wrapping shifty abstraction around their hollow language.

George Michael would eventually grunt acknowledgements to me whenever we passed each other in corridors of power around London. Two years after our interview, Michael could still be summed up the same way – by *The Sunday Times*. An efficient craftsman, of narrow interests and concerns, wrapped up in an unbudgeable, somehow listless ambition to pursue "perfect pop". George Michael represents a whole generation allowed through to the top who are influenced by Elton John, Paul McCartney – the sapped songwriters, the cheerful chaps – rather than Captain Beefheart, Lou Reed, Todd Rundgren, David Byrne, Richard Thompson. And so we find ourselves barely able to avoid George Michael's brand of obedience. Somehow Gilbert O'Sullivan and Squeeze have been bigger influences on new pop than Buzzcocks and Pere Ubu. I still feel it would do us all a bit of good if Michael allowed some anxieties to seep through into his music, and he listened to some Doors, some Van Morrison, looked at some Wenders, some Fassbinder. It is, though, the softest side of pop that has influenced today's charmers, the agreeable rather than the transforming, Bart and not Brecht.

Addition (AL) Three

Notes (continued)

23. Sometimes I feel that the best rock interview ever was when Patti Smith asked Eric Clapton what his six favourite words were. After she submitted the piece, the magazine she was writing for fired her.
24. I did an interview with the guitar player in New Order. What do you want to drink? "Triple Pernod and blackcurrant please."
25. I interviewed The Cocteau Twins, and we dragged through two hours while I asked questions and they looked over my shoulder. They acted like fragile water babies who wanted to spend their lives inside a cork-lined room while they ate marmalade and sticky sweets. I could have pinched them.
26. I asked The Cocteau Twins "Do you want your music to do anything more than just exist?" A standard question. They flinched, dramatically. So I asked them what they had for breakfast, and they reacted like I wasn't treating them seriously enough. What was going on? "Our songs belong as songs, uniquely within the realm that they open up for themselves." Pop music, I decided, is often a very obscure struggle.
27. I blamed myself.
28. Sometimes I feel that the best rock interview ever was the one I did with Siouxsie of the Banshees, after she had failed twice to turn up to be recorded. Third time ... no need to record her, it was certainly the best interview *she* ever did. So what was punk for you? "I was singled out, and I had a sort of second sight. In those days you moved fast and so you didn't want to have much to do with the customary." Joan Collins wanted to know why you were getting down on your knees. "What has that got to do with it?" How do you see yourself now? "Does anything really change?"
29. And what happened to The Cocteau Twins? They ran into the wood, and groaned. Then they frolicked. "I say, a flower!" I could have pinched myself.
30. The longest interview I ever did was with Robert Fripp. It lasted six hours, and could be summed up thus: "Within me arose a storm of blood, a well of sweat and an excessive fuss of mind."
31. I did an interview with Phil Oakey of The Human League. Why do you bother? "I won't stomach that!" What did you say? "Same again please."
32. The pop (i)deal – will you? won't you?

Addition (AL) Four

Yes . . . I worry greatly about what happens to people like Jim Kerr of Simple Minds once they become superstars. Ideals are postponed, they become forgetful, they allow themselves to be rushed about, they sort of disappear. You can't miss them. All that's left is the smile, a couple of dance steps, an even-tempered dullness. Once they threatened to flood the world with strangeness, now they just wave to the crowds. There are those who force us to respect this passage from individualism to invisibility – from nowhere to somewhere, or the other way round? It's the natural way of things, they say. But I worry. I worry that it's hard to illuminate, fictionalise, the trivialities of Madonna, of Tears For Fears, to be involved, because their pretence, their distance, is too well organised. The new pop stars, they even lack humour, or *irony*. But what am I actually *for*? I escaped to tell you.

I worry that everyone - you know what I mean by "everyone" – is getting used to the new gross rock, the clapping together of post-latest effects, ancient justifications, abstract tribal paranoia, towering arrogance, glib assurances, absolute efficiency. This gross rock that is really just the American Way, the fear of growing old, of losing out, of the soft cock, the wrinkled skin, the terror of not touching what it is that's the *thing*. I worry that rock is becoming firm containment, confidently signposted and labelled. So what am I actually *for*? I only escaped to tell you.

I used to think that the way radio and television sorted things out, one day the top 50 would stay exactly the same, because nothing new would be allowed inside. The top 50: same records, different positions. Today I think that record companies will only allow the exact number of singles to be hits during a year, so that they can fill 15 boiled hot compilations every 12 months, with 6 extra at Christmas. Everyone else will be left to struggle for themselves, pleasing a smaller and smaller crowd who read the black and white music papers, repulsed by a rock world made up of the cheerful chaps, the heaven high efficiency, the video veil and market research. Every so often 2 or 3 new acts would be allowed through into this enclosed world of grand enchantment and mass deception, just enough fresh talent to sustain the necessary illusion of novelty. A few regular charity events will persuade most people that pop can be *more than mere entertainment*. A dreadful underground will be created while a royal patronised rock settles into the middle of the road, laced with the occasional cosmetic eccentricity and dark hints. But what am I actually *for*? I escaped to tell you. Something else might happen. Something will happen. It's a question of. . . . I worry greatly. Who's laughing?

continued from page 1

What went wrong? What could happen? Morley had to speak out, or forever hold his peace. In 1978 he moved down to London and wrote more regularly for the *New Musical Express*, starting to talk to the performers, rather than writing around them. It was during 1978 that he interviewed two of that year's biggest stars, Bob Geldof and Debbie Harry, and discovered in himself a ravishing interest in the circumstances of stardom and self-styling, driven on by a curiosity he could only attribute to a northern nosiness and a delight in gossiping over the garden fence. For five years, using up three thirty-quid tape recorders he bought from Boots, he moved through a world of action and folly, week in week out, interviewing entertainers who were off their hinges, or at the hot centre of stardom, or who had been through it all, or seen through it all, or who couldn't wait for their chance. He would listen to the music of A Certain Ratio, Orange Juice or John Martyn, and then fly off to ask Ted Nugent questions. For he had quickly learnt that what went wrong was that very few people agreed with his desire that pop in the '80s – what he had christened, in honour of The Fire Engines and ABC, not Duran Duran or Howard Jones – the "new pop", should be based upon the collective irresponsibility of The Velvet Underground, M.C.5., Syd Barratt, The New York Dolls and Can. The consensus appeared to be that pop should be based upon the agreeable leisureliness of Hank Marvin, The Beach Boys, Bread, Jethro Tull

and Bachman Turner Overdrive. As the man said, there are all sorts of things the general public doesn't want to see or hear. Above all, they don't want to be puzzled. Could this be true? What do people really get out of Phil Collins? Just a complete and beautiful lack of *intrigue*? Three cheap tape recorders helped him to find out not so much what went wrong, or why nobody agreed with him much, but what could be missing. Paul Morley transcribed hundreds of cassette tapes.

If the action he wanted wasn't happening for the moment, he could always gossip.

After five years of intensive interviewing he decided to pause with the questions, but explore further the dilemmas of critical understanding, public appreciation, business condescension and media tranquillising by participating in the general rush for glory and attention. Working as a kind of molester for the Zang Tuum Tumb record label he contributed to the makings of several magical pop/art objects. He was particularly pleased with a joy ride called Art of Noise – comic camouflage and progressive plagiarism – despite it ending in failure, crushed by conventions. After two years at ZTT he noticed that he was talking a lot more than he used to, and was still no fan of facts. He's wondering whether to buy a fourth tape recorder. At the time of writing, he feels a whole new burst of heckling welling up inside. Don't you?

"Yes."